PRAISE FOR VICTOR METHOS

The Silent Watcher

"*The Silent Watcher* is gritty, authentic, and packs a punch. Victor Methos's own inimitable style is addictive."

—Robert Dugoni, *New York Times* bestselling author

The Secret Witness

"A red-hot suspenser aimed at readers for whom a single serial killer just isn't enough."

—*Kirkus Reviews*

An Unreliable Truth

"A straight-A legal thriller with a final scene as satisfying as it is disturbing."

—*Kirkus Reviews*

A Killer's Wife

An Amazon Best Book of the Month: Mystery, Thriller & Suspense

"*A Killer's Wife* is a high-stakes legal thriller loaded with intense courtroom drama, compelling characters, and surprising twists that will keep you turning the pages at breakneck speed."

—T. R. Ragan, *New York Times* bestselling author

"Exquisitely paced and skillfully crafted, *A Killer's Wife* delivers a wicked psychological suspense wrapped around a hypnotic legal thriller. One cleverly designed twist after another kept me saying, 'I did not see that coming.'"

—Steven Konkoly, *Wall Street Journal* bestselling author

"A gripping thriller that doesn't let up for a single page. Surprising twists with a hero you care about. I read the whole book in one sitting!"

—Chad Zunker, bestselling author of *An Equal Justice*

THE SILENT WATCHER

OTHER TITLES BY VICTOR METHOS

Shepard & Gray Series

The Secret Witness

The Grave Singer

The Deceiving Look

Desert Plains Series

A Killer's Wife

Crimson Lake Road

An Unreliable Truth

Neon Lawyer Series

The Neon Lawyer

Mercy

Other Titles

The Hallows

The Shotgun Lawyer

A Gambler's Jury

An Invisible Client

THE SILENT WATCHER

VICTOR METHOS

THOMAS & MERCER

This is a work of fiction. Names, characters, organizations, places, events, and incidents are either products of the author's imagination or are used fictitiously. Otherwise, any resemblance to actual persons, living or dead, is purely coincidental.

Published by Thomas & Mercer, Seattle

www.apub.com

ISBN-13: 9781662516252 (hardcover)
ISBN-13: 9781662516269 (paperback)
ISBN-13: 9781662516276 (digital)

Cover design by Laywan Kwan
Cover image: © Nature Peaceful / Shutterstock; © Raimund Koch / Getty

Printed in the United States of America
First edition

3rd Fisherman: I marvel how the fishes live in the sea.
1st Fisherman: Why, as men do a'land;
the great ones eat up the little ones.
—William Shakespeare, *Pericles*, act 2, scene 1

PROLOGUE

A blurred form darted out from the forest, zeroing in on the woman sunbathing on the rocks.

It moved with blistering speed, kicking up dust whirlwinds and breaking the stillness of Ember Lake.

It swerved toward the young woman, whose eyes were still closed, absorbing the last rays of the sun before evening fell. The sound grew louder, stirring her. In a rush of power, it collided violently with her exposed leg.

Ava Mitchell lifted her sunglasses and saw the remote-controlled car that had hit her thigh. Her brother, Adam, walked over, holding the control and a beer, and said with a laugh, "I wanted to aim for your butt, but it's so big it wouldn't be a challenge."

"Do you always have to be so annoying?"

"Pretty much."

She pulled her sunglasses back on and said, "Where's Sarah?"

"Asleep. I gave her some of your anxiety meds so she'd mellow out."

"You can't just give other people's meds to your girlfriend. We don't know how she's going to react."

He shrugged. "She'll be fine. What's with the ghost stuff?"

"She thinks our cabin is haunted."

"That's stupid."

"She's *your* girlfriend."

He raised the beer to his lips. "Yeah, whatever."

She sighed and rose. "I'm going to take a shower. You could make yourself useful and get started on dinner instead of playing video games and drinking my beer if, ya know, you wanted to."

"Nah."

Ava ruffled his hair on the way to the cabin, which sat inside the forest, only ten yards from the dock.

Entering the two-story cabin, she tossed her towel on a chair and shed her flip-flops. She sighed, regretting her decision to chaperone her freshman brother and his uninteresting girlfriend, Sarah. With no cell service, she was stuck with them.

Ava took the creaky staircase and passed the first bedroom, where Sarah lay on her side, her back to the door and the curtains drawn. Normally, Ava would have kept going, but something caught her attention: Sarah's ragged breaths.

"Hey," Ava said, "how many of my pills did he give you?"

The girl didn't move.

Ava stood at the foot of the bed. "You okay?"

There was no movement.

Ava circled the bed and shook Sarah's shoulder. No response. She rolled the girl over.

Blood pooled on the bed, sticky and crimson. The girl's throat had been nearly ripped out, still pulsing a stream of hot blood onto the white sheets. As she attempted to speak, a fresh gush of blood spilled from the wound, silencing her.

Ava wasn't fast enough to scream.

She felt a tingling warning at her neck. Her eyes darted to the room's dark corner. A figure stood, hands at its sides. Even with the shadows, she knew it wasn't her brother.

Ava bolted for the door. The figure lunged, missing her by inches. Her scream echoed off the walls.

Ava leapt down the stairs, tripped, and tumbled, hitting her shoulder and then her head. Wincing in pain, she looked up—no one followed. She scrambled to her feet, dashed past the living room, and burst through the front door, screaming into the warm air.

Sharp gravel bit into Ava's feet, one stone even causing her to stumble. Ignoring the pain, she kept running.

"Adam!"

Adam was sipping beer, annoyed, until he saw Ava's face. Then his eyes widened. "What happened?"

"She's—"

A gurgling sound came from behind her. Ava turned to see Sarah, hand on her bleeding throat, eyes wide and wet, trying to run from the cabin toward the dock.

"Sarah?" Adam said in shock.

Adam tried to grab her, but she fell into him and he lost his grip. She plunged into the water with a loud splash.

"Sarah!" Adam shouted, dodging Ava's grasp to dive in after the girl.

Ava looked back to the house. A shadow moved across a window.

"There's somebody here!" she shouted.

Adam surfaced, holding Sarah, and struggled to backstroke to the dock.

Ava was about to jump in after him when she heard a door creak. She looked back; the cabin door was open.

"We need to go!"

"Help me get her out."

Ava waded in to help Adam get Sarah to the dock. After Adam climbed up, he pulled Sarah out of the water. Her face was pale and her mouth moved, but no words came. Deep bruises surrounded her neck wounds.

"What happened?" he shouted.

"I don't know. There's someone in the cabin."

Sarah's eyes fluttered, and she became unresponsive.

Adam ripped off his shirt and wrapped it around her neck to slow the bleeding.

"Hold the shirt on her neck. I'll go get the truck."

"No, Adam, there's someone here. We have to get help."

"You wanna walk two miles carrying her like this?"

Ava didn't say anything.

"Didn't think so. I'm pulling the truck around to the dock. I'll be right back."

Her voice, laced with desperation, echoed behind him as he sprinted toward the cabin.

—

Ava held her brother's shirt to the wound. Sarah's lips had turned a deep purple. Blood had soaked her clothing and dripped with the water rolling off her. So much blood and she was still alive. Ava had never realized how much blood the human body contained.

Sarah's eyes opened, but she was too weak to say or do anything.

As the sun dipped below the horizon, the encroaching darkness began to shroud the woods around them.

"Hang on, okay? Just hang on."

Ava looked up at the cabin.

"Adam, hurry up!"

There was no response, and it was almost dark. Ava wrapped the shirt a little tighter across the wound.

"I have to leave you, okay? I'm going to be right back. Just keep your hand here, just like this . . . okay? I'll be right back."

Sarah was trying to speak, terror in her eyes, but no words would come out of her throat.

Ava ran to the cabin, the coming darkness making it impossible to avoid the sharp rocks, causing her own injuries to sting with every step.

The cabin was quiet.

"Adam?"

He didn't respond. Only one light was on and it cast a soft glow, darkness puddling in corners she couldn't see.

"Adam?" she said from the front door.

The truck was in the garage, which was through the kitchen, but there was a window around back. She hoped Adam had been smart enough to go that way instead of through the cabin.

Ava cautiously went around to the back of the cabin near the garage without going inside. She paused outside the garage's single window, listening intently. A breeze rustled a nearby tree branch, creating an unsettling scraping sound against the wooden exterior.

"Adam, where are you?"

Ava noticed a shape on the ground a few yards past the corner of the garage. Silently, she edged closer. Adam lay motionless, face down in the dirt.

"Adam!"

She ran to him and rolled him over. What she saw was a horror show. His face was a mask of blood, his skin torn and shredded. His neck was a gaping wound. He tried to inhale, but no air could get in. Instead, a soft gurgling escaped his lips.

She heard footsteps in the dirt behind her as someone approached.

Without looking, Ava bolted deeper into the forest.

She sprinted through the thick underbrush, screaming for help, aware the nearest neighbor was two miles away. Her parents had bought this cabin for isolation.

A camping area wasn't far and, especially during the summer months, was frequented by families. Ava could get there at a good pace during daylight, but at night, with fear and adrenaline pumping through her, maybe she could get there faster.

After being scraped by branches, sharp bushes, and thorny flowers, she got to a campsite with no cars or people around. She saw a few items of trash smoldering in a firepit. Panic was growing. She would have to run all the way to the first cabin to find someone, and if Sarah and Adam were both bleeding out right now, she didn't know if she would make it in time.

"Hello!" she shouted. "Anyone here?"

Running to the next campsite, she spotted three tents circling a dying fire and a discarded ice cooler. The first tent was empty, just a shell in the dim light.

By the time she got to the last tent, she heard the branches crackling behind her as someone made their way toward the site.

She jumped into the tent, quickly zipped it up, and retreated to the corner. Without her cell phone, she had nothing to hold, so she wrapped her arms around her knees. Outside, footsteps approached, and she heard someone closing in. The footsteps paused in front of her tent.

She held her breath and prayed.

1

Piper Danes sat in the chambers of the Honorable Cody Wilcox, a judge who was known to strong-arm attorneys into plea deals one or both sides may not want. He worked to get cases out of his courtroom as fast as possible. The rumor was that he had irritable bowel syndrome and couldn't stay on the bench for extended periods.

The trial had been ongoing for five days, and Judge Wilcox grew less pleasant the longer it went on. He sat at his desk popping antacids as Piper checked the clock on her phone and realized she'd been in court for ten hours today.

As guardian ad litem, Piper was there for a different purpose from the prosecutor or defense attorney. She was the appointed guardian for a few of the victims. Under the Victims' Rights Act, the victims had a say in the plea deal and were entitled to an attorney to represent their interests.

Lawrence Shaw sat in a chair before the judge's desk in his Armani suit. His client, Richard Malone—a Harvard graduate who had swindled a group of vulnerable people out of millions—hadn't been brought back in chambers.

In the other chair was the prosecutor, a man in a simple jacket and slacks with a bad haircut who spoke plainly. The simple authenticity had resonated with the jury, and Piper knew Malone was going to be convicted.

The judge and Lawrence exchanged a glance, and she knew what it meant. Lawrence Shaw had a reputation for getting reduced sentences for his clients. The prosecutor and he had agreed on a deal of time served and no prison, but they needed Piper's approval, and so far she hadn't seen anything to suggest the victims in this case would be satisfied with the plea deal. What she wanted was simple: Malone sells everything he owns to pay back the victims, and then spends five years in prison.

"He can't do five years," Lawrence said. "Agree with time served and he'll pay back all the victims over his lifetime."

The implicit threat was that if she didn't back down, the victims wouldn't get paid.

"I'm sure Mr. Malone can find the means to pay back the victims either way." She knew it was true because he was accused of defrauding a little over $7 million, and his home alone was probably worth that.

The judge sighed and looked uncomfortable, like it pained him to sit in a chair.

"Your Honor, he will die in prison! He's not suited for an environment like that."

The judge looked to Piper and said, "Ms. Danes, you are the only one in this room who feels this plea deal is against the interests of justice. Is there any way we can get this resolved? The trial is scheduled for another three weeks, and nobody seems to want it to go that long except you."

She gave a forced smile of courtesy. "I think the victims would disagree with you, Your Honor."

He looked angered for a moment and then turned to Lawrence as if to say *I tried.*

"Well," the judge said, "however long this thing goes, we're done for today. That jury's about ready to revolt. But I want you to go out into that hall and see if you can resolve this."

The judge rose with a groan and headed back to the courtroom. Piper, the prosecutor, and Lawrence came out of the judge's chambers and went back along the clerk's entrance. Lawrence put his hand on her arm, holding her in place, and began speaking, but stopped when she looked down to his hand and then politely up to his face. He released her and said, "You're being unreasonable."

"Larry, I don't know how much he's paying you, but I'm sure it's more than adequate to cover the next three weeks of work. Just suck it up and do it."

"But there's no reason for this," he said angrily. "Cases this financially complex go right over a jury's head. You're banking on a conviction and it could easily be an acquittal."

"Then you have nothing to worry about, do you?" she said with a pleasant smile before turning away from him and going back to the courtroom.

The courtroom was massive, paneled wood with tables as old as the building itself. Piper went to a pew behind the prosecution table, and Lawrence joined his two associates at the defense table. Malone winked at her as she sat down. He had been smug the entire trial. He was handsome, and it was a problem, as some of the female jurors would engage with him with subtle smiles and looks. But the trial hadn't been going well for Malone. Victim after victim got up on the stand and tearfully told what he had said and done to get them to turn over their life savings to him.

The bailiff announced Judge Wilcox, who said to bring in the jury, and everybody rose to their feet.

"Be seated," he said. "Ladies and gentlemen, today has been a long one and I apologize, but we had some matters to discuss in private. We'll call it a night for now. Court will reconvene at eight tomorrow morning."

The judge got to his feet, and the bailiff said, "All rise."

Piper stood. Her back ached, her legs hurt, and her cramps felt like they were tearing her insides apart, but she didn't show it.

When the judge was out of earshot, she heard Lawrence speaking to his two associates. She couldn't make out a lot of it, but she did hear "She's on the rag today, boys."

Piper gathered her things into her satchel that she'd gotten as a gift from her grandmother after she'd graduated law school. Lawrence came up to her with the most pleasant voice he could muster and said, "No need to be out in the hall. Why don't we find somewhere for a late dinner and talk about it?"

She pulled the strap of the satchel over her shoulder. "Five years, Larry. Wilcox doesn't want to go against the victims. Malone has to take the deal. It's the only way and we both know it."

She began walking away from him and out of the courtroom. A few of the victims would come to the trial every day, but many of them were infirm and couldn't stay the entire time. One woman, Cleo Bell, always sat in the front. She was dying of leukemia and had to have oxygen. She had told Piper that the money that was stolen from her was for her funeral, so her children wouldn't have to pay for it.

As Piper got to the double doors leading out of the courtroom, Lawrence said behind her, "He'll take it," with a resignation as if he had just accepted a firing squad.

She had to suppress a grin and then turned to him and said, "Get this continued so he can get the money together. I want some of the victims paid first before he enters a plea. Especially Ms. Bell."

Lawrence nodded.

Piper saw Cleo Bell smile at her from the gallery seats, and she smiled back.

Before leaving, Piper looked to Malone at the defense table, who was staring at her with venom. She winked at him and then left the courtroom.

Her beat-up Dodge sat in the far reaches of the parking lot. It was well past nine, and the jury typically had their own parking spaces right next to the building to avoid accidental, or sometimes not so accidental, interactions with any attorneys. Empty parking spaces always gave her a shot of adrenaline, and she reached into her purse and took out her keys and held the largest one between her fingers like a small blade, though she doubted she could hurt someone with it.

The surface roads in Las Vegas were wet from a light rain and empty. It was dark enough that she could see the ever-glowing neon fires emanating from the Strip. She stopped at a fast-food joint and got a sandwich. They'd only been given fifteen minutes for lunch today, and all she had time for was some Tic Tacs. She then drove across town to the home she shared with her grandmother.

Lake Danes was a woman in her sixties who looked older than she was from a lifetime of hard living. She had raised Piper's mother and her two siblings by herself after her husband, Piper's grandfather, passed away from a genetic heart condition.

A twinge of guilt went through Piper as she thought about her grandmother taking Piper in at such a young age: it must've been a relief to see all the kids out of the house and finally have some time to herself, and then she had to adopt her granddaughter and start the process over again.

The home was flat and in front of a golf course, with no fence to separate them. The driveway had her grandmother's old Buick parked on it. Piper got out of her car. The home was always immaculate and smelled like apples from an air freshener that her grandmother had been using for decades.

After ensuring her grandmother was already asleep, Piper retreated to her own room. Overcome with exhaustion, she fell asleep instantly, not even managing to change clothes or brush her teeth.

Piper woke up the next morning with her neck even stiffer than it had been when she had gone to bed.

She got dressed in a gray suit with black pumps before running a brush through her hair. The tangled mess refused to do anything she wanted, so she pulled it back with an elastic instead.

The county's government services were mostly piled into Clark Place, a building meant for middle-of-the-road businesses but that had been bought by the government on the cheap and renovated to hold all the county services.

Piper took the elevators to the third floor and the guardian ad litem's office. It was a hive of activity, the buzz of conversation punctuated by the rhythmic tap of shoes on cheap floors and the rustle of endless paperwork.

Two types of attorneys were visible. Those destined for a weekend chained to their desks sat hunched in their cubicles, wearied by their relentless case files. Others, the lucky ones spared from weekend duty, exuded a lightness, their relief coming out in jokes and laughter.

Some states had contracted attorneys who handled the guardian ad litem duties, but here they had an established office with their own investigators for use on their cases and several paralegals.

Piper was a junior attorney, having been out of law school less than a year.

Tom Williams, her supervisor, who stuck his head out of his office when he heard her, said, "Piper, can we talk really quick?"

"Sure."

She set her satchel down at the cubicle. The attorneys accurately called the clustered cubicles in the middle of the floor the Lawyer's Dump because anyone without enough seniority to fight for an office was dumped there. The GAL's budget was tight, and every penny had to be stretched. Piper didn't mind. Being a guardian had some advantages that made up for the lack of funding and long hours.

Tom liked to say "The only difference between us and other attorneys is that judges *occasionally* listen to what we say."

As the section chief over the junior GALs, Tom had a reputation for making people learn by throwing them in the fire. Piper herself, on her first day, was given a ward who was involved in a complex insurance fraud case with over twenty thousand pages of documents she would have to read. She didn't know it at the time, but it was a test to see how she would handle it, because it would be impossible to read that many pages in time. Piper bribed the interns at the GAL's office with beer to read all the documents after their normal shifts and write small one- or two-sentence summaries of the main points. From then on, Tom left her alone to do her job.

Tom's office was a picture of how to randomly throw things into a small space and have them land in a somewhat workable order. Boxes of files were stacked against the walls, and the bookshelves were overflowing with law books covered in so much dust she guessed he hadn't opened them for decades.

"You look exhausted," he said.

"I am."

She sat across from him, and he put one of his loafers up on the desk, pushing back a little and tilting his chair.

"You want some coffee?"

"I'm good, thank you."

"Suit yourself," he said as he took a drink out of a pale-blue mug. "So I got something and your name came up. Do you know much about Allen Bishop?"

Piper knew the name from as far back as her undergraduate classes in childhood development. Dr. Bishop had changed juvenile criminal justice theory with daring research where he lived with gangs in the inner cities of Chicago and documented their daily lives, eventually publishing his doctoral dissertation on how to improve the handling of children in the criminal justice system.

His theory was simple but powerful: When kids are labeled as "criminals" at a young age, they start to believe it themselves. It's like they look in a mirror, and all they can see is the "bad kid" label that's been put on them. Each crime they commit, each punishment they get, makes them believe in that label even more. If you want to stop future crime, he said, make sure that kids don't feel like criminals.

This idea caused a big stir in the legal world. Some people thought it was a game changer, while others thought it was too simple. But everyone agreed that it made them think about how the criminal justice system was failing these kids, turning them into the very criminals it was trying to prevent.

"I remember his studies from several classes, yeah."

Tom nodded. "It changed juvenile procedure. Started making people think about how kids are different from adults. My undergrad was in sociology, and there was an entire course devoted to him."

She waited patiently for him to speak, hoping he would get to the point.

"Anyway, there's a new federal grant to test some of Bishop's theories. He thinks that everyone in the juvenile system—the guardian ad litem, juvenile court judge, police, the social workers and probation officers—all working together from the beginning of the case with the child produces better outcomes and less recidivism. Kind of pie in the sky if you ask me, but the government certainly wastes money on stupider things."

Tom ran his hand over his desk, wiping away a large swath of dust from the top.

"They're going to try the grant out with Judge Dawson. Know her?"

"No."

"You haven't heard anything about her?"

"I don't listen to gossip."

He nodded. "I'll just tell you then. She's smart," he said, taking a sip out of his mug like he was drinking a fine wine. "Like crazy smart. She got her medical degree and a JD jointly and was like a surgeon or something. I guess career change and then boom, becomes a judge. Don't you hate people like that?"

"Completely."

"Me too." He drank down more coffee. "She has some odd rumors floating around, though."

"Like what?"

"Oh no, I'm not spreading rumors about a judge. You go ask the judge's clerks like everybody else."

She grinned. "Not to be rude, but I have a lot to do, Tom. What is this about?"

"The judge wants a GAL for the grant. She called me personally and asked, and when a judge asks you for a favor, you do it. I think with your education and background you'd be a great fit. Cara would be good, too, if you don't want it."

"I'm pretty swamped right now. I'm not sure I should put anything else on my plate."

"I'll spread your stuff around. This would be full time for a few months, I would guess. I dunno, if you want some diversity on your CV or something, this would be a good opportunity."

"I'll need to think about it."

"Don't think too long."

She nodded and rose to leave.

"She might've killed her husband," Tom said before she was out of earshot.

"She what?"

"That's the gossip that your delicate ears refuse to listen to. Her husband committed suicide, but the rumor is it wasn't, if you know what I mean."

She nodded, unsure what exactly to say to that. "Just let me check my cases and I'll let you know."

"You do that. But don't take too long. She wants someone by Monday morning."

2

Piper finished her work for the day, and her back was screaming. She tried to correct her bad posture by forcing herself to sit straight backed, but the slouching always returned.

She got her satchel and started heading out when her friend Andi Penny hurried up to her.

"You ready?"

"To go home? Definitely."

"No, we're going to Buzz."

Buzz Junction was a bar that catered to a lot of workers in the criminal justice system. Attorneys, police officers, probation officers, prison guards, and everyone in between would go there to have a few drinks and swap war stories. Piper had never liked bars and liked crowds even less, but she had promised Andi after she begged her to come out with her.

"I really don't feel like it," Piper said as she hit the button for the elevator. "I'm exhausted."

"You promised."

"I didn't promise."

"Yes, you did. Don't be a liar."

She sighed. "Do you feel good forcing your friend to do something she doesn't want to do?"

"Yes."

"Fine. One drink. That's it."

She held up her fingers as though swearing in. "Scout's honor."

They chatted a bit on the elevator down, and then Andi rode it back up because she forgot to gather her things before leaving. Piper normally would have waited for her, but every muscle hurt and a headache was beginning to pound on the inside of her skull.

When she got home to change, she kicked off her shoes, her feet screaming in agony, and wanted nothing more than to have a beer and watch some television, but she really only had one friend, and Andi was it.

She showered and then dressed in jeans and a T-shirt. The temperature outside sweltered at over a hundred, and she took off the jeans and put on shorts. Her grandmother wasn't home, and Piper checked the Post-its on the fridge to see if she'd left a note for her, but there wasn't anything new.

Buzz had a dinner crowd that was different from the night crowd. Dinner seemed to consist of everybody: regular joes coming in for some good food, with a little curiosity toward the cops, GALs, and prosecutors who went there to eat. It had gotten some bad press a few years ago when a man named Henry David Smith killed three young prostitutes, and used to come to the Buzz after and listen in on the detectives and officers talking about it, picking up details of the investigation that weren't made public.

The building was two stories and a VIP area, or just somewhere for people to get drunk without too many prying eyes. Piper had been here a few times and never enjoyed it. Something too casual about the debauchery.

"Hey," she said to Andi and the two men sitting across from each other in a booth near the bar.

Mark Davidson wore a sleek jacket and had his hair primmed and proper. Tom looked like he had just woken up. The scent of alcohol emanated from his breath.

"So," Andi said once Piper had sat down, "I was telling Mark how you were on the news the other day and how hot you looked."

She hoped she wasn't blushing as she said, "It was nothing."

Mark said, "I wanna hear it."

"A man tried to shoot his stepdaughter with his shotgun, but she had taken out the shells the day prior when she sensed something was wrong. When he pulled the trigger and only heard the dry click, the daughter ran and went to a police station. I was her guardian."

"Wow, his own daughter?" He shook his head as he took a sip of beer. "Wish I hadn't asked."

Andi said, "Talking about work was a bad idea, never mind. We came here to get drunk." She rose and held out her hand for Mark and said, "Come dance with me."

"There's no one else dancing."

"We're trendsetters. Come on."

They left Piper and Tom alone. They gave each other an awkward smile, and Tom tapped the glass in front of him rhythmically and said, "You seem distracted."

"Do I?"

"You do."

She shrugged. "I've been thinking about your offer."

"Not my offer. But you know you're gonna ruffle some feathers if you take it. People would step over their own mothers to work with Judge Dawson."

"Why?"

"You need to poke your head out of your cubicle once in a while and actually interact with people, Piper. She's the granddaughter of Warren Dawson, who was one of the founders of Champion Chemical. He died and left it all to his only beloved son, Hope's father, who is going to leave it all to her one day."

"So she's rich?"

"You can't say it like that. She's *rich*. That doesn't begin to describe it. She's going to be a billionaire, Piper. Billion, with a *b*. Do you know if you're a millionaire, you could spend one thousand dollars a day and your money would last you a few years. If you're a billionaire, you could spend a thousand a day for twenty-seven hundred years." He took a long drink and motioned for the waitress to bring another. "But it's not the money, it's the connections. That lady could get anyone a job at any law firm in the country. She's got pull. That's what getting ahead is all about, getting to know people with pull."

"I'm not into politics, Tom."

"If you ever want to climb out of the Lawyer's Dump, you should be into politics."

"I'm too tired to think about it now."

Piper chatted a few more minutes with Tom and then a few more with some detectives she knew from Special Victims, and she managed to last a good half an hour after that. Enough to say that she was there. When she left, her head was pounding and a pain was radiating down her leg from being on her feet so much.

"Where you going?" Andi said when she told her she was leaving.

"My head is killing me."

Andi glanced back to the men and said, "So you might be working with Judge Dawson?"

"I haven't decided yet. And how'd you hear about that?"

"Oh, please. Everybody in our office knows everything about everybody. You've been in front of her, right?"

"No, I've been assigned to Judge Wilcox since I started."

"Oh, well I did a rotation in front of her. You can never get a read on her if she likes you or not. I saw her make a detective cry on the stand. Just break down like a baby and cry. But she's got serious juice in getting her clerks and interns jobs with the fat paychecks. You should kiss her butt for a few months. Never know what it could lead to."

"I'll think about it."

That night, Piper sat with her laptop on the couch and read everything she could find about Hope Leila Dawson.

She had graduated first in her class in both medical school and law school, completing a JD/MD in a little under two years, an unheard of time to finish both degrees simultaneously. There were a few newspaper stories of cases that had appeared in front of her that had gotten media attention, one legal article mentioned her in passing and called her the "Billionairess Judge," but other than that, there was nothing. The judge had no social media, no blogs, no published papers. For someone so prominent, it appeared the judge knew how to stay out of the limelight.

Piper set the laptop down and leaned back on her couch. Sweat trickled down her neck from the heat. She thought about going to the thermostat and turning on the air, but it sounded like too much work right now.

She thought about the judge. If what everyone had said was true, if working with Judge Dawson could help her in her career and provide enough money to fix up her grandmother's house and provide some financial stability in her golden years, shouldn't she do it?

With some hesitation, she texted Tom and said she wanted to look at the case file. Just look.

He texted back, Good choice.

We'll see.

3

Piper settled into the chair across from Tom. He leaned back and said, "Got your other cases spread around to the rest of the team. You should be good for a few months."

"Thank you for doing that."

"No problem. You look nervous. You all right?" Tom said.

"Just . . . something new. Change isn't easy for me."

"I get you. But you gotta play the game to get what you want."

He reached down by his desk and came up with a cardboard box. Inside were files, folders, and discs. "You've worked cases involving homicides, right?"

"Yeah."

"Well, this is a double homicide. There was one survivor, Sophie Grace, who's fifteen. I guess the judge wants to make sure Sophie's protected in all this. It's actually the first case applied to the grant, so you're like a legal astronaut or something."

"Great," she said as she stared at the thick folders in the box.

"Don't sweat it. I'm sure you'll be fine."

She rose, lifting the box, which was heavier than it looked, and said, "Have some reading to do I guess."

—

Piper sat at her desk and slowly took the contents out of the box. It was copies of all the evidence in the criminal case, which was still pending. The murder book, a collection of evidence used by the police to keep track of everything in one file, was thick and took her a couple of hours to read through and analyze.

The basic outline of the case was simple: an unknown assailant had gotten past the Grace family's alarm and video monitoring systems and killed the mother, Emily Grace, first in the hallway, then her son, Sullivan, who probably rushed out to see what was going on. Both bodies were then posed by the front door, leaning against the wall.

Sophie Grace was out at the school dance and didn't come home until later that night. She walked through the front door and slipped on her family's blood before seeing someone in the shadows watching her. She ran.

She got upstairs and jumped out a window before the assailant could get hold of her. A family had found her wandering the streets and talking to herself. A note was made by one of the responding officers who said the girl was confused and in shock and couldn't speak at the hospital. The assailant was gone by the time the police arrived.

Piper glanced at the photographs the forensic team had taken while she read the detective's narrative.

Emily Grace's stab wounds were focused on the face and throat. Fourteen in total. The wounds were ragged, not clean entries like a blade. The ME guessed a Phillips-head screwdriver.

Her son was no different. Twelve stab wounds to the face, neck, and shoulders, many of them on the back side. The detective on the case, a man Piper had never met named Lazarus Holloway, conjectured that the boy was running away while the assailant continued to stab him.

Sophie's injuries were inflicted by the shattered glass of the window and the jump down. Forensics had taken photos of Sophie covered in blood at the hospital. One shot had the teen staring into the camera.

The photograph caused Piper to stop and lean back in her chair. She had read that soldiers left for war with the eyes of boys but came back with the eyes of old men. That's what Sophie Grace looked like.

She went back to the forensic reports.

The blood spatter analysis was good; it was done by John Dante at the state crime lab, who Piper had been on one date with. He was a terrible date, showing up an hour late, taking her to Hooters for dinner, and then miraculously forgetting his wallet when it came time to pay. But he knew blood.

Emily Grace's blood spatter analysis showed the general direction of the stab wounds, but it was so chaotic and disorganized it was difficult to make heads or tails of what happened. Some epithelial cells were found on the walls, possibly by the killer leaning against the wall with one hand for support while he stabbed the woman to death with the other hand.

They assumed the killer was nude so he wouldn't have any clothes to get rid of after the slayings. Some traces of blood had been found in the shower.

No fingerprints, shoe prints, hair, or fiber that wasn't the family's. No bodily fluids or signs of burglary or sexual assault. Nothing from the home appeared to be taken. A few glass fragments were found, but may have been from some broken dish or were tracked into the house by one of the family members.

The "listed suspects" form the detectives were supposed to fill out was blank.

She skipped the autopsy photos.

When Piper had a good sense of what happened, she bought a Diet Coke from the machines on the ground floor and went out to a bench in between the buildings. It was tucked in a corner, away from any entrances and exits, and most people didn't know it was there.

Bees were swarming around vibrant yellow flowers. She watched them for a long time, until Sophie Grace's face began to fade in her mind.

After her soda was finished, she went to Tom's office and took a Post-it note and wrote "I'll do it for now" on it and taped it to his computer screen, the only place in the office that didn't have other things stacked on top of it.

She lifted the box and took it home to read again that night.

4

The next day, Piper wore her best suit, something black and plain she had bought at a secondhand store. Her earrings were silver, and she wore an ichthus necklace on a thin chain. Her grandmother had given it to her on her baptism day, which she had when she was ten since her mother wasn't religious and didn't get her baptized as an infant. Piper had worn it ever since. Even to court, where some attorneys thought it was improper for an officer of the court to show their religion.

She had on little makeup and considered putting some more on, but decided it wasn't worth the time. The day was warm, and the drive to the courthouse was pleasant.

The Lloyd George Courthouse stood at the end of Las Vegas Boulevard, a steel-and-glass beacon against the Strip's glitz. The neon lights reflected off the glass windows of the building.

Inside was a vast atrium, sunlight streaming onto a granite floor. The space was filled with light and shadow.

Judge Dawson's chambers were on the fifth floor. Few people went to the fifth floor: it was reserved for the juvenile courts, which weren't open to the public.

The courtroom was hushed and solemn. Whispers echoed off wooden pews and high ceilings as a family sat waiting for the judge to come out. The respondent, what they called juveniles in court rather than *defendant*—a suggestion made by Dr. Allen Bishop—was a young boy in the orange jumpsuit of juvenile detention.

Piper smiled at the clerk, who was busy typing something, and said, "Excuse me, I'm Piper Danes, I'm with the guardian ad litem. I have a meeting with the judge."

"Head through that door and to the right," she said, giving her a nod.

Piper went through the door she had mentioned. It led back into the hallway where the judge's clerks sat at cubicles. The next door was her chambers.

The door was open, and Piper took in Judge Dawson.

She sat upright at a modern brushed steel desk, a far cry from the large wooden desks the other judges had. Her legs were crossed, and her red suit had gold buttons. Her hair came above her shoulders, one side tucked behind an ear. A bright, almost orange color more than red.

She was signing something and said, "Sit, please," without looking up.

Piper sat in the comfy leather chair and waited. After a few signatures, the judge set her pen down and leaned back casually in her seat. She blinked slowly, watching Piper, and it gave her an uncomfortable jolt in her stomach. Her gaze was piercing.

"Good morning," the judge said.

"Morning," she said with an awkward smile.

"I've seen you before. I attended the *Calhoun* appeal upstairs at the appellate court. It was an interesting issue. Does taking an adult and digitally making them look like a minor before filming pornography qualify as child pornography? Your arguments that it should be regarded as actual child pornography were persuasive."

She cleared her throat softly before speaking. "Well, I lost that appeal, so I don't know how persuasive they were."

"I'm certain those judges made up their minds before any attorney spoke in court. You did a good job."

She crossed her legs the other way, the leather of her chair creaking in the silent room. "You've been a guardian now for almost a year?"

"Yes, Your Honor."

"*Your Honor* is for the courtroom. Proper decorum is *Judge*."

She gave a passive grin and said nothing.

"Nobody becomes a guardian to get rich, especially if they have student loans. You have to have a reason for wanting to be there. Did you actually want to work there? You graduated first in your class and were published while still a law student. I assume you had other offers."

"I did, yes. I wanted to be a guardian."

The judge gazed at her a moment and then said, "If I ask you questions, will you be honest with me? Not the type of honesty most people adhere to, I mean actually honest."

"I'll do my best," she said with another grin and hoped she wasn't blushing.

"Most people leave after a few years of gaining experience. Do you plan to do that?"

"No."

"Why not?"

"I enjoy the work. Plus, I've had experience with them."

"How?"

"My mother lost custody of me when I was nine. A guardian was kind to me when no one else was."

"Did you go into foster care when she lost custody?"

"No, I was adopted by my grandmother."

The judge watched her quietly a moment and seemed, at least for now, satisfied. "I assume you read the case files?"

"I did."

The judge put her hands down on the armrests of her chair, her natural-colored nails shiny and new. She blinked slowly again, something Piper had thought she was doing for her benefit as an intimidation tactic, but then realized that's simply how she was.

"It's a unique case. Survivors in home invasion mass murders like this are rare. Why do you think someone would leave Sophie Grace alive?"

"It didn't seem to be done purposely, from the police reports."

"If she escaped and everyone else died, it's not unfair to assume the murderer let her escape."

"I suppose opinions can differ."

"Yes, they can." She paused. "Assume the killer did leave her alive for a reason. What do you think that reason would be?"

Piper inhaled a quick breath and said, "Narcissistic control maybe. Leaving one person alive demonstrates a type of power."

She nodded but didn't show any reaction. The judge said, "Or maybe he didn't get to finish?" She leaned forward now, her hands moving elegantly in front of her. "I assume you have questions for me about the grant?"

"I do. What exactly will be your involvement, Judge?" she said as politely as possible.

"I will be conflicted out of any criminal cases arising from this incident, of course, but I have full authorization to act on behalf of Ms. Grace. So do you as her guardian. She's our priority. Not finding who did this. That's only consequential if it helps Ms. Grace." She leaned back in her seat. "This hasn't been done before, you know. It's quite thrilling. Seeing the entire system come together to work for the benefit of a child. Have you met Ms. Grace yet?"

"Not yet."

"I would go do that as soon as possible. Before the detectives begin showing up and taking statements without anyone else there."

She picked up her pen again, sliding the documents back toward her. "The lead on the case is Detective Holloway. You should go see him before you visit Sophie. He knows you're coming."

The judge resumed signing the documents, indicating the conversation was over. Piper rose and didn't know whether to say goodbye. It was like the judge had already forgotten someone else was in the room.

5

The Las Vegas Metro Police headquarters had a reception desk that spanned the width of the room, manned by uniformed officers. Behind them, the police department's insignia was up on the wall. To the left, a row of elevators moved personnel through the building, their doors opening and closing with a quiet hiss. To the right, a corridor led deeper into the bowels of the building.

Piper was well acquainted with this police station. When she was a child, Family Services had their offices here and regularly pulled her from her mother's home. Late nights in the station weren't as terrifying because her guardian ad litem was there, giving her hot cocoa and convincing the officers to let her watch cartoons in the break room.

She went to the long desk with police officers behind it and said to the first person that looked at her, "I'm looking for Detective Holloway in Juvenile Crimes."

The officer gave her a quick look up and down and said, "Downstairs, bottom floor, to your right."

"Thank you."

She heard them say something about a "dungeon" as she walked away but didn't quite make it out.

She rode the elevator down. The bottom floor had dim lighting and exposed pipes, and she realized it wasn't a floor but basement storage. It was crammed with junk like old water heaters and emergency generators.

A sign on the wall listed various utility rooms, and on the bottom was white tape with handwritten words:

JUVENILE GRANT

Det. Holloway

Det. Riley

TBD

She went into the room and saw a man standing in front of a whiteboard that was littered with drawings, notes, and taped photographs. In the center was the smiling photo of a young boy of about thirteen.

The man stood with his hands resting on his hips. Dark hair, combed back, met a full beard. Deep-set blue eyes focused intently on the whiteboard. His white shirt, sleeves pushed up, showed arms inked with tattoos. His tie was red and loosened at the throat, but everything about him seemed deliberate.

"Detective?"

"You're Danes, right?" Lazarus said without taking his eyes off the board.

"Yes—"

She almost said *sir*.

Seated at a desk against the far wall was a giant in a gray collared shirt with the LVPD insignia over the breast. His head was shaved on the sides and the top buzzed. His arms stretched the sleeves of his shirt, and his belly hung over the desk like it held a beach ball. He looked taller than Piper sitting down. He casually glanced up at her and then went back to whatever he was doing.

"Danes," the detective said, "you know a psychopath, I'm talking a pure psychopath that doesn't know the difference between right and wrong, life or death, do you know they dream in black and white? Why you think that is?"

She stepped into the room and came closer to him to better be able to observe the board.

She stole a quick glance at him. His eyes were the most striking feature. They held an intensity that was almost disconcerting. He gave off heat like a live wire coursing with electricity.

"Maybe their brains process information differently, so they have altered perceptions in dreams."

"Maybe," he said, moving his eyes over the board. "I like the idea of karma. I know it's bullshit, plenty of bloodthirsty dictators die of old age in their palaces, but I like the idea. Dreams are influenced by personal experiences, and a pure psychopath does nothing but harm. Maybe their dreams are sinister because they're sinister?"

He looked at her for the first time, his gaze focused on hers. "I didn't expect anyone from your office to say yes to working here."

"Why's that?"

"You guardians aren't known for taking on more work than you need to."

"My experience with police officers hasn't been much different."

The giant in the corner chuckled.

Lazarus grinned as he picked up a Styrofoam cup of what looked like old coffee and took a sip. "Just to do our job, we have to be willing to die. Because if we're not, some punk wannabe banger with a nine millimeter tucked in his crotch is gonna know it in a second. Do you have to be willin' to die to sit in a courtroom?"

The giant in the corner held out his fist in the air for a bump, and Lazarus extended his arm.

"I don't dodge bullets, no, but my job's not without risk," she said calmly.

Lazarus looked back to the board, his lower lip tucked under his upper as he gazed at the photo of the young boy. "This boy's twelve years old. Almost killed his two sisters. Put rat poison in their breakfast cereal.

When I asked him why, he said he didn't know, but that he would do it again if we let him out." He removed the photo. "He told me he dreams in black and white."

He tossed the photo in a nearby trash bin.

"What'd ya want this crap post for, Danes? You another lawyer climbing up the judicial ladder to get to the bench?"

"No. I want to help Sophie."

He nodded. "Guess we'll see."

"Now my turn," she said.

"Fair's fair," he said, leaning against his desk.

She looked at the giant and then back to Lazarus. "This case is the murder of two people. It should be in Homicide or Major Crimes. Why is a Juvenile Crimes detective the lead?"

"Homicide kicked it."

"Just like that?"

"I used to be Homicide, I'm a good place to kick it to."

"Used to?"

He gave her a cold glare. "Used to."

She looked at the giant. "And who are you?"

"The big man's Riley, he likes goin' by his last name. He don't talk much. He's a floater on loan from SWAT and Robbery and whoever else needs a door knocked down."

"And if I may ask, why do you two want this crap post?"

Riley spoke for the first time. "I go where they tell me," he bellowed in a voice that sounded exactly like what she thought it would sound like.

Piper looked at Lazarus. "And you?"

"Personal reasons."

"See how you did that? I answered your questions honestly, and you deflected. You got the information you wanted, and I got nothing."

He fully grinned now and crossed his arms. "You got something. Now you know Riley only likes to be called by his last name."

"Is there a problem between us, Detective?"

He uncrossed his arms. "You don't wanna be here, and this is too important for some noob to stumble through, so why don't you run back to representing kids in custody battles and we can pretend this didn't happen."

She kept herself calm and smiled at him with no warmth. "But then I wouldn't have the pleasure of your welcoming company."

She glanced at them both. Riley was giving her his full attention now.

She said, "My degree's in childhood development, and I volunteered to work with abused children at a shelter for almost a decade. I worked with victims on cases even you couldn't imagine. Believe it or not, I may have insights to offer that you could overlook. Collaboration gives better insight into a child."

He took a sip of coffee out of the Styrofoam cup. "Quoting the illustrious Dr. Bishop already?"

"Isn't he why we're here?"

"Is it?"

"Judge Dawson seems to think so."

He gave her a mischievous grin. "Who do you think funded the grant?" He finished the coffee and tossed the cup on top of the photo of the boy. "Well, if you ain't leavin', I'm under orders from the judge to keep you involved in everything, so we gotta go meet somebody. I'll drive."

6

Once a vibrant center, the Old Strip now stood as a faded relic of bygone days. A part of Vegas that was exciting back when the city was ruled by the mob rather than corporations.

Lazarus drove his black Chrysler 300 through the streets of the Old Strip with Piper in the passenger seat. The car was clean and empty, almost like no one drove it regularly. Soft bluegrass played through the speakers, and his car smelled like sandalwood or cedar, something woodsy. A rabbit's foot hung from the rearview on a strip of leather.

While Lazarus was on a call, Piper discreetly googled him. The search yielded scant details, mainly linking him to an old murder case involving sex workers, and the crime beat reporter noted his reluctance to speak to any media. His digital presence was almost nonexistent: no social media, no dating profiles.

Piper reflected on their interactions. Unlike other cops she'd worked with, Lazarus seemed driven by something deeper, as if policing was merely a conduit to something else. It intrigued her, and she wondered if it should have unsettled her instead.

"Who are we seeing?" she asked.

"Followin' up on a call that might be relevant."

"You mind telling me what that is?"

He glanced at her. "Two years ago when I was with Homicide, I caught a case at Ember Lake. Triple murder. One of the vics, Ava Mitchell, was chased through the woods and found torn apart in a tent."

He paused and took a hit off a black vape pen. "Her throat had been ripped out by a screwdriver, just like the Graces'."

"So you think the Graces weren't his first?"

"Could be a coincidence. Stranger things have happened. But a quarter mile away in the woods were some German tourists out camping. They said they saw a hiker five days before the killings heading toward the cabin. They couldn't describe much, but they noticed a tattoo on him. A pig on his calf, covered in blood and with an apple in its mouth."

"What does that mean?"

"Not sure yet. Maybe sometimes a pig is just a pig?"

They pulled into an old casino, Black Diamond, and Lazarus parked in front of the valet. The valet came up and exchanged a few words with Lazarus while Piper got out of the car. As a GAL, she did some investigation, mostly follow-ups and hole-filling of things the police missed that impacted her ward, but she rarely worked with confidential informants and she never met them at shady casinos.

Lazarus started going into the building, and she caught up to him. The casino was filled with gray-blue smoke from the cigarettes at everybody's lips. Some casinos had banned smoking, and so the smokers congregated in the places that allowed it.

They threaded through a casino floor of jingling slots and the roulette wheel's clatter. Piper scanned the early-morning gamblers. Some looked newly awake, their disheveled appearances hinting at a quick transition from sleep to booze and gambling. Others had gambled through the night and just looked tired.

They went to a bar and stood waiting for the bartender to finish serving a few customers on the other end. She wore a sleeveless shirt that revealed the myriad tattoos on her arms, and had a looped piercing on her lower lip. When she came over, she gave them a rushed smile and said, "What can I get ya?"

"Not thirsty," he said, motioning to the badge clipped to his belt. "You Misty Gomez?"

She glanced over to the other bartender and said, "Be right back." She turned to Lazarus and Piper and said, "Not here."

They followed her around the bar and through an employee entrance to the kitchen. Another door through the kitchen led outside to the garbage bins. Two employees were outside talking. They gave Lazarus a few glares and then went inside.

She took a package of cigarettes from her pocket, crumpled and smashed, and pulled one out. Lazarus retrieved a small silver lighter on his key chain and lit it for her. She inhaled a long pull, holding the cigarette between her fingers.

"I'm so pissed at Josh for calling you."

"Why's that?" he said.

"He didn't ask me before he told the cops what I seen."

"He owes me. Just tell us what happened, and we'll be outta your hair," Lazarus said.

She nodded. "Just a guy a few nights ago. He was at the bar and we hit it off, and we went up to the room and I told him my prices and he was fine with it. Then he asked for some things I didn't want to do. I said no and he got pissed, but he calmed down and left. That's all that happened. No reason no cops need to be involved."

"What things did he ask you to do?"

"He said he wanted to pretend . . . to eat me."

"Eat you?"

She nodded. "He had like a knife and fork and other stuff with him and when I saw that I was like no way."

"He said he wanted to physically eat you?" Lazarus said again, trying to clarify.

"Yeah, whatever. Pretending to eat me like food. He said he wouldn't hurt me, just pretend. I've had tricks ask for all sorts a' crazy things. Probably woulda said yes except for the knife."

"What happened after you said no?" Lazarus said.

She blew out another puff of smoke. "I got a deal with one of the security guards. If a trick's in my room and I don't text him when they get there and when they leave, he comes up to check on me."

"Smart."

"He takes fifty bucks a night to do it. He's no knight in shining armor."

"No one is. What happened next?"

"I told him a security guard was coming up and he needs to leave. Then he left and that was it."

"You know his name?"

"He said his name was J. J."

"What time did you meet him?"

"Like ten."

Lazarus glanced at an employee who came through a door and dumped a bucket full of something heavy and wet into the dumpster. "I don't care what you do on your own time, Misty. I'm not that type of police. I just want the information on the tattoo. That's what I'm here for."

"It was nothin'. It was some stupid thing he probably picked off a wall."

"How 'bout you tell me anyway."

She blew out a stream of smoke. "It was a smiley face. You know those yellow smiling faces you see on like shirts and bumpers stickers and stuff? It was like that. Except it had teeth and blood on its mouth. And it had one of those chef hats. His other calf had a pig."

"Describe it."

"It had an apple in its mouth and I think had like blood on it."

Lazarus took out his phone and pulled up photos he had saved in a folder. Piper caught a glimpse and saw a circular cartoon face with sharp, somewhat hidden teeth and a red-stained mouth. A white chef's hat sat tilted slightly on the head. Another photo was of a pig's face with an apple in its mouth.

"This?" Lazarus said.

She nodded. "Yeah."

He took his card and held it out to her. "You call me if you see him again."

She took it. "What the tats mean that got the police up here?"

"It means I don't think he wanted to pretend."

7

Lazarus and Piper waited outside the security room at the casino. It was the brains, the part that held all the security personnel carefully watching each game for any signs of cheating, from both the gamblers and the dealers.

Piper said, "I'm assuming the casino knows their bartenders are working as prostitutes out of their bars?"

He nodded. "They hire the girls as bartenders and waitresses to meet johns. The casino gets a cut of whatever they make on the side."

"That's horrible."

"The girls don't have a pimp beating them every day and get a regular paycheck. The casinos give the tourists what they want. It works for everybody. I don't blame 'em. You do what you gotta do."

"What if what you gotta do is wrong?"

"Look around you, Danes. We're in Babylon. What's right and wrong mean out here?"

Several men dressed in short-sleeved button-up shirts adorned with laminated badges strolled past. They acknowledged Lazarus with curt nods but blatantly disregarded Piper.

"What are those symbols?" Piper said. "The smiley face with the chef's hat and the pig?"

He leaned his head back against the wall. "Those bodies I caught in Ember Lake? I couldn't find much about the pig tattoo online, so I ran it by some guys in Vice to see if it's ever come up. They told me it's a long pig tattoo, and the other one that goes with it is a bloody chef."

"What does that mean?"

"It's cannibalism fetish. Long pigs fantasize about being eaten, and bloody chefs wanna do the eating. You get the ink on your calves."

"Do they mean it literally?"

He took out his vape pen. "Vice never saw a real cannibal, but there's gotta be someone out there that wants to do more than fantasize."

"There wasn't any evidence of cannibalism at the Graces'. Was there evidence at Ember Lake?"

"No. But I think it takes time to work up to. Maybe Misty was supposed to be the first one? Either way, I think the next one we'll probably see something."

A touch of revulsion went through Piper at the thought of *the next one*.

She said, "How can you be so sure Ember Lake and the Graces are connected?"

He looked over to the door of the security room.

"Ava and Adam Mitchell and his girlfriend were stabbed to death with a long Phillips-head screwdriver. All the wounds centered on their face, mouth, and throat. What are the odds, you think, of two groups a' people being killed by a screwdriver by two different assailants in the same way?"

She sat quietly a moment.

He took a hit of the vape pen and then said, "I do think it's interesting that Sophie Grace survived when everyone at the Mitchells' cabin and her mother and brother were killed."

"What's that supposed to mean?" she said, glaring at him now.

"I'm saying she survived. That's a fact."

"She barely survived, and only because she jumped out a window and almost broke her legs."

The door to the security room opened, and a pudgy man with a balding head came out. He held out his hand, and Lazarus shook.

"We got everything cued up for you."

"Appreciate it."

They went into the room. Its walls pulsed with the glow of multiple screens. Servers blinked from metal racks and gave off a digital hum.

Behind a desk, security staff monitored the flickering feeds, trained to spot anomalies amid routine. Swift keystrokes selected camera views and zoomed in on suspicious movements.

They were led to a set of monitors, and on one of them was a crystal clear image in high definition of the bar Misty worked at. The date and time stamp were at just before ten o'clock on Saturday. The employee pressed play.

"What you looking for?" he asked.

Piper spotted Misty almost immediately. She didn't look like she had just now. She wore a skirt and had on too much makeup. Heels that she had trouble walking in from being unaccustomed to them. Piper wondered how long she had been doing this, because she didn't look like a pro.

A man came into view and sat down. Tall and thin, shaggy hair, shorts and a collared shirt. White tennis shoes.

"Can you get me a closer look of that tattoo on his calf?"

"No problem. We can zoom these suckers in close enough to see zits on your face."

The image zoomed in on the calf. Piper leaned in a little closer. It was a smiley face. Swaths of the yellow face were taken up by splatters of dark-red blood, and it dripped from the mouth. A white chef's hat sat on top of its head. The other calf had a pig with an apple in its mouth.

Lazarus snapped a photo of the tattoos, and several more of the man's face as the video played. Then he took out another card and laid it on the keyboard in front of him. "I'm gonna have someone from Cybercrimes come out and get all this. If you see this man again, call me directly."

They left. Out in the hall, Piper said, "That's it?"

"What else would you like to do?"

"I don't know. Get his face out to the public and see if anyone knows him?"

"Cops only do that when they're desperate. We're not desperate. Not yet. We're gonna have IU run his face through their database of known felons and see what comes up first."

He glanced at her as they were walking. "You got another idea?"

"I just think there's higher priority people to speak with."

"Who would you have spoken to?"

"Sophie."

"Well," he said, "no time like the present."

8

The Children's Justice Center stood on a quiet street, its brick facade blending in with the surrounding trees bathed in the midday sunlight. The gentle rustle of leaves in the breeze and a few birds chirping in the branches were the only sounds.

The central edifice had gentle hues, a departure from the cold functionality of government institutions. Inside was a play of colors, a conscious effort to soften the blow of having to stay here because there was nowhere else to go.

For a lot of women and children, it was the only place in the city where violent fathers and husbands couldn't reach them. Piper had been here dozens of times as a GAL, and many times more before that when she worked as a crisis counselor at the local children's hospital.

The first time Piper had come here in her official capacity as a guardian, she was visiting a young boy and his two siblings who had been living in a storage shed with their parents. The kids were eating garbage out of some nearby bins when they were spotted by a couple of patrol officers who were at the scene of a car accident.

The parents were too junked up on fentanyl to notice their children were slowly starving to death.

Piper had to recommend to the court whether to abolish the parental rights of the mother and father. She hadn't slept that night and didn't know what to do the moment in court when it was her turn to speak on behalf of the children. But the parents made it easier for her: they didn't come to their children's parental rights hearing. She asked that their rights be terminated, and the judge agreed. With a single judge's signature, the government took away their children. Piper had never forgotten the children's faces when they were told they wouldn't be going back to their parents. Despite the neglect, there was no one else in the world they knew.

A voice startled her.

"Piper, is that you?"

A kindly old woman named Carol who worked at the CJC as a social worker came up behind them in the lobby. She wrapped her arms around Piper, who hugged her back. The woman pulled away and said, "Where have you been? It's been weeks."

"I had a couple cases up north to handle. How's everything here?"

"Puttering along. Who's your handsome friend?"

He said, "Detective Holloway."

"You have a first name, Detective Holloway?"

The bluntness of Carol's comment made him grin.

"Lazarus."

"Oh, I love that name. Now why would you want to hide that for *Detective Holloway*? Be proud of your uniqueness."

"Yes, ma'am."

Carol looked back to Piper and said, "Who are you here for, dear?"

"Sophie Grace."

A look of concern came over her face, and then sadness. "I was wondering who would be assigned to her. I'm glad it's you." She motioned with her hand and turned away without another word.

Lazarus looked at Piper and then followed behind the two women. The halls echoed with their footsteps. Piper passed by a door and saw a young girl playing with dolls. She had bruising around her cheekbones. Piper glanced back and noticed that Lazarus kept his gaze forward and didn't look into the rooms.

They stopped outside a door near the end of the hall on the second floor. It was closed. Carol turned to them and said, "She's not speaking much, of course, but we got her out of her room yesterday, so at least she's mobile a little bit. Now, if you two upset her, I'm going to have to ask you to leave."

"We won't," Piper said with a warm smile. "Thank you, Carol."

She nodded. "Be gentle with her. This one's . . . just be gentle."

Carol opened the door.

Sitting on the bed looking out the only window in the room was a girl who looked younger than her fifteen years. She had long brown hair and a cherubic, pretty face. Her hair was messy, unkempt, and her ankles looked twisted in odd angles from the way she sat cross-legged with Converse sneakers on her feet.

"Sophie," Carol said, "some people are here to see you."

Lazarus stepped farther into the room and said, "Sophie, it's good to see you again. I wanted to come talk to you about a few things we didn't get to discuss the first time we met. You feeling up to it?"

She looked at him, her eyes weary and red. She blinked slowly and then nervously wrapped her arms around her knees.

Lazarus looked at Carol, whose face was a mask of sadness.

"Sophie, we need to know more about the man that did this to your family. We need you to answer some questions. You think you can do that?"

She didn't say anything and looked down to the floor.

"Sophie, I need to hear you say yes. I need your help."

"Detective," Piper said, "can I see you privately a moment?"

They stepped out into the hall. Though Piper took a few paces away from the door, she kept her voice low.

"She's not a suspect," she said.

"I know."

"You're talking to her like she is."

"Her memory will never be as fresh as it is right now. We need to press her and get as much as we can."

"No."

"She's a witness to a double murder."

"She's also my ward and I'm her guardian."

Lazarus took a step closer to her, his voice low. He didn't meet her eyes, instead fixing his gaze on the floor. "You wanna catch this guy or not?"

"That's not my job. My job is to protect that girl, and I will protect her from everyone. Even the police if I have to."

Lazarus put his hands on his hips as he stared at her. She stared back, and then walked around him and went into the room.

"Sophie, my name's Piper. It's a gorgeous day outside. I'd like to take a walk to that store on the corner and get a Coke. Would you come with me?"

She looked to Carol, as though for approval, and then started getting off the bed.

—

The day really was gorgeous, with a light-blue sky and puffy white clouds scattered from horizon to horizon. They walked along the sidewalk and Piper strolled slowly, getting Sophie's rhythm and pace down so they could walk in a way that made her more comfortable.

"The first time I came here," Piper said, "I went to the little garden in the back and I read a book while I waited to meet somebody. It was one of the most pleasant hours reading I've ever had."

She swallowed and then said nervously, "It's quiet back there."

"It is. But what I like most is that it smells like apples there in the fall." They stopped at an intersection. "Have you explored the center at all?"

Sophie kept her gaze low as she said, "No."

"That's a shame because they have a pretty cool library. Do you like to read?"

She nodded as the light turned and they began crossing the street.

"What do you like to read?"

"Fantasy," she said softly. "I like Percy Jackson."

"I haven't read much fantasy. I liked *Lord of the Rings*."

"It's all right. Kinda too much singing."

They resumed their path on the sidewalk, heading toward a Chevron. Under the store's bright fluorescent lights, Piper thought their skin looked a different tint.

Piper went to the sodas and got two cups, handing Sophie one. She filled her own and waited while the young teen got something fruity. She seemed younger than she was, and Piper couldn't picture her driving a car, though her sixteenth birthday was only a couple of months away.

Piper paid for the drinks, and they went outside. They stood in front of the convenience store, watching a man on a Harley pull up for some gas. The bike was loud and Piper didn't want loud around Sophie right now, so they strolled across the street to a small park. They sipped their drinks slowly in the hot sun.

"I lost my parents, too," Piper said. The girl looked up at her. "I guess more accurately they lost me. My father left when I was young, and my mother lost custody of me, so I went to live with my grandma. She's the one who raised me. I don't know what happened to my dad. He never reached out to me. Do you know where your dad is?"

Sophie shrugged and left it at that.

There was a pause in the conversation before the girl said, "Why did your mom lose you?"

They walked past a small fountain that had the water turned off.

"There's something called neglect, where a parent doesn't meet the needs of their child. Doesn't feed them or clothe them or provide a place to live. She didn't do that for me."

"Do you talk to her anymore?"

She shook her head. "No. If she wanted anything to do with me, she would've let me know by now." She watched the girl. "Your mother and brother weren't like that. They loved you very much. I can tell."

She didn't respond.

"Sophie, you don't have to talk, but I'm here to listen to you. I'm a lawyer appointed by the court to represent you. That means I'm only here to help you. Not to judge you, or to tell you what to do or what to feel. I'm here to listen."

In front of them, a playground bustled with children, watched by mothers chatting on park benches.

Piper settled on a worn bench, Sophie following her lead.

Piper looked at the teen and felt a tug in her heart that almost pained her. She knew exactly what the girl was about to go through.

Her nervous system would have dissociated on the night of her family's slayings and put her in survival mode. She wouldn't feel the full impact of what had happened for a long time, and when it came, it would come in pieces that wouldn't make sense until the whole was revealed in one painful moment. A mess of all the emotions her body wasn't letting her feel would pour out, which could easily lead to addictive behavior, even suicidal behavior if untreated. One young boy Piper had worked with had gone catatonic when he saw his parents die in a car accident that he survived. The boy never spoke a word. The fact that Sophie could even function was amazing, and Piper was impressed with her strength.

"What's going to happen to me?" Sophie said.

"Well, me and you are going to spend some time together, and I'm going to talk to your teachers and friends and follow the investigation into finding the person that did this to your family. That police officer that was with me is going to try to catch whoever this was, and we can talk later about where you can go until you turn eighteen and can live on your own."

"Where would I go?"

"Most kids go to another relative. Your father has no known address or employment, and I only saw your uncle Bill listed, but he won't be able to take you."

"I wouldn't want to go with him anyway."

Piper didn't have the heart to tell her that Bill had told Carol he wasn't interested in seeing his niece, much less taking custody of her.

"Was there anybody else your mom mentioned taking you if anything happened to her?"

She shook her head.

There was a long beat of silence, and Sophie, her arms folded tightly over her chest with her drink set next to her, was unable to look Piper in the eyes when she said, "I saw him. The man that killed my family."

9

Piper sat with Sophie on the bench as she talked. She didn't push or prod, just as she had promised, only listened.

The girl gave descriptions of blood and horror Piper could barely imagine. Remarkably, Sophie spoke without tears, a sign to Piper that she hadn't yet begun to truly process the ordeal.

When she was done speaking, Piper walked the girl back to her room. Sophie's arms weren't folded anymore, and she was talking about how Carol had said when she was ready someone would drive her to school, but she wasn't ready to see anyone from her school yet.

When they got back to the center, Piper walked her to Carol, and before she left, Sophie asked, "When will I see you again?"

Piper smiled warmly at her. "I'll come by tomorrow."

Piper was going to take out a card and give it to her, but it felt too impersonal, so she got a small Post-it note and a pen from the front desk and wrote her name and cell phone number on it. She handed it to Sophie and said, "If you ever need to talk to me about anything, text or call me. I can come down if you need me."

"Thanks," she said shyly.

Piper watched the young girl go up the stairs, and Carol had a wide smile.

"That's the most lively I've seen her since she got here. Thank you for doing that."

Piper glanced up at the teen as she disappeared upstairs. "She's not grieving yet. Will you just keep an eye on her?"

"Of course."

They hugged again, and Piper left the complex and went back to Lazarus's car. He leaned against it with one hand in his pocket and another sucking on the vape device that looked like a small black pen. The scent was smoky leather.

Piper lifted her phone and showed him the notes she had taken. "There was only one assailant. He's about her height, and it was too dark for her to make out any tattoos or skin color. He's right handed, and she thinks he was nude when he attacked her. He had something in his hand that she said could've been a knife or something like it."

Lazarus glanced at the notes and said, "All that from a walk, huh?"

She put her phone away. "You don't know how to talk to children, Detective. What are you doing in Juvenile Crimes?"

He opened his car door. "Let's get a drink."

It was barely lunchtime when they got to the bar. Lazarus maneuvered his sleek car into the dust-covered lot of the Last Chance Saloon. The building was sun bleached, secreted away in the city's corner. It had the scorch marks of too many summers under the desert sun.

It smelled like heated asphalt as she got out of the car.

Inside, the bar was lit by slats of sunbeams slicing through cracks in the blacked-out windows. The creaking floorboards sighed under their weight. Somewhere in the back, a jukebox played Zeppelin.

Lazarus got a place in the corner. The booth was old and the upholstery torn. The bartender, a man that looked like he was part of some biker club, gave him a nod. Lazarus nodded back. The table was sticky as Piper sat down and set her bag next to her.

Lazarus observed her thoughtfully. He had encountered many new attorneys who, like her, dedicated themselves to a cause they felt a deep connection with—the abused, the neglected, the overlooked. They were usually idealistic, driven, kindhearted, and gentle. But he knew that the world didn't discriminate in its cruelty, breaking the gentle and the kind just as easily as the cruel and the wicked.

A server came over with two beers. A brand Piper had never heard of, Midnight Porter. The server was a middle-aged woman with a large burn scar on her hand.

"Where you been, Laz? I haven't seen you in a minute."

"Just tying up some loose ends before summer. It's our busy season. Crime goes up in the summers."

"For real?"

"For real," Lazarus said.

"Well, I'm glad we got you out there protecting us. Lemme know if you need anything else, sweetie."

"Thank you, Kate."

He pushed a beer over to Piper. "Rude to let a man drink by himself."

She lifted the beer and smelled it and read the label: there was coffee in it. A lot of coffee. "You always drink on duty, *Laz*?" she said with a hint of humor.

He guzzled half the beer. "I drink two Midnight Porters every day and have for seventeen years, since before drinking age. I'm not stopping now 'cause a desk jockey sergeant might give me a tongue-lashing."

Piper took a sip of the beer, and her eyes widened in disgust. The bitter taste punched her in the mouth, making her gag and cough. It tasted like stale, fermented coffee with a side of salt. The bitterness was excruciating.

"It's an acquired taste," Lazarus said.

She read the label. "This has more caffeine than two energy drinks. Can you even sleep?"

"No," he said, taking out his vape pen.

They chatted a minute as he finished the first beer and took hers.

Piper said, "So are these people friends or enemies?"

Lazarus leaned back in the booth, resting his head against the upholstery in a dreamy state. "What makes you say that?"

"If they know you well enough to bring your usual, you're either a friend or someone they need to keep an eye on. My guess is they're friends."

"Good guess."

"I was a waitress at a dingy bar through law school. Pay was horrible but tips were okay."

Lazarus subtly nodded his chin in the direction of the bartender. "That's Bass, he owns the place. His son was killed a while back and I caught it. His head had been caved in with a hammer. The kid was only sixteen. Not old enough yet to really piss people off."

"Did you ever find out what happened?"

He nodded as he took another drink of beer. "The universe happened."

"I don't understand."

"Randomness happened. Someone saw him and decided it was a life they wanted to extinguish."

"You never found who did it?"

"No."

"What a waste of youth."

He nodded and stared down at the can of beer. "It's all will to power. Whoever killed him expressed their power, and when I find them, they'll be overtaken by a greater power."

"That's why laws were written."

"Laws were written to benefit the people who wrote them."

"Seems like everyone benefits."

He gave a little shrug. "Some benefit more than others."

The waitress came back and asked if Lazarus needed more beer, and he told her two was enough without the sun setting yet. Piper asked for a Sprite.

"You haven't told me much about Ember Lake. What was it like?"

He hesitated and then spoke. "The two younger kids were bad enough, but Ava was . . . I've never seen a human body so . . . mutilated. Her parents couldn't have an open casket for her 'cause the ME couldn't stitch her together well enough."

He continued to stare down into his half-finished beer as he sucked smoke from the vape. "Odd she's dead but Sophie's still alive, ain't it?"

Piper refused to respond.

"That was good work with her," Lazarus finally said.

He didn't seem like he was used to giving compliments, and Piper didn't embarrass him any further by saying thank you.

Lazarus took a deep swig of his beer before speaking. "So," he began.

"So."

"What's next for you?"

"I've got a slew of interviews lined up with Sophie's teachers. You?"

"I need to have a word with my man that's got the tattoos." He guzzled the remnants of his beer and said, "I think it's time we left. I gotta visit someone that ain't gonna be happy they're seein' me."

10

Lazarus Holloway sat inside a bar at the Black Diamond on the other side from where he had interviewed Misty. He sipped coffee while he waited for the evening shift change.

Misty cleaned up her section of the counter and went into the back before coming out with a handbag. Lazarus rose to follow her. He stayed tucked behind a crowd of Japanese tourists and followed them past the fountain, where Misty took a phone call.

The air outside had a metallic taste from the exhaust of the glittering cars lining the Strip. Drag night, when they could get away with it, which with neighborhood CCTV cameras on the corners and drones in the air wasn't as likely anymore.

Misty went to the silver Ford truck in employee parking, and Lazarus came up to her as she was taking out her keys. She turned off her alarm and opened the door just as he put his hand on it and shut it. It startled her, and she gasped.

"That was some nice bullshit you fed us earlier. Not remembering his name and just giving us J. J."

She tried to open the door, and he held it closed.

"Smart girl like you who pays the security guard to protect her, no way you don't know more about him. I would guess he even took an STD test before you saw him. That's because you're not a real walker, you're a bored housewife. Real walkers don't have a choice in who they take."

"What do you want from me?"

He kept his hand on the door. "Why don't you wanna give me his name?"

"You know what would happen to my business if they knew I gave up their info to the cops? These tricks are all part of their forums and whatever. They all talk. I would have zero. Nothing. No one would see me."

"That sounds like a *you* problem. I want to talk about *my* problem. My problem is I got dead bodies, and the man you took up to your room is who I need to speak to about it."

"He got a little rough. That's it. Tricks do that all the time. All the things they can't do with their wives they want to do with me. It ain't nothin'. And I haven't heard from him since."

"If this man is who I'm looking for, he might see you as a loose end, and men like him, they tend to tie up loose ends."

She took a step back now and leaned toward one hip. "What do I get out of it if I tell you?"

"You'll get busted one day and need someone to ask for. Ask for me."

"Why?"

"You take care of me, I take care of you. That's how it works. Talk to Josh. He'll tell you I always keep my word."

She folded her arms and thought a moment. "Jayden Camden."

"He a regular?"

"I seen him a few times."

"You know where he works?"

She shook her head. "I know he's big into church. Quotes the Bible and stuff. Told me I should come to his service."

"Where at?"

"That big church on the hill by the bus station. I don't know what it's called."

He watched her a moment, seeing if she would open up and say anything else if he kept quiet, but she didn't. He let go of the door and opened it, then held it as she got in and shut it for her.

"If you're lying to me—"

"I'm not."

He backed away as she started the truck, rolled in reverse, and then glanced at him one more time before driving away.

Lazarus gave a quick wave and headed toward his car, which was parked around front.

11

Piper rose early in the morning, her waking thoughts heavy with the fact that the killer was still out there and knew that Sophie had survived. It cast a shadow over her morning, and she had to force herself to put it out of her mind.

She wanted to try to catch the teachers and administrators before school began so she wouldn't have to ask them to come out of class or wait around until class ended so they could talk. People were more receptive in interviews when it was set at a convenient time for them.

Palmwood High School was in the heart of the neon-lit landscape. The school was small and the parking lot packed. Piper had to find street parking.

The interior of the high school had white floors, and trophy cases were lined along each side. Sophie's parents had both gone to high school here, and Piper wondered if there were any photos of them in the display cases.

There was still time before classes started, but some students were already there. Huddled against the walls with earbuds in, preparing for the day of reckoning that was about to begin.

She remembered her own high school experience, and it left an unpleasant taste in her mouth.

She took two wrong turns and then found the teacher's lounge where Sophie's homeroom teacher had agreed to meet her. A man in a collared shirt and slacks sat at a table in the small room. He was older than Piper, but not by much.

"Mr. Tate? I'm Piper Danes. I'm from the guardian ad litem's office."

"Right. Thanks for meeting me before class."

"It's not a problem. May I sit?"

"Of course."

She sat across from him at the small round table with four chairs. A fridge was pushed against the wall, and what looked like a bar, complete with stools, had two coffee makers behind it and small bins of snacks like peanuts and pretzels.

"How is Sophie?" he said.

"She's as good as can be expected."

He shook his head. "It's sickening. She's such a vibrant girl. I doubt she'll ever be the same after this. Do they know who did it?"

"No."

He nodded and looked down to his coffee. "Tell her I'm thinking about her, will you?"

She gave a half smile and said, "I will."

"So," he said with an inhale, "what did you want to know?"

"I'm trying to get a sense of Sophie and everyone in her life. Did you know her well?"

"Somewhat. I had her in several classes, but she wasn't the type to go out of her way to talk to anybody."

"What do you mean?"

"She was painfully shy. When I'd call on her for something, her face would turn bright red."

"How did she seem to you in the few weeks preceding her family's murder? Did she seem distracted at all? Maybe hostile, or the opposite, withdrawn?"

He shook his head. "No. She was great. Always was. Quiet and did her work."

"Who did she spend her time with at school?"

"You can't just ask her?"

"Yes, well, sometimes children don't give you full answers, as I'm sure you know."

"Oh, yeah, I know. Talk to Chloe Ard. I think she's Sophie's best friend. She can give you more info about her than I can."

Piper wrote the name down in a small pocket-size notebook with a blue pen. "Um, I've looked at Sophie's records and didn't see any behavioral issues that needed to be addressed."

"No, when I say she's great, I mean it. She does her work and keeps her head down. Texts a little too much in class, but what teenager doesn't?"

"Did you ever get to see Sophie under stress? Perhaps she was failing or something along those lines and you spoke to her about her grades?"

"Yeah, there was one class she struggled with last year and I talked to her about it."

"How did she respond to that stress?"

He shrugged. "Fine. She cut out some activities and focused more on the work and pulled her grades up. I'm telling you, if you're looking for some troubled kid, it just isn't there."

"No, what I'm looking for is to maximize her well-being given the circumstances. Speaking of which, when she is ready to come back to school, do you have adequate academic and emotional support for someone in her situation?"

"It's a small school with an even smaller budget thanks to the county, but yes, I will personally make sure she has counseling and that a counselor will be monitoring her."

"Thank you."

He nodded. "I've never dealt with a guardian before. I thought this would be more like a deposition or something."

"No sir, I'm just trying to get a sense of who she is and how best to help her."

"Well, in that case I'll do whatever I can. You need anything from the school, reach out to me and I'll get it done."

She gave him a pleasant grin, though something had gone off in her. A little pinprick in her gut that what he had just said somehow wasn't what he had meant. "You cared for her?"

"Yeah, I guess. She was a great student. Some of these kids wouldn't cross the street to spit on me if I were on fire, and some of them are these sweet souls you don't want to get hurt. She was one of the sweet ones."

"Did you know her family at all?"

"I didn't know Sullivan. I would've had a class with him next year. I knew Emily and Paul. We went to school here together."

"Really? You didn't mention that on the phone."

"You didn't ask." He sipped his coffee. "We went to a couple dances and I asked Emily out, but she wasn't into me. She always liked Paul. He was kinda the wild one. When she met him, I was happy for her, but I really didn't think they should be together. I knew it wouldn't end in a happily ever after."

"What do you mean by Paul being a wild one?"

"Just sneaking in liquor to the school, smoking joints in the bathroom, drag racing, stuff that today kids do all the time but back then didn't happen much."

"Did you stay in touch after graduation?"

He shook his head. "She ended up getting some administrative job for the government, and Paul went to college up north. We didn't talk after that."

"Do you know much about what happened between Paul and Emily?"

"Just gossip. I do know Paul didn't take anything when he left. Just woke up one morning and ran off."

"Do you know why?"

"Why does anyone do anything?"

"Can you share anything about her parents that might not be in the case file?" she asked.

He took a moment, fingers tightening around his mug. "Emily was an addict, struggled with Oxy her whole life." His voice trailed off as he shook his head. "Makes me think . . . maybe someone she got pills from . . . I just don't know."

Piper felt a wave of sadness wash over her. The scars of her own mother's addiction had deeply etched into her being, its tangled roots embedded in her psyche. She had watched addiction consume her mother, coloring every subsequent experience of her she ever had. She wondered if Sophie had endured a similar pain.

"Did she ever mention that she was worried about Sophie at all?" Piper said.

"For what?"

"I don't know, it's why I asked," she said with a pleasant smile.

"I don't know. Like I said, we didn't talk anymore."

He finished his coffee and then stood up. "I have class in a minute. Maybe we can finish this later?"

"That's actually all I had for now. Um, would anybody mind if I wander around the school a bit?"

"Not at all. Grab a visitor pass from the front desk."

"Thank you for your time, Mr. Tate."

"Call me Bryce. And let me know if you need anything else."

Piper left and wandered the corridors, her mind awash with childhood memories she had briefly suppressed during the interview. Now, they surged back, unstoppable. Her grandmother's words echoed in her thoughts, teaching her not to shun these memories, but to acknowledge them, to name them, and to move forward.

Her experience had showed her that often, beneath the surface of violence lay the core issue of drugs. Violence was a by-product. She knew she had to discuss with Lazarus tracking down Emily Grace's dealers. It was entirely possible this was retribution, a deal gone bad, or who knew what else.

Classes were getting ready to start, and students were piling in through the doors of the school. The metal detectors would occasionally go off, and the school officer would have to search a backpack or bag. How different, she thought, these kids' high school experience was from her generation's.

She stopped at the front office for a hall pass and asked in which classroom she could find Chloe Ard. The receptionist looked it up for her and said it was customary for the school officer to be at any interviews with students that didn't involve their parents.

"He'll be done in a minute," she said. "You can just have a seat."

"Thank you."

The school officer, a large Polynesian man with beautiful tattoos on his forearms, came in a few minutes later and said, "You page me, Nancy?"

"Would you mind taking her to see a student in Ms. Yen's room? Chloe Ard? She's Sophie Grace's lawyer."

"Sure."

Piper rose, and the officer shook hands and smiled. He opened the door for her as they went out into the hall.

"Thank you."

"No problem. So you're a lawyer, huh?"

"I am."

"This all you do? Work with kids?"

"It is. You?"

"Yeah," he said as the final students who were lingering in the halls ran to class. "Some officers, they don't like it. I like it. The kids are funner than adults."

They came to a classroom not far from the front office and he poked his head in and waved to a young girl in the front. She had a blond streak in her brunette hair and wore a jean skirt with a white blouse.

"How you doin', Chloe?" the officer said.

"I'm okay."

"This is a lawyer helping Sophie. She wanted to talk to you." He motioned with his head toward a small alcove with vending machines. "I'll be over there if you need me."

"Thank you."

Piper took a few paces away from the classroom, and Chloe followed her. She had a look Piper had seen dozens of times: when an authority figure—or at least who the children thought was an authority figure—came to speak to a child, the child always thought they were somehow in trouble.

"Chloe, my name's Piper, and I'm Sophie's appointed legal guardian. I'm trying to understand what she needs so I can help her. I was told you were her best friend?"

"Yeah. Is she okay? She doesn't answer my texts."

"I would maybe give her some time."

She folded her arms as she strolled next to Piper. "I miss her."

Piper kept her gaze down to the floor. The school had quieted now.

"When it's time, she's going to need you, Chloe. She doesn't have anyone else left."

The teen nodded but didn't look at her.

"So Sophie hasn't talked to you since it happened?"

She shook her head. "No. We held like an assembly to talk about what happened. I texted her right after and told her I loved her and she never texted back."

"Do you two hang out in a group or just the two of you?"

"Just us. Sophie doesn't like the other girls here."

Just as she said that, they passed a classroom where a group of girls were standing at the front hanging out because the teacher wasn't there. They could've been clones of each other, dressing and acting exactly like everyone around them. She knew the type and could understand Sophie better by the fact that she wanted nothing to do with them.

"Have you talked to Jason? He was her date."

"Not yet. Why?"

"He's homeschooled, so he doesn't go here. I don't really know him."

"How did Sophie meet him?"

"I think they took some class together or something. Her mom was always putting Sophie into those art classes after school."

They had circled the hall and kept walking.

"How long have you known Sophie?"

"All her life. We went to elementary school together."

One of the main risks Piper had seen in a situation like Sophie's was of self-harm and suicide. It was always on the forefront of her mind whenever dealing with children that had been through massive trauma.

"Has she ever hurt herself that you know of? Maybe cutting or burning herself?"

"She wasn't like that. I know a lotta girls that cut, but she wasn't like that."

Piper asked a few more questions and then left the school. She sat in her car and was about to call an investigator at her office but stopped and instead took out the card Lazarus had given her. She called him, and he didn't answer. She didn't leave a message, but a second later he called back.

"Hey," she said. "Did you talk to Sophie's date for that night? Jason Graff?"

"Yeah, not much there."

"What do you mean?"

"He dropped her off in a car with four other people inside. It's not him."

"That wasn't what I was asking."

"What were you askin' then?"

"I want to know how to help her, and the only way to do that is to talk to everybody that knows her. I need to be kept apprised when you interview people in her life."

"Well, we gotta go do somethin', so come down and meet me at the Dungeon in an hour and I'll keep you *apprised*."

"Do what?"

"We're goin' to church."

12

Piper pulled up to her grandmother's house around noon with take-out sushi. Her grandmother, isolated in her own world, had barely any friends and even fewer relatives who kept in touch. Piper was her lifeline—without her, her grandmother often neglected to eat, lost in the solitude of her days.

"Grandma?" she called out.

Her grandmother's voice carried from the patio. Piper followed and came out to the backyard, which showcased the sprawling golf course.

The HOA had decreed that no homes in the area could be more than one level to preserve the view. The sky unfolded like a vast, clear canvas.

Piper eased into a chair at the outdoor table, the cool breeze ruffling her hair. Across from her, her grandmother clicked her laptop shut. The sight of her grandmother's gnarled fingers, succumbing to the early stiffness of age, gave her a tug of sadness.

"You really don't have to bring food all the time like I'm helpless, dear."

Piper passed over a container of sushi and chopsticks. "I don't want you overexerting yourself in the kitchen. I'd rather you take it easy."

"You're too young to spend your time with an old woman. You should be out there looking for a good man to spend your life with."

"It feels like it's not worth it sometimes."

"What happened to that man your friend set you up with?"

She shook her head as she put a piece of sushi in her mouth.

"He mentioned a book I like, and I started talking to him about it and he got uncomfortable. It was like he didn't want his date knowing as much as him."

Her grandmother moved the laptop aside with a knowing grin. "To some men, everything is a threat."

Piper exhaled and stared up at the blue sky. She used to lie out here on the golf course when she was a kid, hoping there was someone staring back at her up in the stars. The idea that they were alone in the universe never sat well with her. *Someone* had to be there—God, aliens, someone.

She shoved another piece of sushi in her mouth and stood. "I have to run. I'll be back for dinner."

"Where you going?"

"Apparently church."

Piper went back to the police station and waited by the elevators. There was a line, and she preferred getting exercise anyway, so she took the stairs the three flights down to the Dungeon.

The custodian, Henry, was near the elevators getting something out of a utility closet.

"Hello," she said.

"Hello yourself, young lady."

She entered the Dungeon and stared at the three desks arranged inside. It looked like college students occupied the space.

Better than a cubicle, I guess.

She looked at the whiteboard. Everything that had been up about Lazarus's previous case had been taken down and the board wiped cleaned.

In the center of the board now were two striking images: Sophie's school portrait and a snapshot of Ava Mitchell, her arm lovingly draped around her younger brother, both radiating joy. Surrounding these were contrasting images: pre- and postmortem photos of Ava's brother and his girlfriend, grim crime scene snapshots, and in one corner, unsettling digital renderings of the long pig and the bloody chef. Sophie's mother and brother were captured in a single, poignant photo. It showed Emily Grace clutching her son close, his face alight with a broad smile even as he wriggled in her embrace.

Piper's experience with cases of cannibalism or similar fetishes was nonexistent. To her, it felt as distant and improbable as lightning striking: a bizarre anomaly in some far-off place. The absence of cannibalism at the crime scenes bolstered her belief that this case was something else.

The sound of the elevator doors opening broke her train of thought. Lazarus entered, sharing a brief exchange with the custodian before stepping into the room.

"It's like riding an elevator to the gallows, ain't it?" he remarked.

"I've seen worse." Piper turned from the haunting images on the board and perched on the edge of her desk. "I need a favor. I need you to find someone for me."

"Who?" Lazarus asked.

"Emily Grace was hooked on oxycodone, and probably had a dealer."

Lazarus pondered for a moment. "No criminal or drug treatment record on her."

"Addiction's a hidden disease," Piper said, "and people can be masters at hiding their diseases."

He nodded. "I'll find 'em for you."

"Thanks."

He grabbed his jacket off the back of his chair and put it on. "You wear that Gospel guppy around your neck every day, Danes? You a woman of faith?"

"I am."

"Good," he said while straightening his tie. "'Cause I don't know how to talk to these people."

The church sat outside downtown Vegas up on a hill overlooking the valley below. As Lazarus drove up the hill, the silhouette of the church came into view against the backdrop of the midday sun. The building was brown and off-white, and the wooden cross at the top looked like a skeletal remnant.

"I know this church," he said as they parked in front. "The Good Lord dropped the roof on some of his worshippers 'bout ten years ago. They rebuilt it and came right back worshipping what saw fit to crush Grandma and Grandpa under wood and brick."

"I can see why you'd want me out here talking to these people."

Piper followed him up to the church. He stood out front with his hands on his hips, staring at the cross.

One of the doors was held open by a brick on the floor. A man worked on something down the hallway, and he noticed them and came out. He looked haggard, tired, with dark circles under his eyes. He smiled warmly.

"I was surprised you called from Vegas. Usually they ask the local police to do whatever they need done," the man said.

"I like to look people in the eye when I'm speaking to 'em."

"I know exactly what you mean. It's a lost art with all this technology mucking up our brains."

"Amen to that, Reverend."

He glanced at Piper and said, "Reverend Jack Husso. Nice to meet you."

"You as well."

He looked at Lazarus. "So you said you needed to talk about one of my congregation?"

"You have somewhere we can sit?"

"Sure. Come in."

They followed him into the church.

It was still and quiet, not even creaking wood. The stained glass windows, probably majestic at some point, looked like faded mosaics now. The pews were worn out. The entire place smelled like dust. Piper liked the old church.

Behind the podium was a small door that led to some offices. The reverend went into one that had a nameplate on it that said "Reverend Husso."

Two chairs were set before his desk, and he motioned for the pair to sit. He sat behind the desk. There were photos up on the walls, the reverend with various figures from around the city. Paintings of scenes out of the Bible.

"So, what can I help you with, Detectives?"

"She's a lawyer."

"Oh," he said, looking at Piper with just a hint of disappointment in his face.

"How well do you know Jayden Camden?" Lazarus said.

"Fairly well. He's been coming here for seven years. Quiet man, keeps to himself. Have you been out to see him?"

"I went to his apartment. No one was there, and all the blinds were drawn. There's no employment listed for him. What does he do?"

"He's on disability. He can't work. Occasionally the church helps him out with some cash here and there."

Lazarus grinned.

"What is it?" the reverend said.

"You should ask him what he spends that money on."

Reverend Husso looked like he took offense, and Piper quickly spoke up. "Does he have any family that you know of?"

The reverend took his eyes off Lazarus and turned to her. "His mother, but other than that I don't think he's close to anyone."

Lazarus said, "I noticed a few convictions on his rap sheet."

The reverend watched him a moment. "Detective, whatever it is you're looking at him for, you're wrong."

"And why's that?"

He ran his fingers softly over the desk. "You a man of Christian values, Detective?"

"I was raised as such, but I'm not, no."

"Then you may not understand the power of redemption."

"Oh, I understand power, Reverend."

"How do you mean?"

"There's eight billion people in the world, which means there're eight billion perspectives all fighting for power."

"You don't sound like someone raised with Christian values."

"Values are like laws: created by the people they benefit most."

Piper tried to interject, but Lazarus quickly got in, "Christian values began with slaves in Rome who pushed charity, humility, and kindness 'cause those values empower the weak."

The reverend smiled and said, "Luckily we've come a long way since then."

"You certainly have. You take the most hardened atheist and you ask him 'What's morality?' They'll spit words like charity, humility, kindness—all Christian values. It doesn't even cross their minds there's other types of morality. The Romans thought a man was entitled to kill his family if he desired. A Viking who refused to rape and murder was told they wouldn't be allowed into Valhalla. Their morality wasn't more wrong than ours, just different."

The reverend looked him in the eyes. "Sometimes, Detective, the people that have the most faith reject it the hardest."

"You got me wrong, Reverend. I don't reject it. I'm a great admirer of Christianity. When even atheists are Christian, I'd say Christianity's just about won the power game, wouldn't you?"

Reverend Husso gave a weary smile and said, "Someday, Detective, you'll find that cold logic isn't enough of a reason to get up in the morning."

Piper glanced between the two men.

"We just want to talk to this man, Reverend Husso," she said, trying to get the conversation on track. "He has information we think might be useful. We're not looking to get him into any trouble unless we have to."

The reverend gave a single nod. "I think you're barking up the wrong tree, but if you think it'll help to talk him, I won't stop you." He brought a notebook near and took a pen out of a cup on his desk that had "World's Best Dad" etched on the side in a child's handwriting.

"This is his mother's address," he said as he wrote. "It's where he stays."

"What about his apartment?" Lazarus asked.

"He's just running out his lease. He's on the sex registry and can't stay there anymore because there's children in the complex now. But you already knew that."

He slid over the piece of paper with an address and name on it. Lazarus glanced at it and then folded it and put it in his pocket.

"Appreciate your time, Reverend," he said, rising.

They began to leave when the reverend said, "Detective Holloway . . . the scriptures tell us that a man who dwells in unbelief stumbles in darkness. Just something to keep in mind."

"Don't kid yourself, Reverend. We're creations without a creator. We're all stumblin' in darkness."

13

Piper sat in the passenger seat of Lazarus's car. I-215 was at a standstill because of an accident, and Lazarus turned on some soft bluegrass music.

From her work, she had friends in the police department and had reached out to one, asking about Lazarus. Her friend had texted her back just now and said Lazarus kept to himself, but she knew something had happened that got him kicked out of Homicide, though she wasn't sure what.

"Do you really believe what you said to him?" she said. "All that about morality and power?"

"It's not about belief, it's about truth."

"Even if the truth makes you miserable?"

"Especially if the truth makes you miserable." He changed lanes to get off the freeway. "I haven't eaten since yesterday."

They pulled into a diner meant for people driving through Vegas to California. Truckers and families and residents who drove hours for work because they couldn't find anything closer.

The diner had a neon sign that didn't work. Inside was checkerboard linoleum and red vinyl booths. It smelled like frying bacon.

They were seated by a young woman in jeans and a tank top. She kept glancing at Lazarus and asked him if he was doing anything fun today.

"No," he said flatly without looking at her.

They were by a window that looked out to the dirt and gravel, the dust kicking up in thin puffs as a truck rolled out of the lot and headed back to the freeway.

Lazarus ordered black coffee and fried eggs and bacon. Piper asked for a soda and a tuna sandwich.

"You didn't seem like a fan of the reverend," she said.

"The priestly class has always taken advantage of the desperate. I understand why they do it, but that doesn't mean I have to like 'em."

"I don't know, I think he believes in what he preaches."

"Every priest in history believed what they preached, they just didn't know why."

The server brought their drinks.

"I had a ward who ended up taking her own life," Piper said. "I went to her funeral. Her father wasn't religious. He was down on his knees crying over the casket. He thought he would never see his daughter again. The mother was still a believer. She sat quietly in her chair with tears running down her cheeks, but she had this grin on her face. Like she just knew she would see her daughter again. You would say that father was accepting truth, but I just saw needless suffering."

"You drank the Kool-Aid, too, Danes? Why do you assume suffering is bad? Maybe that's all we're meant to do?"

"I refuse to believe that."

"The truth don't care what you believe."

The food came. The lettuce was wilted and the mayonnaise on her sandwich looked yellowish. She pushed the plate away from her.

"You get anything from the teachers?" Lazarus said, biting into his greasy bacon.

She shook her head. "Not really. She didn't seem to interact with them unless she had to."

"Anybody say or do anything odd?"

"Odd? No. There was one teacher that tried to date Sophie's mother in high school and got rejected, but that's about it."

"Get me his name. I'll check him out, too."

Lazarus shoved half an egg in his mouth with a fork and then took a bite of toast and leaned back in the booth as he chewed. He didn't seem to enjoy the food. It was more like he knew he needed sustenance and took some in.

"So you really think this man might be a cannibal?"

"I don't know," he said with a shake of his head.

"Why haven't you let it out to the public yet?"

He took another large bite of egg and toast before putting his fork down.

"Saying you got a cannibal isn't like saying you got a murderer. It touches something deep down. Something primitive. The thought of being eaten. People get scared, and when people get scared, they do dumb things."

"What else do you know about this cannibal-fetish community?"

He took a bite of bacon and then, as though some switch inside him had said he'd had enough nutrition, he placed the rest down.

"The fetish is called vorephilia. *Vore* from the word 'carnivore.' It's not literal—usually. Most people see it as something new and kinky to try. I talked to a married couple that have a spit in their basement and pretend to roast each other over it, but no one's hurt."

He wiped his hands with a napkin and tossed it onto his plate.

"I don't think he's worked up to the act yet, but he will."

14

The address the reverend had written down was in a town not far over the California border. Lazarus knew he had no jurisdiction there unless he was in hot pursuit across state lines, but it didn't matter. When he flashed the badge and began asking questions, few people asked if he was a cop in the state where they lived.

Lazarus's car rolled through the worn-down neighborhood, past faded houses hunched with neglect. He pulled up to a house in a cul-de-sac. Its picket fence was weathered and gray. A leafless oak tree stood to the side of the house.

Gravel crunched underfoot as they crossed the driveway and got to the sagging porch that creaked under their weight. A rusted swing swayed with a breeze.

Lazarus knocked and stared at the porch as he waited. Piper glanced up at the old home. Prefabricated and falling apart.

The sound of a chain sliding from its groove and then the door opened. A frail, elderly woman stood in a blue nightgown.

"Afternoon," Lazarus said.

"Afternoon," she said, her voice steady and calm.

"We'd like to talk to Jayden if we could, please."

"He ain't here."

"When will he be back?"

"He won't. He—"

Lazarus didn't hear the rest of what the woman was saying. His attention was on the sound of something sliding across metal and catching because there was friction. A window. He leaned over to Piper and whispered, "Keep her talking."

He wandered off the porch, and Piper stumbled with her first couple of words before she asked the mother about where they could possibly find Jayden.

Lazarus rounded the house. There was a dilapidated chain-link fence in the back. He could see a taller man in shorts and a T-shirt with bare feet heading toward the fence. Tattoos on his calves.

"Police, stop!"

Jayden Camden looked back, his eyes going wide as Lazarus and he locked gazes.

Jayden burst into a sprint, his arms churning as he tore through the backyard. With youthful agility that Lazarus knew he himself didn't have, Jayden vaulted over the fence. Lazarus pursued him, swiftly shedding his jacket and discarding it onto the lawn before jumping the fence.

Between the houses, a dirt path led to a cracked sidewalk. Lazarus tracked Jayden's sharp turn onto it and kept going, pumping his arms and pounding the pavement.

Cars stretched along the road, and families populated the sidewalk, immersing themselves in the Rockville Zucchini Festival. Festive carts and vibrant tents adorned the streets, forming bustling queues of people waiting in long lines.

Jayden shoved two men aside, their shouts trailing behind him. Lazarus sprinted through the crowd, chest burning. He zeroed in on the tall figure ahead. Jayden tossed a display case behind him, forcing Lazarus to leap over it. Close enough to shoot, he kept his gun holstered.

By the curb, kids were looking at toys. Jayden grabbed the stand and knocked it down hard, making moms and kids shriek. The big stand and the children and families blocked the way. Lazarus went through a taco tent and came out the back.

Jayden made a break for an open bus with Lazarus right behind him. As the rear doors began to close, Lazarus lunged and managed to leap on the steps just in time. The doors clamped onto his arm, sending a sharp pain through him. With a forceful push, he pried the doors open with a crunch and jumped onto the bus.

Jayden, unaware of Lazarus entering through the back doors, was shoving his way toward the rear of the bus. When he saw Lazarus, he had no time to react before Lazarus charged, tackling him around the waist. They crashed onto the grimy floor.

Lazarus cuffed Jayden's wrist to a nearby seat's metal beam and stood, watching him intently, breathless. Jayden briefly struggled with the cuff before relenting and reclining on his back, his breaths labored.

All eyes, including the wide-eyed, silent bus driver, were fixed on Lazarus. Lazarus nodded toward Jayden and said, "He didn't pay for a ticket."

15

The Dungeon had no spare rooms for interviews unless they wanted to do it in a utility closet, so Lazarus chose an interview room tucked on the second floor. Few went to that section of the floor because it was reserved for Major Crimes and Homicide, which consisted of only a handful of elite detectives, so the hustle of other floors wasn't evident there.

Piper rested against the wall of the elevator and watched Lazarus. He was leaning with one shoulder and staring at the floor, lost in thought. The elevator doors opened, and they stepped off.

An officer with wide shoulders and gray hair stood above a desk flipping through a file.

"Got your man in interview two."

They walked by the detectives' offices. Piper quickly peeked into one. A man sat quietly, looking out the window, his desk and chairs buried under a mess of files and papers. He looked like he had a hand-tailored suit and an expensive watch.

The interview room was better than Piper expected. A clean carpet covered the floor. A big table sat in the middle, with lots of black, comfy chairs around it. Through the windows, she could see the busy streets below.

Jayden Camden sat at the end of the table, shackled to the floor's O-ring used for security during interviews. The one-way glass didn't draw his attention.

"I need to talk to him alone," Lazarus said, his eyes never leaving Jayden, who was sitting with his arms folded.

Lazarus went into the room. He ran his fingertips over the top of the table, but his eyes never left Jayden's. He sat down across from him.

"I have this recurring dream, Jayden," he said in a low whisper. "I'm walking and there's this hole in the middle of the world. I'm right at the edge and the hole's getting bigger, and it feels like I'm spending my life just tryin' not to fall in."

Jayden lifted his eyes. He tried to seem calm, but his fear was loud in the quiet room.

Piper saw a camera in the corner on the ceiling but couldn't tell if it was on or not.

"That hole don't leave. It follows you . . . and whenever you look back and think you're gonna see blue skies, you see a bigger hole. And now it's looking to swallow you up." He stared the man in the eyes. "I bet it's been looking to swallow you up for a long time."

Jayden looked down.

"It was just you and your mama growin' up, wasn't it?"

He didn't respond.

"I didn't see anything about your pop other than his rap sheet. Did you know him?"

He glanced up at him now and said softly, "No."

"My father was the opposite. He was always there, always willing to spend time. It was my mother that ran off on him. Probably hard to picture with your mother. She seems like a tough lady. Willing to stick it out for the people she loves."

"She is a tough lady."

One corner of Lazarus's mouth lifted in a small smile. It was quick, barely there.

"Must've been hard for her to see you in juvenile court so much."

He kept his head down. "They told me—"

"That those records are sealed? They are for most people. I have permission to see things like that. I'm not judging you, Jayden. What's youth for if not to act like an idiot?" Lazarus reached into his pocket and came out with some cigarettes.

"You want one?" Lazarus said.

"No."

He held the cigarette out for him. "Give it a try. If ever there was a time to calm your nerves . . ."

Jayden stared at it but didn't move.

"Take it, Jayden."

His hand came up slowly and took the cigarette. Piper could see what Lazarus was doing; establishing a power dynamic where he had subtly forced Jayden to do something he didn't want to do.

Lazarus lit the two cigarettes. He seemed at ease with a cigarette in his hand, though Piper had never seen him smoke anything but a vape pen.

Jayden brought it up slowly to his lips, concern etched on his face as he inhaled a drag and coughed.

Lazarus waited for him to stop.

"Did your mama ever get remarried?" Lazarus asked.

He shook his head, staring down at the cigarette, which he didn't seem to know what to do with.

"Why not?"

"She said she didn't want to. She just wanted it to be us."

"That's a good mama right there."

"Is she here? I wanna see her."

"Yeah, we'll get her down here for you."

"Thank you," he said with relief.

Lazarus blew out a stream of smoke from his nose. There was no ashtray, as smoking in a government facility was banned now, but there was a watercooler in the corner with paper cups. He got two cups and placed one in front of Jayden. He set the other one down in front of him and ashed into it.

"Did you see that new Jeffrey Dahmer show on Netflix?" Lazarus said.

Jayden swallowed and looked down into his cup without moving.

"No," he said.

"It was good. See, I always thought he was just insane, but now I'm thinking he didn't have a choice. He liked what he liked and no one, not even him, knew why."

He inhaled softly on the cigarette.

"I noticed the tattoos on your calves. What are they?" he asked.

"Just anime characters."

"Now that ain't true, is it, Jayden? I've seen 'em before."

He said nothing.

"It's all right. I understand. But tell me about 'em. What do they mean?"

"You already know that."

Lazarus nodded. "So, is the fantasy you getting eaten or doing the eating?"

"I'd never really do it. I just acted it out a few times."

"With prostitutes?"

He nodded. "I'm on the forums. No one really does it. *No one.* It's just fantasy. Like when people have foot fetishes, nobody looks at them for stealing shoes or whatever. But because of what we like, everyone thinks we're into hurting people. We're not."

"You on the forums a lot?"

He nodded.

"Let's assume for a second you're tellin' the truth. The man I'm after, I think he's a chef but not like you. It's not fantasy for him. I think he's going to do it. Can you think of anyone I should be looking at in the forums?"

He shook his head.

"What about Reddit and 4chan? Anyone ever talk like that? In a way that maybe has other people wondering if they're serious or not?"

He didn't respond for a second and then nodded.

"Who?"

"I don't know his name. He just has a screen name. BloodyChef77."

"What is it about BloodyChef that made you think of him?"

"He doesn't talk like it's a fantasy. He talks like he's done it before. Just, like, detailed stuff about what he's done. He lives here, it's a Vegas forum."

"I'll need to know everything about that forum and him." Lazarus slid over the legal pad and said, "Start writing." He rose and came outside. He stood next to Piper as they watched Jayden writing down information.

"He could be lying," Piper said.

"I don't think so. He's too scared. I'm gonna send Riley to check out where he was on the dates we're lookin' at, but I don't think this guy could kill anybody. He doesn't have the fortitude." He looked at her. "I need to get BloodyChef's information."

"I can draft a subpoena and get it from the ISP providers."

He said, "You sure you wanna see how deep this rabbit hole goes, Alice?"

"I'm here, aren't I?"

16

Piper drafted a subpoena that night. She sat in her grandmother's office with a beer next to the computer. When Lake Danes had quit her career as a pediatric nurse to spend more time with her granddaughter, she'd worked from home. The job wasn't great, medical data entry, but the pay wasn't bad, and a flexible schedule meant Lake could go to all of Piper's school performances and softball games when she was growing up.

"What are you doing?" a voice suddenly interrupted Piper, causing her to jerk her head in surprise. The abrupt movement startled her grandmother as well.

"Oh my goodness," Lake exclaimed, her hands flying to her mouth before they settled over her heart. "I'm terribly sorry, dear."

"It's okay," she said, letting out a long breath. "I know it's late."

She sat down on the couch with a groan, her knees creaking. "You haven't worked late in a long time."

"Haven't I? Guess I didn't notice."

"That's when you know you've found something you really love. When you don't keep track of the time."

Piper printed off the subpoena. "I wouldn't say I love this. I've just never seen anything like it. It's so . . . tragic."

She gave a dismissive wave of her hand. "The world's always been a mess, dear. You're not going to fix it. Just fix yourself."

She sighed and leaned back in the chair. "Did you take your arthritis medication, Grandma?"

"It makes me nauseous."

"You have to take it."

She grinned. "Your mother never worried about me like this."

Her mom coming up gave Piper a shock, like a cold shiver running through her. Lake's eyes were already showing that she was somewhere else, lost in a memory. Piper could tell she had taken her pain medication.

"You remind me of your mother in a lot of ways, before she got into the drugs. You should have seen her, Piper. She was so full of wonder. She would run outside chasing butterflies until she couldn't run anymore. The world held nothing but fun for her." Her eyes glistened with tears now. "I don't know what I did."

Piper had seen this before. When her grandmother was having a particularly exhausting day, it was like her defenses came down. Walls crumbled, and the pain medication loosened her lips and brought up memories she kept locked away during the day.

"You didn't do anything, Grandma."

"I tell myself that, but who knows? No one in our family ever got involved with drugs. Your grandfather didn't even take ibuprofen. I just don't know how it happened."

"You did everything you could," Piper said.

Lake's eyes were drifting closed.

Piper took the subpoena and put it carefully into a manila sheath and then put that into her satchel. Then she turned to Lake and said, "Let's get you to bed, Grandma."

—

When her grandmother was in bed, Piper went back to her office and googled information on the death of Ava Mitchell. Something she had already done but had only given the information a cursory glance because she hadn't decided whether it had any relation to Sophie and her family.

The young woman was twenty-one and in college. Ava had long brunette hair and a pretty smile that lit up her face. One photo showed her out on a track in high school, and she looked like Sophie.

The killer had murdered her younger brother, Adam, and his girlfriend, Sarah, at the family's cabin, but Ava got to the woods and hid at a campsite of some German tourists who had driven to a lookout spot to see the glimmering lights of the city from a higher vantage point. Her body was found torn apart in one of the tents. Piper saw one of the photographs: blood coated the interior and ran down the sides, even dribbling out to the exterior.

There were mentions of the murders on local news sites, one blog written by a family member in remembrance, and a few articles. The governor had even mentioned it as the type of tragedy his new drug initiative was meant to prevent.

One particularly salacious true crime website had autopsy photos. Piper quickly skipped those and kept reading.

The lead detective on the case, Lazarus Holloway, had written extensively on the possible implication of the tattoo and its meaning. His research filled the report to the point that the narrative became a lesson in modern cannibalism fetishes. She pictured Lazarus's lieutenant reading this; he must've thought Lazarus had lost his mind.

Before she turned off the computer, she pulled up all the crime scene photos of the Grace family and stared at them. The images were revolting, but she couldn't look away from the chaos in the hallway—the victims' bloody, ragged wounds like open sores on their flesh.

Sophie had jumped out the window and saved her life, but what would have happened if she hadn't? Would she have a similar number of injuries, or would it have been much worse, like Ava Mitchell?

Piper's eyes grew heavy with impending sleep. She shut down the computer, the last image being Ava Mitchell's blank gaze.

The next morning, Piper wore a gray suit and checked on her grandmother. She was out gardening, and the sunlight was warm and the sky clear. Lake was pulling weeds in shorts and a large brimmed hat with a flower-print blouse. Dirt caked onto her work gloves, and her face was pale and sweating from the heat.

"Need help?" Piper said.

"In your suit?"

"I can change."

"No, it's fine, sweetie. Thank you. I enjoy doing it myself." She took off her hat and wiped the sweat on her brow with the back of her arm. "Where you off to?"

"Seeing a judge."

A smile came to her lips. "I love when you say things like that. You know how proud of you I am, don't you?"

A pinch of embarrassment went through her. "Thanks, Grandma." She kissed her grandmother's cheek and told her she didn't know if she would be back in time for dinner.

The courthouse was busy today, and Piper had to wait in line at the metal detectors to get in. She went to Judge Dawson's courtroom and saw her on the bench, speaking softly to a young boy in an orange jumpsuit.

The judge asked the parents if there was anything they'd like her to know, and the father rose, his cheeks red.

"I'm sure you hear this a lot, Judge," he said, "but I just wanna say he's not a bad kid. He's done some bad things, but he's a good kid. I'm hoping this whole thing'll get his head straight. But I'm gonna watch him as best as I can. Anyway, that's all I got to say."

"Thank you," Judge Dawson said passively. She looked to the young boy. "Dustin, you are eleven years old and already have a criminal history that I see in boys much older than you. I know it's minor things like shoplifting, but minor things turn into big things quickly without you realizing it. I haven't sent you to juvenile detention because I think it would be counterproductive at this point, but do you want to be locked up?"

The boy said nothing until his guardian said, "You can answer."

"No," he said. "I wanna go home."

She nodded. "I'm going to give you that chance. But make sure you stay out of trouble."

"Okay," he said quietly.

"The respondent will meet with P&P upon release and will be monitored for the next year. We will hold a review hearing three months hence. Court is adjourned for a brief recess."

"All rise," the bailiff bellowed.

Everyone in the courtroom rose as Judge Dawson went to the back entrance. She glanced at Piper and motioned with her head to follow.

Piper rose and went out back, stealing a quick glance at the bailiff to make sure he wasn't about to tackle her for getting too close to the judge.

Judge Dawson went into her chambers and said, "Shut the door," as she took off her robe, revealing a black suit, and hung the robe on a coatrack that looked like the branch of a white aspen tree.

Piper shut the door and sat down. Judge Dawson took a moment, one leg crossed over another, and she stared out the window for a bit. Piper took the chance to take the subpoena out of her satchel and placed it on the desk. The judge turned casually and looked at it. She picked it up and read it in what seemed like a few seconds. Piper thought there was no way she read it that fast, but then the judge asked, "There's a new case out of the Tenth Circuit, *Harvey v. Rosenblum*, dealing with internet service providers and subpoenas. Have you looked at it?"

Piper nodded. The primary issues with subpoenas to internet service providers was that the appellate courts found they were too broad, giving the government too much power to track citizens. Piper had made absolutely certain that the subpoena in this case wouldn't be overturned on appeal by keeping her request limited and specific.

"Yes, Judge. It can be distinguished. It was dealing with subpoenas in civil matters, and that ISPs are entitled to an expedited hearing if they object to the subpoena on grounds that it's overbroad. The Court didn't extend that protection to criminal subpoenas. Anyway, it's moot because I made absolutely certain that the subpoena wasn't overbroad."

The judge nodded, and Piper knew she just wanted to see if she had actually read the case.

"Cannibalism . . . interesting topic."

"You don't seem surprised, Judge."

"Should I be?"

"I don't know."

She gave a mysterious smirk. "What do you think of Detective Holloway?"

"He's . . . very passionate about what he does."

"He is that." The judge kept her gaze on her, and it made her feel uncomfortable, but Piper didn't fidget or squirm in her seat.

"How do you feel when you think about this? About a man seeing other people as food?"

"I don't know. I don't feel anything. Revulsion maybe."

"It's our darkest taboo. Academics avoid even researching it."

Piper hesitated. "You could have told me."

"Told you what?" she said, genuinely curious.

"That this case involved suspected cannibalism. You selected Lazarus for this because of Ava Mitchell. You knew where it was going, Judge."

"Yes, I did know. Does that bother you that I kept it from you?"

"No. It's just you selected him purposely for this grant. I'm guessing you selected me purposely, too. I just would've liked to have known why."

"You're wondering what I saw in you that would make you a good candidate for a case like this?"

"Yes."

She thought for a moment. "The *Calhoun* case we spoke of before, it was quite brutal. I saw you on an interview in the news. They tried to elicit salacious details and you kept taking it back to the child, what it meant for her and how to help her. I was impressed. Not many guardians allow themselves to empathize with their wards."

"It's a necessity."

The judge watched her a moment and then took a gold pen and signed the subpoena. Piper picked it up, thanked her, and rose. She was nearly to the door when she heard the judge say, "I did choose you for a reason. Show me that I was right in doing so."

17

Piper went to the office but found she couldn't work because they were doing construction today on the unfinished portion of the basement. Hammers and drills and the occasional sound of something breaking. She took it for as long as she could but eventually left and went to a café down the street. The type of place only open for breakfast and lunch that always smelled like grease.

She sat at the counter and watched the cook, the owner who ran the place with his wife, frying up potatoes and eggs on a massive grill. Piper ordered coffee and pancakes and set her laptop down in front of her. She glanced behind her to make sure no one would be able to see over her shoulder. She was on a flight once and left some photos out that she had been looking at—a young boy that had been severely physically abused by his stepfather—and the teenage girl in the seat behind her had seen them, and the mother asked Piper to put the pictures away.

She pulled up the police drawing of the man's calf that the German tourists had described. None of them spoke English, and there wasn't an interpreter immediately available, so Lazarus had used Google Translate and noted that some of the minor details might be skewed because of the language issue.

It looked like a round face with teeth and blood and a chef's hat.

Piper ran it through both Google and an AI images program, trying to discover if it could possibly mean something else. She found a few references to some earlier cartoons, but that was about it. She then turned to reading articles about cannibalism fetishes.

One article by a psychiatrist that dealt with the fetish said that many of his patients pointed to a single memory of when the fetish began showing itself: Porky Pig. Apparently there was a scene in an old *Looney Tunes* cartoon where Porky got roasted over a spit with an apple in his mouth. The psychiatrist stated that many of his patients with vorephilia cited that episode as an awakening for them.

A male voice said, "Never really liked Porky Pig."

Piper looked over her shoulder and saw a man with messy blond hair. He wore jeans and a white T-shirt, the only decoration a silver watch on his wrist.

"I always thought he was kinda dense," he said.

"Who did you like?"

"Pepé Le Pew was interesting."

"He was basically a rapist."

He chuckled. "Interesting doesn't mean good."

Piper watched him leave, mulling over the brief, unsolicited interaction. She found it mildly intrusive, but his offhanded comment lent an unexpected lightness to a topic she didn't want to be reading about.

She turned back to the screen and the image of Porky Pig and decided she didn't want to read about that anymore. She checked the time; her grandmother would be getting hungry, and though she hated Piper fussing over her, Piper knew she had a hard time cooking anymore with her arthritis and she had a sensitive stomach that required certain foods. Piper left some cash on the counter and went home.

Lake was sitting outside in a lawn chair, letting the sunlight warm her bare legs, as Piper came inside to the kitchen.

"What are you doing, sweetie?" she called from outside.

"I thought we'd eat together. Be out in a minute."

She made two servings of rice and plain chicken breast and took them out to the patio. Her grandmother sat up in her seat as Piper set the plates and silverware down.

"This looks delicious," she said.

"Just rice and chicken, but it'll hit the spot."

They talked about trivial things, what they'd done during the day, things they'd seen, rumors they'd heard.

"You dating anyone?" Lake said as subtly as possible.

"No."

"No one at work? What about Tom?"

"My boss?"

"What's wrong with that? You spend all day at the office. Where else are you supposed to meet somebody?"

"No, I'm not dating at work."

Her grandmother lightly squeezed her hand. "I don't want you to be lonely, Piper. That's why I'm always so curious."

"I'm not lonely, Grandma. I have you."

Her grandmother was from a generation where compliments embarrassed them, and she stopped asking about it and unfolded her napkin across her lap.

"What are you working on at the office?"

She cleared her throat. "Same old stuff."

"Oh, that's good. To have something familiar."

"Yeah, it's definitely something," she said with a forced smile.

They finished and Piper cleaned up so her grandmother could take a shower.

Piper decided the fatigue was straining her ability to think, and she took a nap on the couch in the living room. It felt like only a couple hours, but the sun had gone down when she awoke, and she had that slight panic from waking up at a time of day she didn't expect.

She went down the hall and saw her grandmother lying on the bed. It was a moment of unguardedness, and she looked frail. Old and tired.

Piper wondered how much of what she saw during the day was a mask her grandmother wore for her benefit.

"Grandma, I'm going to work at the office for a bit," she said from the hallway.

Lake sat up, hiding the old woman that had been lying on the bed in pain, and Piper heard a small groan. She sat rigid and said, "When will you be home?"

"I don't know. Not long."

"Okay, dear. I'll see you when you get home."

Piper watched from the hallway awhile longer as her grandmother pushed off the bed and went into the bathroom.

It was dark when she went outside to her car. The air was warm, and she could hear traffic from the nearby freeway that cut across the landscape like a blanket of veins and arteries.

She got into her car and drove the streets. It was sparse, but there were cars. Enough that she could zone out, let her mind drift, and she would see nothing but an ocean of red taillights in front of her.

The station was quiet, with just a few people moving around or chatting softly in the hallways. She took the elevator to the Dungeon. The doors opened on the small lobby.

The office lights were switched off, and she reached to turn them on when Lazarus said, "Leave them off, please."

Light from the lobby spilled into the room, casting some illumination, but the area where Lazarus's desk sat remained veiled in shadow. In front of him, a tumbler and an open bottle of whiskey rested. "I thought only two beers?" Piper said as she set her satchel down on her desk.

"Whiskey's more like candy. Don't count." He poured a little more into the glass, then said, "Have a drink."

"I'm not a big drinker."

"Everybody's a big drinker."

Piper sat across from him as Lazarus handed her a tumbler with a few fingers of whiskey. She took a small sip: it tasted like fiery oak wood. She slid the glass back and cleared her throat.

"You ever heard of Sawney Bean?" he said, his voice slightly slurred.

"I don't think so."

"Him and his kin lived in a cave in Scotland. For decades, families takin' the roads would disappear, and they could never figure it out. Then they found their cave one day 'cause someone got away. Inside were strips of dried flesh hanging from the ceiling and dishes made of bones. But that ain't the interesting part. What's interesting is the young kids in the cave. They killed for forty years before they got caught, so an entire generation had grown up not knowing cannibalism was considered wrong. It was nothing to them. They didn't understand why people would have a problem with it."

Piper didn't interrupt him or respond. It didn't much seem like he was really talking to her anyway.

New photos were up on the board, some of them of Sophie. Photos of her arms and legs on the night of the attack.

Her flesh bore the brutal aftermath of her escape: streaked with blood, laced with cuts ranging from shallow scratches to deep gashes.

"Any luck finding Emily's dealer?" she asked.

He took a sip of his whiskey. "She had a valid prescription for chronic back pain. No dealer. You get anywhere with the teachers?"

"Not really. They'll have support for her throughout the year because if they don't, I'll drag them to court, but after I'm no longer assigned, that'll stop, and she'll be on her own way before she should be."

"You sound like you know what that's like."

"I would figure we all do."

He took a long drink of whiskey.

"Why you really here, Danes?"

"You first."

"What'd you say I was doing before? Deflecting?"

Piper leaned back in the chair, slinging one elbow over the back as she crossed her legs. It was the most comfortable she had felt down here, and she wondered if it was because the lights were off.

"When my mother lost custody of me, my guardian was a woman named Ms. White. The first day, I couldn't stop crying. She stayed with me. When I woke up, not sure where I was, she was there telling me it was going to be okay. It's because of her my grandmother even found out I existed. My mother had never told her she had a child. I wouldn't have anyone if it wasn't for Ms. White. Next to my grandmother, she was the most important person in my life."

"That's a great reason for being a guardian, not a great reason why you're in this basement with me."

Piper paused briefly, then extended her hand for the tumbler and took a small sip before placing it back. "People say the eyes are the windows to the soul, but I never understood that until I started working with abused children. Kids who've endured real trauma get this distant stare because their minds shut down to cope. Sophie has it, but she's fighting so hard to not let it consume her. I can relate to that, I guess."

Lazarus stayed silent as he refilled the tumbler and took another drink.

"Now you," she said. "Why did you leave Homicide?"

He looked down and remained silent for what felt like a while, but his expression showed he had something to say. Piper waited without speaking.

He retrieved his vape pen from a drawer and brought it to his lips, taking a deep drag. The smoke looked gray in the dim light. "When I caught Ava Mitchell, I thought it's a simple B and E, breaking and entering, that went bad. Then I see the tent . . . I'd never seen anything like it. Not even a sexual sadist tearing up prostitutes in a dingy motel room came close. Takes a helluva lot to rattle me."

He drew deeply from his vape pen, the vapor briefly clouding his expression.

"She fought. Her hands were covered in defensive wounds. She tried to rip open the tent with her fingers and teeth . . . she wanted so badly to live."

He paused.

"I couldn't get it outta my head. Couldn't stop thinking or talking about it . . . I stopped sleeping. When you can't sleep, you know it's bad."

He took the vape pen out of his mouth, as though disgusted, and put it away.

"I trudged along another six months in Homicide and then took some time off. When I came back, I asked for a transfer. First opening was Juvenile Crimes."

"Did your lieutenant know how bad you suck with kids?"

Lazarus grinned. "No. He didn't ask too much. They hated my guts in Homicide anyway. They got the reputation as the elite of the elite, so when someone tells 'em they ain't so elite, bruises the ego."

"You talking about them or you?"

"I don't know. I'm drunk."

Piper grinned and took another sip of whiskey. "So that's a great story of why you're in Juvenile Crimes. Not why you're down in this basement with me."

Lazarus leaned back, and she could see his profile in shadow.

"I'm puttering along in JC and I get a call from Judge Dawson. She tells me about this grant, that they're trying something experimental in juvenile justice and she thinks I would be perfect for it. I said no."

"How'd she convince you?"

"She sent me those crime scene photos from the Graces'. She knew they were similar to what happened at the Mitchell cabin and that I couldn't say no to that."

The elevators dinged. Henry got off and poked his head through the open door and said, "Sorry to interrupt. Just grabbing some toilet bowl cleaner. We got a mess up there."

Lazarus said, "Have a drink with us, Henry."

"Nah. You cops are too doom and gloom for me."

18

Cybershield Systems was housed in an office building downtown near a Whole Foods.

Lazarus parked in visitor parking while Piper finished her cup of coffee. Last night she had stayed up late and only gotten a few hours of sleep. As she lay in bed and stared at the ceiling, she kept thinking of what Lazarus had said: *When you can't sleep, you know it's bad.*

They went into the atrium and toward the row of shiny silver elevators. Cybershield was on the eleventh floor.

The doors opened, and they stepped off with a group of people in suits or shirtsleeves with fancy ties. In front of them, they saw the Cybershield office area, which had a receptionist and desk made of glass.

"This isn't some mom and pop, these guys are legit," Lazarus said. "Emily Grace was shelling out almost five hundred bucks a month for her alarm."

"Why?"

"I don't know. Maybe you should ask Sophie."

They let the receptionist know they were there. A bit later a man in a suit came out, short-cropped blond hair and a look on his face that said he had far better things to do than talk to the police.

"Detective Holloway?"

"Yeah," he said.

He held out his hand, and Lazarus shook. "Timothy. Good to meet you. You didn't go into much detail on the phone."

"I prefer talking in person." He glanced around. "Quite a setup you got here."

He nodded. "Top of the line. Even the government's a client. We like to say Fort Knox relies on us."

"Clever," he said.

"Yeah, well, anyway, I did look up the name you gave me. Emily Grace. I'll get you everything you asked for on a drive. But was there anything specifically you wanted to know?"

"I saw a bill. She had some expensive security."

"It was our top-of-the-line home system."

"Not top-of-the-line enough apparently."

Timothy looked to both of them and then cleared his throat. "Yes, well, what can I do for you today exactly?"

"I'm trying to find out why a single mom who makes fifty grand a year is spending six of that on an alarm system."

"That's not our place to ask why somebody wants an alarm."

Lazarus moved over to an old-time map of the Las Vegas tunnels underneath the city. "What about the person that installed it?"

"What about them?"

"I wanna talk to 'em."

He looked to his receptionist and then checked his watch. "Lucy, please get them whatever they need." He turned to Lazarus. "I have a meeting to get to, but if there's anything else you need, please don't hesitate to call."

Timothy rushed away. Lazarus got the information for the installer. It was a man named Barry Watson. He was out on a call, but Lazarus got the home where he was currently at, and they left.

The address was in a section of the city that had almost no retail or restaurants. It was a series of homes pushed up against a cliff with only one road running past them. Lazarus took a phone call, and Piper listened as he told someone on the other end that the answer was no and they needed to find someone else. He hung up and didn't say anything about it as they got out of the car.

A blue van with "CYBERSHIELD" written in white letters on its side sat in the driveway of the flat, tan house. A man wearing a Cybershield shirt and jeans was stowing away equipment in the van.

"You Barry Watson?"

The man turned to him, facing him squarely. He was much larger than Lazarus.

"Yeah."

Lazarus flashed his badge. "I need to talk to you 'bout one of the customers you installed an alarm for. Emily Grace."

Barry's expression slackened as he regarded them both. "I saw it on the news. She was a really nice lady."

"She was paying a lot more than she could afford for protection. I was hoping you could tell me why."

"Tell you why she got an alarm? I don't know if she said anything about it. If she did, I don't remember. I do like ten of these a day."

"Well she was scared a' someone getting past it, and someone did."

"I know. We talked about it back at work. There's no way. This is next-generation stuff. We're talking eight cameras, six motion detectors, an alarm on every entrance and exit, plus satellite monitoring of the street, which is new. It'd be like trying to break into a police station. No one could get past it if it's working correctly."

Lazarus said, "Assume I do want to get past it. What would I need?"

"I mean, a lot of technical knowledge. You'd have to know all the latest updates and all."

"You know all that?"

Barry glanced between him and Piper, who simply stood and watched. "Yeah, and so do the twenty other installers we have, plus all the installers and former installers from every company in the state."

"But you're the only installer that's been in her house, Barry."

The two men locked eyes. Piper glanced past Barry and spotted a woman peering out of the house, watching the strangers interrogate her alarm installer on her front lawn. "Is there a device?" Piper said.

Barry looked at her. "A device?"

"Something that a person without technical knowledge could use to get past the alarm?"

He nodded. "Yeah," he said, glancing at Lazarus. "Yeah, there is. It's called a POD."

"What is that?"

"It looks like a remote control, but it tricks the alarm into thinking it's still on when it's off. I don't really know how it works. We don't use them and they're like five grand, but that's what I've heard."

Lazarus said, "Where would I get one?"

"I don't know. Maybe I can ask some of the IT guys back at the office. They might know something."

Lazarus took out his card and slipped it into the man's breast pocket. "You handle it and get in touch this afternoon, not tomorrow."

As they walked back to the car, Piper asked, "What was that about?"

"Little dog psychology. Gotta shake things sometimes to see what falls out."

"Have you ever heard of a POD?"

"No."

Piper got into the car and googled it.

"Sounds high-tech. It interferes with 'modulation of the system using an EMP pulse,' whatever that means."

He shifted the car into reverse and rolled back off the driveway, glancing at Barry, who maintained an unwavering stare.

"You want to dig deeper into him? He seemed fine to me," Piper said.

"You weren't looking for what I was."

19

Piper sat at her desk in the Dungeon, occasionally hearing someone come down there, only to realize it was the wrong floor and go back up.

Lazarus paced and had the phone glued to his ear. She heard him say, "There's no one else that would have access to somethin' like that?"

Riley was silently typing away at his computer. Piper knew he was currently splitting his time between the grant and the Gang Task Force. Today, she noticed bruising on his knuckles and wondered who would have been dumb enough to challenge a giant.

The elevator dinged and opened. Heels echoed in the hallway, and then Judge Hope Dawson stood at the door in a blue suit and black stockings.

Lazarus said, "Lemme know as soon as you know," and hung up. He looked at Judge Dawson and said, "Careful. You're classin' the place up."

"Not sure it needs it. It's quite charming for an underground chamber."

Lazarus leaned against his desk and watched her quietly. Piper gave her a smile and kept the surprise out of her face, or at least tried to. Riley glanced at her, uninterested, and went back to his work.

"Detective," Judge Dawson said as she noticed him in the corner.

"Judge," he said in his deep voice without looking away from his computer screen.

"Talkative as always."

Riley grinned.

The judge walked around the space. "Just thought I'd come by and see how everything's going. How's Sophie?" she asked Piper.

"She's doing better. Talking more. She didn't interact with the kids at first, but Carol told me her best friend comes by now and they take walks together sometimes."

"Have you been visiting with her?"

"Yes. Nothing dramatic, but she's opening up more."

The judge nodded, directing her attention to the board. It displayed photos secured with small magnets, adorned with blue marker drawings alongside names, dates, and a table of tasks. The judge approached, calmly absorbing the information. "How are you doing, Detective Holloway?"

"You asking 'bout me or the case?"

She turned and gave him a small grin. "Both."

"Well," Lazarus said with an exhale, "the main thing is the alarm system. It never went off, and the cameras didn't catch anyone in or out. But there's a device that disrupts the alarm system and turns it off without the company being informed it's off. So I'm tryin' to narrow down who could get their hands on somethin' like that."

The judge turned back to the board. "What about before? A houseguest that was missed perhaps?"

"I looked. Their last visitor was a neighbor three days before they were killed, and the neighbor left after half an hour. Whoever killed them got past that alarm somehow. We find out how, we find him."

Judge Dawson stared at Sophie's picture. "I think I know someone that can help."

Green Meadows was a planned community marketed to people near retirement. It was set on thirty acres of desert with a man-made pond.

Its prominent feature was the small casino, reminding everyone that they were still in Vegas.

The judge had gotten them in touch with a security systems expert, Erik Toby, who used to be with the Las Vegas Metro Intelligence Section. He was retired, and the judge said he was *interesting*, and Piper didn't know what that meant.

Seeking a brief escape from the office, Riley slid into the car's back seat, causing the entire vehicle to dip down from his weight. He had to settle into the middle seat, the only spot that could somewhat accommodate his frame. Even then, he was forced to slump down, his head bowed to dodge the car's low roof.

"You ever worked with the Intelligence Section before?" Lazarus asked Piper as he drove.

"I didn't even know there was one."

"They're more like support. Analyzing evidence and threat assessments, making sure we don't get our asses blown off running into an escort agency that turns out to be a meth lab."

"Did you know this man?" Piper asked.

"No, he was before my time. You know him, big daddy?"

Riley grunted and shook his head.

Lazarus said, "One thing I know, they're the smartest guys in the room."

They parked in front of a tan home with a pointed roof nestled next to the pond. A trail surrounded the water, offering a path for people walking their dogs or jogging. The neighborhood looked like someone had gone through and polished it with a toothbrush. No grime or dirt, no real life. Piper didn't like it.

The front door was large and had a placard that said "COVERT OPERATIONS UNIT."

"At least he's got a sense of humor," Piper said.

They knocked and waited. Erik Toby answered in boxers with a robe hanging off his shoulders and flip-flops on his feet.

"Who the hell are you?" he said.

"Detectives Holloway and Riley, and this is Ms. Danes."

Piper said, "Judge Dawson should have called."

"Good Lord, you brought a giant with you."

"He's harmless," Lazarus said coolly.

"Well, if you're with the judge, come in."

He had been holding a silenced pistol and placed it on a decorative table near the door. Lazarus glanced at the gun. "Silencers are illegal."

"You ever read the criminal code? Everything's illegal. To hell with it. Choose your sin, I say. You guys want some pot?"

Piper said, "Um, no, Mr. Toby, we were just hoping—"

"*Dr.* Toby. I didn't get a PhD to be called 'mister.'"

"*Dr.* Toby, we were hoping to get some information on—"

"Wait." He halted abruptly, hand raised. The room fell silent as he cocked his head toward the ceiling, while Piper briefly observed Lazarus staring at a small sculpture on a pedestal. Riley looked around the home.

"My damn ferret gets in the air vents," Toby said, lowering his hand. "Ex-wife takes the BMW and leaves me her ferret. I think she trained it to cause me stress to kill me. What were we talking about again?"

"Judge Dawson's request to help us?"

"Oh, right, yeah. She said you'd have some security data for me to review."

Lazarus held up a thumb drive. "This is what the alarm company gave us." He tossed it to him, and Toby caught it and turned it over in his hand.

"You sure you guys don't want some pot? I've been smoking since I retired for my arthritis and I'm telling you, there's nothing that helps more."

"Really?" Piper said.

"Yeah, and I tried everything. I even went to some revivalist tent to get a blessing from some preacher who said he could heal the sick. Only thing I got was a heat rash on my butt cheek. Forget it. Give me the drugs and leave me be, I say. What were we talking about again? Oh right, the data. I'll look at it and get back to you. Give me some time."

"How much time?" Lazarus said.

"I don't know. Time. It'll be done when it's done. And don't give me lip, son. I was wearing a badge while your daddy was in diapers. Just kidding, you're beautiful. Don't tell your giant to hurt me. Now get the hell out of my house."

He wandered off down a hallway, mumbling something about giants and disappearing into the bowels of the home.

"I guess we're done," Lazarus said.

"You sure you want to hand all that data over to him just like that?"

He lightly touched the statuette on the pedestal. "I think he's crazy enough to actually know what he's doing."

20

The next day, Piper was at the office, feeling restless. She contemplated revisiting her pending cases at the GAL, but she didn't want to seem like she was trying to micromanage from a distance. With nothing else to do, she immersed herself in summarizing her interviews with people who knew Sophie Grace.

Piper had interviewed several teachers, the principal, and some of Sophie's peers, but few seemed close to her. Her main task was ensuring Sophie's safety, a complex job given teens' ability to hide their emotions. Spotting the warning signs was crucial, since their outward behavior rarely reflected their inner thoughts.

Piper couldn't ignore the physical threat to Sophie either. If the killer thought Sophie could identify them, she was in danger.

Her phone rang. It was Lazarus.

"Hey," she said.

"I found him."

"Who?"

"Paul Grace, Sophie's father. Thought you might wanna join me to have a chat with him."

"I do. Where can I meet you?"

"I'm outside."

—

Paul Grace lived nowhere near where she thought a tax attorney, or apparently former tax attorney, would live. Across the border into Utah, at the base of swooping canyons and mountains.

Concealed behind trees and boulders, cabins were scattered throughout the area, all enveloped by dense pine forests.

"Looks like we got a hike," Lazarus said as they stopped in front of a trail leading up.

It was a tranquil day, cloudless and blue. A faint haze hung over the valley from desert dust kicked up from strong winds.

They almost missed the first cabin because it was concealed by dense foliage. Rows of trees surrounded the home, almost entirely blocking it from sight.

"Can I ask you something? What do you know about Judge Dawson?" Piper said as they continued up the trail, a breeze blowing through the pines and creating a soft whisper.

"Like what?"

"Like her husband."

"You wanna know if there's any evidence she killed him?"

"Just making small talk."

"No, you're curious, be honest about it. No, I don't think she killed her husband."

"Why?"

"I caught a body once that they were going to clear as an ulcer that caused the vic to bleed to death. Judge Dawson read the autopsy report and found an error in the way the ME tested the ulcer, and we had the vic examined again. Turned out his wife had been feeding him crushed glass in his food for weeks and the ME missed it, and she picked it up in five minutes of reading a report. She's too smart to push him over a balcony and be the only suspect."

"How'd she even read a report on a pending case?"

"I showed it to her."

By his response, Piper could tell this wasn't an area he wanted to discuss further.

"That's the cabin," he said.

The cabin sat back from the trail but was visible. Unlike the previous one, it had fewer trees around it. The roof was worn, but the rest of the cabin looked fairly new.

Before they even reached the door, it opened and a man stood there with some fishing gear and a camo hat.

A few similarities in facial structure, but other than that, Sophie had gone toward her mother.

"Who the hell are you?" he said loudly.

"Easy, partner," Lazarus said. "You Paul?"

"You from the county?"

"I'm police."

"Hmm," he grunted. "What you want to talk to me about?"

"How 'bout the murder of your wife and son?"

"Ex-wife. And I wasn't anywhere near there. I haven't been to the city in five years. She got the house and everything else. I didn't want any of it. And I told her to leave cities because the country's gone insane. But she didn't listen."

"You're gettin' worked up pretty good, Paul. You got yourself a temper there."

"I never laid a hand on her. She made all that up to get more in the divorce. But I didn't care, I let her have all of it. I sold everything, bought this cabin, and keep the hell to myself. Now I got things to do."

He tried to brush past them, but Lazarus blocked his way. The two men glared at each other.

"Thing is, Emily was shelling out some serious money for the best alarm she could get. Someone had her spooked."

"I don't know anything about that. And you know I didn't have anything to do with it because you'd have the handcuffs out right now if you did."

Lazarus didn't respond.

Piper said, "Have you talked to your daughter?"

They exchanged a glance, and the anger in Paul's eyes started to dissipate. He swallowed hard and cast his gaze downward. "How is she?"

"She's alone."

He was quiet a long time.

"Everyone's alone," he finally said before pushing past them and heading farther up the trail.

21

After dropping Piper off, Lazarus called a few contacts he had around the city. Men who worked in the right bars and casinos and escort agencies who had their ears to the ground. None of them knew anything about the murder of the Grace family other than what they had heard on the news.

Paul Grace was about what he had expected, though he had some insight. He was right that Lazarus had nothing. He had already investigated Paul. He had been drinking at a hunting lodge the night his wife and son were murdered, and both the bartender and a couple of regulars confirmed he was there until closing time.

The saloon's parking lot was scorching and covered in desert dust, with the sun beginning its gradual descent behind the mountains. Lazarus kicked the dust off his boots before entering the bar.

Midnight Porter wasn't a common beer, and there were only a few places that served it regularly. The saloon kept it stocked for him.

He went to his booth near the back. The view out the window was of the parking lot, and he liked watching the people coming and going. He played a game when he didn't feel like going home. He would watch people leave the bar and guess how much they'd had to drink just by the way they walked and talked.

He'd confirmed it with Bass several times and found himself to be accurate. Eventually he grew bored and stopped asking about it.

Bass came over and set his two beers down, his large frame making the wooden floors creak.

"This seat taken, brother?"

"It is not," Lazarus said, leaning back and popping open one of the beers.

Bass took a pill wrapped in cellophane out of his pocket and swallowed it down with a swig of Lazarus's beer. "Don't know why you drink this piss."

"I don't like sleeping. But here's the question, did I really choose the beer? Since before I was born, since the moment the universe came into being, I was always gonna sit right here at this time and drink these beers. Did I ever really have a choice in it?"

"You usually talk like this when you got something pissing you off."

Lazarus smirked and took a long drink of his beer. "The past. Just when you think you've put it behind you, it shows up again."

"Nothin' ever leaves, brother. I know."

Lazarus gave a nod. "How's Stacey doin'?"

"Some days better than others. She got rid of most of the clothes, but kept some. A blanket and some shirts. I caught her smelling them one day a while back."

Lazarus tapped the top of the beer slowly with his finger. "I'm a find who did it one day, Bass. I promise you that."

"What's it matter now?"

Someone called for him behind the bar.

Lazarus said, "Before you go, lemme ask you somethin'. When you were with the club and doing dirt, you know anybody that did a lot of B and Es? Maybe business burglaries? Good with alarms?"

He thought a moment. "Yeah, but he's still with the club."

"It's cool. I need some advice. I don't need to know his name."

Bass exhaled. "I must really trust you, brother, 'cause he's not the type of dude you send a cop to."

Bass made the call, and they agreed to meet near a taco truck in an old Sears parking lot that was vacant now.

Lazarus went out to the lot before the meeting and parked down the block. He took some binoculars out of a black case in the trunk of his car. Then he sat in the driver's seat and surveyed the parking lot.

He scanned from left to right and then went around the perimeter of the lot and then up on the roof. No one there.

The taco truck had a line of people. Lazarus lowered the binoculars and then surveyed the land in front of him with his bare eyes. Across the street was a porno shop, advertising half off all DVDs.

Two men on Harleys sat in front of the shop smoking. Suntanned skin, greasy hair, and some homemade tats.

"There you are," Lazarus whispered.

Another biker came up the street on a black chopper with flames on the side. He had long gray hair pulled back into a ponytail and thick black sunglasses. A cigarette dangled from his mouth, and he flicked it away when he pulled into the lot. He stopped near the taco truck and got in line.

Lazarus drove over and got out. The biker eyed him as he approached, and Lazarus said, "Manny?"

He looked him up and down. "Bass said to look for a good-looking white dude that don't know how to dress. He's right."

"Bass should talk. All he wears is his vest, and he's not even in the club anymore."

"You a one percenter once, you a one percenter for life. Ain't no retirement plan."

"Is that going to be you? Dead or in prison before retirement?"

"Road takes you where it takes you."

Lazarus noticed the man's boots. They were black and went up to his knees. Mud was caked along the tips.

"So what you wanna know?" Manny said.

"I got a friend whose house was broken into. Cops can't figure it out, 'cause she's got top-of-the-line security and no one was in the house except her family."

Manny turned to face him, his sunglasses so dark that his eyes remained hidden. "Only people that would come up here askin' me all this and sayin' it that way is a cop."

Lazarus glanced in the direction of the two men across the street. They weren't talking to each other anymore but now staring fixedly at the two of them.

"I told Bass not to mention it."

"Man," he said with a click of his tongue against his cheek, "you think I don't know how a cop talks?"

"I need advice and I'm willin' to trade for it."

"Trade what?"

"I'm a detective with the Metro PD. Wouldn't be a bad thing to have me owe you a favor."

"Don't let your mouth write checks your ass can't cash."

"When I owe a favor, I pay it back. Bass'll vouch for me."

"How you know him?"

"I was the detective assigned to his boy's case."

Manny looked squarely at him now. "I never wanted no kids and got six. Bass and his old lady only wanted kids and they got none. Life got a shit sense a' humor, don't it?"

"Sure as hell does."

A few people left the line with their food, and Manny and Lazarus stepped closer to the registers and waited.

"What type a' system?"

"Cybershield. Fortress model. The newest one."

"That's some serious gear."

"She was scared of someone." He glanced back to the two men across the street, who were eyeing him quietly. "How could you get past somethin' like that?"

"If it's workin' right, you can't."

"You ever heard of a POD?"

"Yeah, but only time I seen 'em is back in the army. Too hard for civilians to get."

He shook his head. "There's gotta be a way to get past it."

"Guess you could dig."

"Dig where?"

"House have a crawl space?"

"Yeah."

"Might be able to get in from there. Cut a hole out on the bottom of the floor from the crawl space and get in."

He shook his head. "Forensics went into the crawl space and searched. They would've seen a hole."

"Man, there wouldn't be no hole left. This is why the cops can't catch nobody. You put it back on and fill in the edges with epoxy resin. No way anyone in a crawl space with a flashlight'd be able to tell."

Lazarus hadn't thought to go into the crawl space himself. He knew the forensic techs and criminalists in the way a mechanic would know his tools. Forced himself to get to know them, to learn if they were the type of person to make a mistake and take responsibility or cover it up. The type to get on hands and knees in a dirty, damp crawl space or skip it because the victims were already dead.

The forensics team at the Grace home had been decent, but he could never really be sure unless he checked himself.

"So I go into the crawl space and look for repairs for a hole big enough to fit someone through."

"If this dude knows that much about breakin' into a house, bet he hid the cut real smooth."

"I gotta try . . . I got nothing else."

22

Piper drove to the Children's Justice Center and found Sophie standing outside waiting for her. She wore a summer dress with Converse sneakers. She still didn't smile or look people in the eyes, but at least she was able to come outside without Piper having to go in and get her.

The girl got into the car and put on her seat belt.

"I love your dress."

"Thanks. Carol got it for me."

Piper pulled out of the parking spot and merged onto the surface road. She made a turn past a Greek restaurant and used a gas station to change direction on the street.

"Where we going?" Sophie asked.

"It's a surprise."

They drove in silence for a few minutes before Piper started asking simple questions to establish a rhythm. Eventually, she asked about school. Sophie discussed how differently everyone treated her and how all she wanted was for people to forget, but it was all they talked about with her.

"They don't know how to act," Piper said.

"I know," she said with her eyes out the window.

"You don't have to see anyone you don't want to. No one can tell you how to start healing, Sophie."

The girl remained quiet, observing the passing business landscape and greasy diners as they exited the freeway. The humane society was located up a narrow road, surrounded by industrial spaces. The building had a modern design with a front entirely made of glass. A woman with purple hair came out to greet them.

"Hey, cutie," she said as she gave Piper a hug.

"Thank you so much for getting us in, Holly."

"Anytime. And who's this?"

"This is Sophie."

"That is a beautiful name, Sophie. You ready to have some fun?"

She glanced to Piper with a shy, curious grin. "What is this?"

"Follow her and find out."

They went inside to a private room. Three lively puppies were in there, tails wagging. One jumped up on Sophie, paws on her shin. She had a smile but was hesitant to touch him. Holly picked one up and gently put him into Sophie's arms.

"This is Bruiser. He's a rottweiler mix and came to us from the streets actually. He's a rescue."

Sophie got a shocked look on her face. "Someone lost him?"

"We don't know, he didn't have any tags and he was starving, but look how healthy he is now."

Sophie looked down to the dog and rubbed his head.

"I'll leave you to it," Holly said with a quick squeeze of Piper's arm as she left.

Piper stood against the wall, watching Sophie happily playing with the puppies on the floor. It was the first time Piper had seen her smile.

Sophie held Bruiser in her arms while the other two dogs, which appeared to be Labs, played and tumbled around. Then, they spotted a chew toy in the corner and dashed toward it. One of them managed to sink its teeth into it, and the other one bumped into the first, emitting a playful bark, trying to assert dominance, which made Sophie giggle.

Her laughter was soft and sweet but evoked sadness in Piper.

Sophie gently rubbed Bruiser's head and whispered, "You're alone just like me, aren't you?"

Suddenly, the young teen lowered her head over the puppy, clutching it tightly. She closed her eyes in an attempt to hold back tears, but the sobs overtook her, and she couldn't stop them.

As Sophie wept, Piper joined her on the floor and wrapped one arm around the girl, and they sat with Sophie crying and the puppies wrestling.

23

It was a Tuesday when Judge Dawson's clerk called Piper on her cell phone and said the judge wanted to meet for lunch.

Piper hadn't seen Lazarus today. Riley had popped in briefly in the morning and actually spoke to her. He talked about his wife and two kids and then said something about enjoying kicking down doors more than paperwork.

Up on the board now were crime scene photos from both scenes. Another photo was up of Ava Mitchell, what looked like a high school yearbook photo. It sent a shock of discomfort through her.

She looked like Sophie.

She looked like Piper.

Piper got her satchel and rose to leave for lunch. Henry was down in the basement again riffling through the utility closet and looked at her as she passed and gave him a quick smile.

"Your friend's a lot different than you," he said. "He's here all night sometimes. I don't think he sleeps."

"Don't know how. I can't function if I don't get my eight hours."

"Me neither. The great free pleasure in life."

The elevator doors opened, and Piper said, "Have a good day, Henry."

It was a clear and pleasant day, so she rolled down her car windows, letting the breeze flow through. Her lunch with the judge was at a country club. The club's golf course appeared lush and green, and as she drove up, a gate with a teenager checking passes came into view.

They had free valet, but she felt self-conscious at the state of her car and drove the extra distance to self-parking.

Going inside the extravagant building, she instantly felt out of place. Most of the women looked like they could be ripped from magazines, and the men were dressed like movie executives or CEOs. She wore a plain suit she had picked up at JCPenney.

She found the hostess and said, "Excuse me, I'm meeting someone here."

"Sure, go on in."

The tables were immaculate with thick tablecloths and spreads of colorful food laid out before the different guests, some of them sipping mimosas and Bloody Marys.

Judge Dawson occupied a secluded table on the veranda, her chin resting on her hand as she gazed out over the grass. She was dressed in an elegant blue suit that seemed like it would cost more than a rare piece of jewelry.

"Please, have a seat," the judge said without glancing in her direction. It caught Piper by surprise since the judge's eyes were averted.

She then shifted her attention to Piper, who felt a small discomfort at the judge's gaze.

"Have you eaten here?" the judge asked.

"I haven't."

The judge signaled to one of the servers, who hurried over as if responding to their boss.

"Yes, Judge?" the young man said.

"Can I presume to order for you, Counselor?"

"Sure," she said with an awkward grin.

"Two smoked salmons and two glasses of Prosecco, please."

"Of course. Good choice."

He left without trying to upsell anything, and when they were alone, the judge said, "I don't usually drink so early, but the acidity of the wine cleanses the palate to offset the richness of the salmon."

"You certainly know your food."

"The great pleasure in life. With all the various compulsions people engage in, they forget some of the best ones nature has given to us."

"Someone told me the same thing about sleep this morning."

"I prefer being awake when I experience my pleasures."

Her hands were as smooth as cream, and she moved with grace. As if she were gliding through water. "Your basement brought back memories of an office I occupied during my brief tenure as a lecturer."

"Where?" Piper said.

"The FBI Academy at Quantico."

"Really? Doing what?"

"Teaching search and seizure at the request of the director. Most federal agents are former police officers, and law enforcement tends to have an atrocious understanding of the Fourth Amendment. So he asked if I could give some primers to the incoming cadets. They had my office in the basement away from everybody else. As though they had to hide their shame that they were having trouble understanding the Constitution."

"I have a feeling they understood it just fine. People in government tend to ignore the Constitution when it stops them from doing what they want to do."

"Touché." The wine came, and the judge closed her eyes, savoring a sip. She let it linger in her mouth briefly before swallowing and opening her eyes.

"Do you know Napoleon refused to go into battle without his favorite wine? He believed he would lose any encounter if he didn't have a bottle with him. He couldn't get his wine at Waterloo. Didn't turn out so well for him." She took another sip. "Do you have anything like that? Beliefs that defy logic that you are certain are true?"

"Yes."

"What?"

"My faith in God."

She grinned. "I would be careful saying that around Detective Holloway."

Piper felt a little more comfortable with the judge's grin and leaned back in her seat. She still felt awkward among all this affluence and didn't quite know what to do with her hands, so she put them in her lap. "He has some curious views on the subject."

"Oh, yes, I'm familiar with Detective Holloway's views."

"How long have you known him?"

"We've had a few cases together."

The server brought an extravagant shrimp cocktail with the wine, though she didn't recall the judge ordering it. Piper was hungry and wanted to try some, but the judge wasn't taking any, so she waited.

"Does he still carry a photograph of Ava Mitchell in his wallet?"

"I don't know. I didn't know he did that."

"Whatever she meant to him, he couldn't let go of it."

"Then why did he leave Homicide?"

"There's a subtle difference between *leave* and *leave before they ask you to leave*. He couldn't focus on anything else, and everyone knew it. But it came full circle for him with this case."

"You think the two are linked as well?"

"What does the detective say?"

"He thinks it's the same person."

She sipped her wine before saying, "Similar circumstances, similar deaths. It's a fair conclusion."

"He's certain it's somebody with a lot of alarm security experience."

"Or someone that wants him to believe they have a lot of alarm expertise."

"I don't know. I'm not convinced they're linked. Lazarus certainly is."

"Detective Holloway enjoys working with theories. The problem with theories is that you have them first, and then look for evidence. But it leads to making the evidence fit your theories rather than the other way around. When it works, it's brilliant. When it doesn't, innocent people get arrested and the guilty go free."

The food came out. The judge took a linen napkin and folded it into a perfect triangle before laying it on her lap. Piper tried to do the same thing and felt like a child fumbling with a toy she didn't understand.

Judge Dawson took a small bit of salmon on a fork and tasted it. She ate slowly and chewed purposefully. Piper just wanted to wolf it down, so she had to restrain herself and take small bites. The salmon tasted like smoked honey and almost melted in her mouth.

They ate silently for a few minutes before the judge said, "What does he think of Sophie?"

"Doesn't talk about her that much."

"When he does, what does he say?"

"He wants to interrogate her."

"Interrogate, not just interview?"

"She's already been interviewed."

"So he thinks she was involved somehow?"

"He at least thinks she knows more than she's saying." Piper set her fork down and took a sip of the wine. "I try not to blame him for it. He has little experience with kids, and she's the only one to survive."

"Why do you think that is?"

"I think it was a miracle she got away, and I'm not going to let anyone interrogate her with any other assumptions."

The judge took another bite before sipping at her wine. "In my experience, detectives are too quick to accuse and guardians too quick to trust."

"I'd rather trust and get hurt sometimes than not trust at all."

"Depends on how much you get hurt if you're wrong."

24

Piper sat with the therapist Dr. Alexandra Foster, who Sophie had consulted last year, in the small office on the outskirts of North Las Vegas.

Emily Grace, Sophie's mother, had clearly recognized the toll her worsening addiction was taking on her kids. In a desperate bid to shield them, she had sought help, her motherly instincts fighting to save her children.

Piper tried not to, but couldn't help contrasting it with her own childhood memories. By the time she had grasped the reality of her mother's addiction, it had already consumed her. Piper had only known her mother through the lens of addiction, never experiencing any other facet of her.

Lazarus called. She sent it to voicemail.

The young therapist had raven hair and a tattoo of a tree on her forearm, the branches spreading like it were wrapping slowly around her.

"Sophie's one of my favorites," Alexandra said. "I just can't believe it. Sullivan was only twelve years old. It's inhuman."

Piper just nodded. "Dr. Foster—"

"Alex is fine."

"Um, Alex, I know that patient confidentially prevents you from disclosing anything very personal, but my job with Sophie is to make sure she gets through this. What can you tell me that might help me take care of her, that doesn't violate privilege?"

"That's clever," Alex said.

"I'm sorry?"

"You're trying to convince me you're not attempting to violate privilege by making it sound like you're concerned about it."

Piper grinned bashfully. "You have a lot of insight."

"I have to. Children don't want to talk about their problems with a stranger. If I can't read people quickly, I would never get them to open up."

Piper said, "I just want to know how best to help her."

"You can be there for her. Everything she ever knew about the world was taken from her in the worst way possible. She needs to know there are still people that care about her."

A text came through on Piper's phone, and she saw it was Lazarus. All it said was Call me.

"Can you excuse me a second?" Piper said as she rose and went out into the hall.

She called Lazarus who picked up and said, "We got a name on BloodyChef."

"Who?"

"Robert Darrell Grimes. Forty-one, unemployed pipe fitter that's on disability from a back injury he got on the job. Lives out in a trailer park on Rattlesnake Ridge. All the BloodyChef's posts came from the computer in his trailer. I'm goin' out to watch the trailer tonight."

She paced in the hallway a moment. "I want to come."

"Why?"

"I want to be involved. You might need me to draft a warrant anyway, so I should know what's going on."

"Your dime."

Piper's grandmother was napping on the couch with the television still on. Piper switched off the TV and gently covered her grandmother with a quilt. Afterward, she went outside to wait for Lazarus.

When Lazarus arrived, night had already fallen. Piper hopped into the car, and he pulled away from the curb. He was dressed in jeans and a black button-up shirt, soft bluegrass playing on the stereo.

"You done ride-alongs at all?" he said as they drove.

"No. We had a chance at the GAL to see what it was like, but I didn't do it."

"No reason to. Cops are on their best behavior during ride-alongs. You don't get to see what really happens."

They merged onto the freeway and left the city behind, entering the vast expanse of desert that stretched between Las Vegas and the next major city a couple of hours away. Through desert so barren even animals didn't inhabit it.

"You ever take that Christian fish off?" Lazarus said.

"No."

"Why?"

"Why do you have a rabbit's foot hanging from your rearview mirror?"

He grinned as he changed lanes. A soft sapphire light emanated from his dashboard, casting his face in blue shadow.

They eventually exited the freeway and drove through desolate, dust-covered fields. There weren't many houses, but the few there were prominently displayed "NO TRESPASSING" signs.

As they approached a trailer park, Lazarus nodded toward a trailer adorned with front string lights and a Confederate flag hanging from the side. He parked nearby but not too close.

"That's Grimes's trailer."

The trailer was run down with rust caked around the windows, the wooden porch looking rickety and unstable.

Piper said, "Don't you have a team for this kind of work?"

"The Intelligence Unit. But we're not on great terms at the moment."

"What did you do?"

He smirked. "Why assume I'm the one at fault? Maybe it's on them?"

"Is it?"

"No." He sighed. "It's frustrating. I've got a crawl space to inspect and I'd rather just get it over with."

"Crawl space?"

He nodded. "Got a tip about bypassing the alarm system. Involves cutting through the floor from underneath."

"Didn't CSI already check there?"

"I need my own look."

Piper redirected her attention to the trailer. She leaned down, adjusted the seat, and pushed it back. "Have you done this a lot?"

He nodded. "I was with the Intelligence Unit before Homicide. Pretty much everybody would use us, so it was a good education, I suppose. I'd sit for hours listening to phone calls between drug dealers, human traffickers, pimps and their girls . . . Got to really hear what people are like when they think nobody's listening."

"What made you want to go into Homicide?"

A song came on, an acoustic guitar and banjo strumming a slow tune as a mournful voice echoed over the instruments. Lazarus turned it up and didn't answer.

Piper leaned her head back and listened to the soulful music. She had never heard bluegrass before meeting Lazarus—in fact, she didn't listen to much music at all, and she wondered why.

After about an hour, she started to feel claustrophobic. She had already examined every trailer, played out various scenarios in her mind, and caught up on her emails and messages from the office.

"Did you ever lose someone you were watching?" she said, more to break the silence than anything else.

He took out his vape pen and rolled down his window a crack. "We were watching this guy for Financial Crimes 'cause he'd been passing off fake C-notes. Top-notch fakes. We had to go to the Secret Service to get confirmation they were even fake. Guy was an artist."

"How'd he get away?"

"He lived in an apartment complex and made us somehow. I still don't know how. But the complex had one of those underground lots, and we couldn't see down there. So he got a mannequin, dressed it up in his clothes, and then summoned an Uber and got the driver to take the mannequin to the airport from the underground lot. We followed the Uber, and the guy took off the other way."

"You're kidding?"

"No."

"You don't sound too disappointed."

"You think he happened to have a mannequin in his apartment? He had that planned out long before we ever showed up. He outsmarted us. He deserved his freedom."

Time ticked away slowly. They chatted, but eventually Piper felt weary and stopped talking. They sat for several hours before Lazarus said, "I'm taking you home."

"I'm fine. I can stay."

He started the car. "This isn't what they pay you for. Might as well get some sleep."

25

Lazarus dropped Piper off and waited until she was in the home before leaving.

He played music loudly on the way back to the trailer but turned it down as he got near. He parked closer to the trailer than he had with Piper.

He'd lived in a trailer when he was younger, after his mother ran out on his father.

He remembered little of that night other than his mother telling him it was time to go. A single backpack was filled with whatever clothes she had hastily grabbed, and they left the house at three in the morning. He didn't get to say goodbye to his father, who was asleep upstairs.

Time passed slowly in front of the trailer park. He didn't mind. A lot of problems in the world could be solved if people could do what he had taught himself to do: sit still and do nothing. Sometimes, doing nothing solved problems in a way concerted effort couldn't.

Lazarus spotted the first sign of movement behind Grimes's windows. A silhouette of someone with a man bun and a large belly appeared. The door creaked open, and the man emerged, holding a garbage bag. He tossed it into a nearby bin. Lazarus ducked lower in the seat.

Grimes lingered near the trailer's lights, inspecting something on the ground in a neighbor's yard. Lazarus couldn't make out his face.

Grimes answered a call, prompting Lazarus to check the dashboard clock, which showed it was almost one in the morning.

Now who'd be callin' you at one in the morning, partner?

Grimes went back into the trailer. A few moments later all the lights turned off. Lazarus waited. No lights were on anywhere else in the trailer park.

He popped the trunk and got out of the car. Tucked underneath the spare tire, completely hidden except for a single screw that had to be lifted, was another compartment. Inside, he had stashed a handgun, some lockpicks, two military utility knives, a forensics kit, and some gloves and other tools. He took out a pair of gloves and a flashlight and tucked them into his knapsack that he slung over one shoulder. He scanned the area, making sure no one was out, and then ran across the street to the fence of the trailer park.

Lazarus stealthily entered the park, guided only by the pale glow of the moon. The dim light cast eerie shadows, turning the trailer park into what looked like an aluminum graveyard.

Lazarus stayed low and moved swiftly, the gravel crunching beneath his feet. His heart raced and he slowed down, cautious not to alert anyone.

Grimes's trailer was the second down the row, easily visible from the street but offering multiple blind spots for anyone inside. Lazarus guessed Grimes had firearms; many residents in this area were hunters and had rifles and shotguns.

The garbage bin was about ten feet away. He stayed close to the trailer and hurried over to it.

He slowly lifted the lid and folded it back. The garbage was full, and the stench of rot hit his nostrils. He opened his knapsack, put on the gloves, and tucked the flashlight under his arm. Then he began sifting through the layers of discarded waste.

Each rustle of a plastic bag or rattle of a can made him stop and listen for any movement from the trailer. He had no reason to be sifting through this man's trash at one in the morning. A first-year law student could get anything he found thrown out of court. If he was caught, his best bet was to run. He wished he'd thought to bring a mask.

The bag Grimes had thrown away was filled with refuse. Lazarus took it out and put it on the ground and dug deeper into the can.

Underneath were layers of beer cans and pizza boxes, bags of fast food with dark grease stains soaking the bottoms. He stuck his hand in something that felt like warm pudding against his gloved fingers and he grimaced.

The door to the trailer opened.

Lazarus flicked off the light and swung behind the garbage can. He held his breath.

Grimes came out barefoot and looked up at the moon as he tapped a package of cigarettes upside down on his palm. Then he took one out and lit it with a lighter. The ember tip glowed in the darkness as Lazarus watched the man smoke. His hands were shaking, and he was pacing and mumbling. Lazarus wondered if he was on some type of stimulant. Meth use had begun dwindling in the drug communities and was being taken over by synthetic cathinones and Adderall. Grimes was acting too peculiar to not have something coursing through him.

Grimes smoked the entire cigarette and then tossed the butt on the ground and went back inside. Lazarus didn't move for a while, then came out and grabbed the bag Grimes had thrown away and hurried back to his car.

—

Lazarus parked his car at his apartment complex, grabbed the bag, and entered his apartment.

His living space was sparsely furnished, mainly because he preferred to keep the lights off at night and wanted to avoid bumping into objects. But he turned them on now and proceeded to his balcony. Carefully, he emptied the contents of the garbage bag onto the floor, revealing a substantial collection of used sandwich bags.

Lazarus ran his pinkie over the inside of a bag and then smelled and tasted it before spitting it out. A strong, bitter, chemical taste. Unpleasant. Crushed Adderall. Crushed because dealers liked cutting it with filler to squeeze every penny out of their buyers.

He gathered the garbage up again and then went inside and washed his hands before going to his home office.

The large room, which was the master bedroom, was painted a dark navy, and against the wall was a desk with only a laptop on it. Rows of bookshelves took up the other walls. The room held a single decoration: a replica of the painting *Gaze into the Abyss*, by Natalia Petrovna. A lone wanderer standing at the edge of a chasm that looked like it went down forever. The wanderer was staring into it.

He opened a form on his laptop and filled it out:

AFFIDAVIT FOR SEARCH WARRANT

STATE OF NEVADA COUNTY OF CLARK

I, Detective Lazarus Holloway, swear under oath:

1. I am a duly appointed detective with the Las Vegas Metropolitan Police Department and have been so employed for the last 15 years.
2. I am investigating the unlawful possession and sale of Adderall, a controlled substance under Nevada law.
3. I respectfully submit this affidavit to request a search warrant for the premises at 487 Desert Bloom Lane, Rattlesnake Ridge, Nevada, a single-family dwelling, owned and occupied by Robert Darrell Grimes.
4. On May 27 of this year, while conducting a routine follow-up patrol near Mr. Grimes's residence, I noticed a small sandwich baggie in plain view, protruding from the publicly accessible trash can outside his trailer home.

5. Upon closer examination, the baggie appeared to contain a crushed powder, which I suspected to be Adderall, based on my training and experience.
6. An initial field test of the powder tested positive for amphetamine, the active ingredient in Adderall.
7. I believe the substance was discarded by Mr. Grimes and that further evidence of the possession, use, or sale of illegally obtained Adderall may be found within his home.
8. Based on the foregoing, I respectfully request that this court issue a search warrant authorizing the search.

Lazarus Holloway, Detective, Las Vegas
Metropolitan Police Department

He printed out the document and then called Piper.

"Hello?" she said groggily.

"I'm insulted you don't have my number programmed into your phone."

"Do you know what time it is?"

"No. I need a warrant to search Grimes's trailer."

"Why? What happened?"

"I'll send you over the affidavit, it's all in there. Can you get it in front of Judge Dawson right now?"

"You're really going to make me wake her up now?"

"I need that warrant. I think she'd be more likely to sign it without too many questions if you take it to her. Please and thank you."

He hung up before she could object and realized he smelled like spoiled milk and rotting meat. He stripped and threw his clothes away in his garbage can before getting into the shower.

26

Piper drove on the quiet roads to Judge Dawson's house, her stomach filled with butterflies. She'd never had to wake a judge in the middle of the night before.

The house was shaped like a circle and had a view of the valley.

After parking her car in the driveway, Piper took a moment to lean against her car and admire the sparkling cityscape in the distance.

"It's a marvel, isn't it?"

She flicked her head around and saw Judge Dawson approaching her. Silk robe with silk pajamas on underneath. Slippers and her hair pulled back. No makeup. And yet she still made Piper feel like she was the one that was underdressed.

"It started as a railroad town until Bugsy Siegel dreamed of a glittering city in the desert. The day after his dream, Nevada legalized gambling. They were going to postpone the vote until the next session. If they had, Bugsy might not have remembered his dream, and the city wouldn't exist. How much of life, do you think, hinges on pure chance, Counselor?"

"Probably more than we care to admit."

"I would agree. Come around back."

When they got to the patio at the back of the house, the judge gestured to a chair and table with a view of the city. Piper took her seat. The house was surrounded by a balcony overlooking the cliff, a sheer drop on the other side. She hoped the judge hadn't noticed her brief glance at the precipice.

"I'm sorry for waking you," Piper said.

"I was up reading anyway. What do you have for me?"

Piper retrieved a copy of the warrant she had prepared, along with the affidavit Lazarus had sent her, from her satchel. She placed them on the table. Though she couldn't make out the writing clearly in the dim light, Judge Dawson read it in a few seconds, extracted a gold pen from her robe's pocket, and signed the document. "Rather interesting he'd be doing a routine patrol at that hour in that area, isn't it?"

"He's an interesting man."

"He is that." She pushed the search warrant toward her on the table. "Has he told you we briefly dated?"

She almost blurted out *You're freaking kidding?* but held herself back and just said, "No, he hasn't mentioned it."

"We saw each other in court, and after the case was over, he asked me to have a drink with him. I probably should've said no, but there was something that made me say yes. Curiosity, perhaps."

"What happened?"

She thought a moment. "I believe he's the type of man that enjoys the comfort of misery. It's difficult to be in a relationship with someone like that."

Piper looked down at her signature. She couldn't see it clearly, but the swooping *D* dwarfed all the other letters.

"Would you like something to eat or drink?"

"No, thank you, Judge. I'm going to check on Sophie in the morning, and then I have to finish the interview with her therapist. I better get home."

"Has she opened up about remembering anything new?"

"Only a little, but we're getting there."

"Is Detective Holloway still trying to get you to allow an interrogation?"

"He is."

The judge leaned back in the chair, placing her arms on the armrests like some Victorian aristocrat. "We have enough time in this life to become exceptional at one thing. So we have to choose our one thing carefully. Lazarus didn't choose his carefully. Now, he sees the whole world as a puzzle to be solved rather than something to be experienced. Don't make the same mistake."

Before Piper could reply, the judge had already stood up. She tucked her hands into the pockets of her robe and made her way back to the house.

27

Lazarus had the signed warrant in his hand and was sitting outside the trailer park as the sun started to rise. He hadn't called in Tactical. Members of the SWAT team had trigger fingers that flew a little too freely for his taste, and he needed Grimes alive.

Riley stood next to the open trunk of his Chrysler, securing his Kevlar vest with the LVPD logo displayed on the front and back. Lazarus fastened his own vest and meticulously inspected the magazine and chamber of his pistol. "Don't shoot unless you have to," Lazarus said. "And even then, try to wing him. I need him alive."

"You think this guy's a cannibal?" he said, checking his Remington. "I don't wanna go in and see someone hanging off a meat hook."

Lazarus closed the trunk. "You seen cows hanging off a' meat hooks. What's the difference? Meat is meat."

"This is why people don't like you."

"People like me fine," he said, holstering his weapon. "Cheer up. You're gonna have a real story to tell your kids now."

Lazarus stayed low, hugging the side of the entrance, while Riley approached from the opposite side. They both reached the front of the trailer park. Lazarus wiped the sweat from his face with the back of his arm.

They rushed into the park.

Lazarus positioned himself on one side of the door, with Riley taking the other. They paused for a moment before Lazarus swung in front of the door and shouted, “LVPD, search warrant!”

With one forceful kick, he burst through the door. Grimes, dressed only in his underwear, jolted awake. Lazarus aimed his gun at Grimes while Riley rushed past him to secure the trailer.

“Don’t move,” Lazarus said.

“I won’t,” he said, blinking away the sleep in his eyes.

The trailer was a hoarder’s paradise: dirty dishes and utensils, bills and discarded trash covering the floors.

“We got someone,” Riley said. He came out of the back of the trailer with a young teen, maybe fifteen, in boxers. The boy was trembling.

“It’s okay, Walk,” Grimes said. “Just remember what we talked about.”

“Keep your mouth shut,” Lazarus warned Grimes, causing the man to avert his eyes.

Lazarus lowered his weapon. Past the boy, behind him, he could see a room with a setup that included two monitors and a massive hard drive, something used for advanced online gaming or programming. Robert Grimes looked about twenty years too old for a rig like that.

Lazarus checked the boy over. He had bruises on his upper arms from being grabbed too hard, and Lazarus could see circular scars over his forearms where someone had put cigarettes out on him.

“Riley, you and Grimes go have a smoke. Me and Walk will hang out here.”

Riley led him out of the trailer. Grimes turned back and asked if he could get dressed, but Riley yanked him outside the trailer with one hand like a doll.

When the door closed, Lazarus sat down across from the boy in a breakfast nook. “I’m guessing Walk is short for Walker?” Lazarus said. There was a package of gum on the table, and Lazarus grabbed it and unwrapped a piece and put it into his mouth. Then he took another one and offered it to the boy. At first he shook his head, and then Lazarus said, "It helps calm you, take it."

The boy hesitated and then took the stick of gum.

"You know what your dad does for a living?" he said.

The boy met Lazarus's gaze, his eyes a mixture of fear and defiance. He had already learned that he needed to hide his fear when dealing with the police, but he hadn't quite mastered it yet.

"Your daddy taught you not to talk to the police, but I ain't regular police."

The boy swallowed. "What are you gonna do to my dad?"

"Depends what you tell me."

"I wanna see him."

"Then talk and we'll leave. Don't talk, and I gotta search everything, including that computer. You know you can't permanently delete files, don't you? My tech guys at the station told me that. What are they gonna find on there, Walk?"

The boy stayed silent, his gaze to the floor.

"I know either you or your daddy are BloodyChef77. Look up at me when I talk to you, son . . . I know it's either you or your daddy, and I think it's you. Am I right? Think carefully before you answer."

After a moment of hesitation, the boy finally nodded.

Lazarus leaned back, scrutinizing the boy's face. "Don't know much 'bout teenagers, but I know they like to shock folks. This what that was? Or you actually interested in eating people?"

He shook his head. "No. I was just . . . playing around."

"By telling people you'll cook and eat them?"

He shrugged and looked down to the floor. "Me and my friends would post stuff. It was funny."

Lazarus motioned to the rig with his chin and said, "I'm taking all that gear. I wanna know everything you've been doing and with who. But if you're being honest with me, I can let this go as curiosity. Lie to me, and then I can't let it go."

"I'm telling the truth. We were just messing with people. I would never do anything sick like that."

Lazarus rose and picked up the computer's hard drive. "If there's video of you eating people on here, I'm gonna be royally pissed off."

He went outside and handed the hard drive to Riley and told him to put it in the car. Robert Grimes was smoking and shivering though it wasn't cold. He was weak. Lazarus could almost smell it on him.

"Sit down."

He sat quietly on the dirt across from Lazarus and waited.

"You don't seem shocked the police raided your trailer. Happened before?"

"No."

"Then why you not scared 'bout the dope I'm gonna find in there?"

"I'm thinkin' maybe we can work something out."

"You got nothing I want."

"I got cash."

"Don't want money. People that have it do nothin' but spend their days trying to keep it. But answer honestly, and I'll leave. Can you be honest?"

"Sure, if it keeps me outta lockup. I just got out and got my boy back."

Lazarus noticed his cigarette was done. He pulled the package of cigarettes and lighter out of his pocket. He took out two cigarettes and gave one to Grimes and took the other one. He lit both. He inhaled the smoke and let it soak into his lungs before blowing it out through his nose.

"I used to go through three packs a day. Everything I ate tasted like ash, and I still didn't stop. That's like you, Rob. You can't help but get trouble stuck to you. The world tastes like ash and you don't care."

"I don't know what that means."

He inhaled and blew it out. "Whose rig is that?"

"Me and Walk's."

"You and him or just him?"

"I don't use it much. He likes to play games and make those apps and things."

"He do anything else on that computer you know about?"

He shook his head. "What does this have to do with anything?"

He blew out a breath of smoke. "I'm looking for a man that maybe thinks other people are food."

"What?" he said with a nervous chuckle.

"Somebody's been posting about cannibalism from that rig right there. I think it's your boy, but I gotta make sure it ain't you."

"How?"

Lazarus lowered the cigarette. "Me and you, we're gonna get to know each other real well."

28

Sundays were usually reserved for church with Lake, but today was different. Piper was accompanying Sophie to her church for the first time since the murders, responding to Sophie's text from the night before asking if she could go with her.

Piper picked up Sophie around nine in the morning. Sophie was wearing a slightly ill-fitting dress with just a wisp of makeup on. She stood nervously in front of the CJC building with Carol next to her. After exchanging waves with Piper, Carol gave Sophie a hug before she climbed into Piper's car.

"You look so pretty," Piper said.

Sophie blushed. "Thanks."

"You excited to see your congregation again?"

"I guess. I just don't want everyone to talk to me about it."

Piper pulled away and out of the complex.

"How about we wait until it starts and then go in and sit in the back? People won't talk during the service."

"Okay."

Sophie didn't say anything on the drive down to the church. It was an imposing building of stone and wood. She was Pentecostal, and Piper had never been to a Pentecostal service. She had heard of things like speaking in tongues and faith healing and had watched some of those programs on television. Her own Lutheran church claimed no such spiritual gifts.

They waited in the car until ten minutes after the service started. The building smelled like old pews and dust. Hymns echoed in the hallways. They found a few empty seats in the back with an elderly couple next to them.

"We used to sit there," Sophie whispered, nodding to the front rows. She reminisced about her family's past church visits, a smile on her face as she pointed out where her brother used to struggle to play guitar during worship. Piper observed the early signs of an impending emotional breakdown as Sophie's hands trembled and her foot tapped incessantly on the floor.

"Do you want to take a minute and go outside?" Piper whispered.

She shook her head, but her foot continued to tap anxiously. Her breathing became shallow and erratic. Piper observed tears streaming down her cheeks as the congregation sang a hymn titled "It Is Well with My Soul." One particular verse got to Sophie:

"When peace like a river, attendeth my way,
When sorrows like sea billows roll;
Whatever my lot, Thou hast taught me to say,
It is well, it is well with my soul."

Unable to contain it any longer, Sophie shook with the first tremor of a sob, and her face twisted in agony.

"Let's get some fresh air," Piper said.

They sat on the church lawn, and Piper leaned back on her hands and lifted her face to the sky, enjoying the sunny day. The shade of a nearby tree was pleasant and cool.

Sophie said, "I'm remembering some of it."

Piper said nothing as she stared at the girl.

"There was so much blood . . . I slipped on it when I ran."

"Could you see who was chasing you?"

She shook her head and wiped away tears. "No. I didn't look back. I didn't know if I had time to open my window, so I just jumped out of it. I cut myself pretty bad. I have scars now."

Piper wanted to tell her they weren't noticeable but didn't say anything.

The police re-creations showed a scenario where the attacker cornered Emily and Sullivan in the hallway, killed Emily, and then chased Sullivan into the living room, where he collapsed and bled to death. Then the killer dragged both bodies back to be displayed near the front door.

Piper really didn't want to ask her this question, but knew she had to. "What did you see when you opened the front door, Sophie?"

She swallowed. "My mom and Sully. I thought they were sitting down, and I didn't know what the blood was. I thought maybe they spilled something."

"What did you see then?"

She shook her head, her gaze down. "Like . . . a shadow. It was in the dark in the hallway, kind of in the corner where you turn into the kitchen, but it was different than the dark. It moved."

"Could you make out anything? Hair or face or clothes?"

"I saw his feet. He wasn't wearing shoes."

"What color was his skin?"

"I don't know. His feet were really dirty. Like muddy almost."

Piper sat quietly a moment, watching the girl rip grass out of the ground and twist it in her fingers.

"How about we finish the service?" Piper said.

Sophie nodded, and Piper helped her to her feet.

29

Lazarus disliked Sundays. The days were slow and heavy. They reminded him of death. Not that his death much interested him—the randomness of the universe made any prediction impossible—but he was curious about the day before his death. What would he be doing the day before he died? How would he spend his final twenty-four hours? He wanted to believe he would be doing something worthy of the final day, but he doubted it. He would probably be doing nothing in particular.

Rolling out of bed took more effort than he wanted to expend, but he did it anyway. He got into the shower and turned the water cold. He stared into the showerhead, gasping as the frigid water pounded him, but he didn't move. Not until his skin numbed and the cold didn't bother him anymore.

Afterward, he dressed in slacks and a white button-up shirt and red tie, loosened at his throat. He rolled down his sleeves and buttoned them before getting his keys and heading to the Dungeon.

The day boiled, and he turned up the air conditioner. The drive took longer than expected on a Sunday because of traffic, and then he remembered he lived in Las Vegas and it was no different here on the Sabbath than any other day. He used it as his day to catch up on paperwork.

Unfortunately, everything he did on any case that he wanted introduced into court later had to be documented, which meant mountains of paperwork. Narratives, supplements, affidavits . . . they seemed to never end. He had a partner once, a young woman who loved the minutiae, the details that he never thought about, and she would keep their paperwork up to date. She would hassle him until he got his overtime together, vacation filled, retirement accounts straightened, and everything that Lazarus at least thought a spouse was supposed to do.

One day, while effectuating an arrest on a parolee, she was struck in the jaw when he spun around and clocked her with his fist. While she was on the ground, the parolee struck her again and again, saying, "Sorry, baby, but I can't go back to jail."

She had to have her jaw wired shut, and eventually healed, but she never came back. Lazarus heard she became an accountant. Now, because some punk couldn't do a few weeks in the can, Lazarus had to do his own paperwork.

He caught up as quickly as he could and then left. By four in the afternoon, he was sitting at the saloon drinking his beers. He'd left three messages for Erik Toby and hadn't heard back. His phone finally rang.

"This is Holloway."

"This is Erik Toby. Dr. Toby. I took a look at everything."

"And?"

"I can say with near certainty this alarm was not interrupted on the night of those people's deaths."

"What about any other nights?"

"No. No POD was used. But I looked at the false alarms like you said, and there was one that stuck out to me."

"How so?"

"There was an anomaly two weeks before. This system isn't like other systems. Moore's law applies to alarm systems just like computers. They advance very quickly."

"Dr. Toby—"

"I know, I ramble. You're young. You can put up with some rambling by your elders. Anyway, this system uses machine learning and pattern recognition. They work together to analyze sensor data in real time and a bunch of other hogwash you don't care about. But it's highly unlikely for this system to malfunction and there be no record anywhere. I would say with ninety-nine percent certainty it was working and armed at the time of their deaths."

"All machines fail occasionally, even if it's unlikely. So what's the number? One in a hundred chance it fails?"

"Probably closer to one in ten million."

Lazarus reclined against the booth's cushions and gazed at the ceiling. "He got in somehow, Doc."

"Not my circus, not my monkeys. Have a good one, Detective."

Lazarus hung up with Toby and then tried to get in touch with the CSI shift supervisor, but it went straight to voicemail. He had requested CSI to join him for a second examination of the Grace home's crawl space, knowing the value of an extra set of eyes. But their response was still pending. The delay was typical of the bureaucracy he often navigated, but it didn't lessen his impatience.

Lazarus finished his beers, nodded to Bass, and left.

Lazarus arrived at Judge Dawson's home in the evening and parked in the driveway. The setting sun cast a glint off the house, making it seem new. It was an elegant bit of architecture, but there were others like it all over the city. He wondered why she chose to stay here after her husband took a header off the balcony.

Getting out of the car, Lazarus heard the front door unlocking as he approached. He nodded once in gratitude to the camera above the entrance.

The house blended in with the desert. It had a large staircase, beige floors, and walls that looked like the red earth outside.

"In here," she called from deep inside the house.

Lazarus took a few wrong turns before finding her in a room transformed into an art studio. She wore paint-splattered jeans and a white T-shirt. The space was filled with paintings, and the lighting was dim.

She had her back to him, looking at a painting of a naked woman reaching up with both hands. The woman looked like a ghost, with the night sky visible through her body.

"I can't stand that cologne," she said without turning around. "I think it has pine trees on it if I'm not mistaken?"

"It reminds me of the woods."

"I forget you're a country boy."

She made a small brushstroke and then stepped back for perspective.

"What are you painting?"

"Nyx devouring Helios while he devours her. What do you think?"

"I hate it."

She grinned. "I can always rely on you to be honest."

"Honesty's easier."

She reached toward the painting and darkened a small portion of Nyx's breast, making it appear more in the flesh than the rest of the body.

"How's Ms. Danes working out?"

"I like her fine. She's smart."

"Oddly optimistic all the time, isn't she? Not a common trait in a guardian."

He stood beside her, observing the painting.

"Why are you here, Lazarus?"

"I can't figure out how he got into the house."

"So? Why come here?"

"This is why we didn't work. You got a heart like ice."

"It's not about heart. You're here to discuss ideas and emotions and theories. That's what you do with a spouse, or your partner. I am neither."

She let out a sigh, placing her brush and paints down. "I'm sorry. The futility of it occasionally gets to me. Does it get to you?"

"No."

She grinned again as she washed her hands in a sink and dried them with a white rag. "You have an amazing flair for self-deception. Just be careful, the easiest person to deceive is ourselves."

He glanced up to the ceiling, where there were spatters of paint on the plaster. "I think that girl knows something. She gets ambushed and walks away with some cuts and scrapes? How?"

"Ah, and there it is. The real reason you're here. The answer is no," she said, beginning to rinse off her brushes.

"To what?"

"To giving you permission to interview her over her guardian's objection."

"I didn't ask you to."

"No, you're not that stupid. You'll make a subtle plea. Something that I might actually say yes to. And then later, when you do what you want, you'll say that my instructions were vague. No, you do *not* have permission to interview that girl unless her guardian allows it."

"She might know how he got in."

"Tough. Figure it out without her."

She turned off the light as she left the room. "I'm not going to cheat for you, Lazarus."

He followed her down the hall. "Yeah, that girl's alive, but the dead are important, too, 'cause this life is all we got, and whoever killed 'em took everything they ever had and everything they were ever gonna have."

"See yourself out," she said, turning a corner without looking back at him.

He stood for a moment with his hands on his hips, and then left.

Lazarus got into his car as his phone rang. It was Piper.

"What's up?"

"What are you doing for dinner tonight?" she said.

"Why?"

"My grandmother insists on meeting you. She wants you to come over for Sunday dinner."

"I can't."

"You have to."

"Why?"

"Because she already spent the time and money to make a meal for three."

He had nothing to say to that.

"See you at seven."

30

Piper sat on the back porch while her grandmother finished making dinner. She was an amazing cook when her arthritis allowed it, a skill she humbly attributed to necessity and not talent.

The doorbell rang, and Piper answered it. Lazarus stood there looking uncomfortable. "Come in," she said.

"I like the house. It's comforting."

"Odd thing to say, but thanks."

"Is that him?" her grandmother hollered from the kitchen.

Piper led him to the kitchen, where Lake dried her hands and then came over to Lazarus. He held out his hand and said, "Nice to meet you, ma'am."

She put her arms around him, hugged him, and said, "We're huggers in this house."

The surprise on Lazarus's face forced Piper to look away so he couldn't see her suppress a chuckle.

They sat in the dining room to eat as the setting sun cast an orange glow across the sky. Piper and her grandmother joined hands. Lazarus followed suit, holding hands, and her grandmother offered a blessing for the meal. Afterward, she began serving the food, starting with Lazarus. They ate pasta and salad with a good red wine.

"Lazarus is a unique name. Do you come from a religious family?" she said as she speared some salad with her fork.

He took a sip of wine. "Yes, ma'am. My parents were what you would call devout."

"Oh? Do they live nearby?"

"I don't know. I don't know if they're still alive."

She stopped midbite and looked at him. "I'm sorry."

He drank another sip of wine. "What about you two? She never talks about her life."

She looked at Piper with a grin. "She's always been good at keeping things tight lipped. I think she doesn't like people to know much about her. That's why she doesn't have a boyfriend."

"Grandma!"

"Well, it's true."

Lazarus smiled as he sipped some more wine.

"I think you've had enough wine tonight, Grandma."

"Oh, don't be embarrassed. How else are you going to find someone if you don't put yourself out there?"

Piper blushed and glanced at Lazarus, who was grinning over the edge of his wineglass.

Lake asked, "So were you raised here in Vegas?"

"No, ma'am. I was born in Point Pleasant, West Virginia, but raised in a small town in the desert of Utah. A polygamist community."

Her gazed fixed on him as if he had admitted he was from another planet.

"Your parents were polygamists?"

He finished his glass and poured another. "My parents were religious, but apparently my father wasn't religious enough. When I was a kid, my mother met someone more passionate about it and left him. That's the thing 'bout using crazy as a measuring stick. There's always someone crazier."

He drank more wine while Lake watched him.

"My mother and the man she ran away with had plans to get married. Only turned out she was wife number three. Something he didn't tell her until she was standing in the desert with only her child and the clothes on her back."

"Goodness. What ended up happening?"

He shrugged. "She married him out of necessity I suppose, or weakness, but I left the second I turned eighteen. Last I saw, they were still married and miserable." He looked at Piper. "What about her? What was she like as a kid?"

"Oh! I've never seen another child like her. Curious about everything and with a giant heart. She didn't like that anthills would get stepped on, so one day she made a little cover to put over them so people could step over the hill. Some boys came by and thought it would be funny to jump on it, and Piper cried all night. She couldn't understand why someone would do that."

Lake's eyes suddenly glistened as she said, "Her mother was the same way. For a time."

"Must've been hard taking on a child you didn't know you'd be taking."

"I didn't mind. In some ways . . . I don't know. I didn't mind," she said, looking at him with a warm smile, the glistening in her eyes fading away. "Do you have any children?" she asked as she took a sip of wine.

"No, ma'am. Was engaged once, though."

Piper said, "You were?"

"I can commit to things occasionally."

"What happened, if you don't mind me asking?"

Lake interjected, "Piper, that's rude. We can find nicer things to talk about."

"I don't mind," Lazarus said. "Police, see, we have this syndrome. Next-case syndrome. That the next case'll be the one where things go back to normal and get better, but they don't. And something's gotta break. Either your mind or your marriage."

Lake took a bite of food and said, "You know, you're probably not very fun at parties, are you?"

"I wouldn't know. No one ever invites me."

She smiled and softly put her hand over his. "Then your next birthday we're having here at the house, and I won't take no for an answer."

They continued eating and talking, finishing all the pasta and an entire bottle of wine. Piper, her cheeks flushed from the wine, began clearing the dishes, but her grandmother insisted that Piper stop and join her friend outside. "I'll bring dessert outside on the patio," she said.

Piper nodded toward Lazarus, and he stood up, following her outside. They settled on the patio, gazing at the pine trees behind the house. There was no wind, so everything was as still as a painting.

"It's quiet here," he said. "It's hard to find quiet anymore."

"I love it. I moved out once, but why stay in a crummy apartment if I can stay here and save money?"

"Can't argue with that."

She hesitated and then said, "I'm sorry about dinner. My grandma puts it in everybody's head that people have to be married. Not everyone does."

"You ever been close?"

"Once. In law school. He was a professor actually."

"You were hooking up with the professor? I never pegged you as having questionable morals, Ms. Danes."

She grinned as a moth landed on the patio near her foot and then flitted off.

"We were the same age, it wasn't weird at all."

"What happened?"

"He was married. I found out from another law student he had dated. He didn't even hide it when I confronted him. He wasn't embarrassed at all."

"You loved him?"

"I thought I did, whatever that means." She looked at him. "What about you? Is there going to be a Mrs. Holloway one day?"

"I got close enough to know it ain't for me."

"You don't think you should try it before deciding you don't like it?"

"I don't need to eat a rhino's ass to know I wouldn't like it."

Piper laughed.

For a brief moment, they fell silent, enjoying the soothing sounds of the breeze rustling through the trees.

"You get anywhere with the therapist?" he said.

"She had to reschedule. I don't think she's going to open up and tell me much, but I set an appointment for Sophie, so I'm hoping she allows me to be in there with her. What about you? Any luck with the alarm?"

He shook his head. "Nope. CSI ain't takin' my calls apparently, so looks like I'm goin' into the crawl space by myself. Unless you wanna join me."

"Um . . ."

"I'm kidding."

He closed his eyes and leaned his head back in a way that reminded her of Judge Dawson.

"So when were you going to tell me you and Judge Dawson dated?"

"Never."

"Why?"

"Exactly because we're going to have this conversation."

"Oh, come on, don't be that way. What's she like? She never talks about herself with me."

Lazarus paused a moment. "She's brilliant, refined, and the most dangerous person I know."

"What's that supposed to mean?"

"Exactly what I said."

"Well, what else?"

"That's it."

"That's it?"

"What else do you want?"

"You have to know more about her than that."

"Some people, isolation breaks 'em, and some people it makes 'em stronger. She's one a' them. I don't know any more about her than you do."

"I don't believe you."

"Ain't my job to make you believe."

A breeze swept through the pine trees and made a whispering sound.

Lazarus, his eyes fixed on the sparkling black canvas above them, said, "What went through your head as a kid lookin' up at this sky?"

"That there were peaceful alien races staring back at me. I liked that idea. That someone, somewhere, has it figured out."

Lazarus took out his vape pen. "I would think about galaxies moving farther away."

"What about it?"

"All our knowledge of the universe comes from studying galaxies, but they're speeding away. Eventually we won't be able to see 'em, won't even know they're there. We'll need a new truth, and humanity's never been good at abandoning old ones."

He took a hit off his vape. "One thing I do remember my piece of garbage stepfather saying right was 'Humanity's a blind man feeling an elephant's trunk and calling it a snake.'"

Piper was silent, and then Lake, who had come out there at some point, said from behind them, "Well, that is just horseshit."

Lazarus grinned. "Probably. He was insane." He checked his watch. "I have to go. Thank you for dinner."

"We haven't had dessert yet."

"Another time." He nodded to Piper and said, "I can see myself out."

When he was gone, Lake said, "What a pleasant young man. Seems lonely, though. Those souls always make me the saddest."

31

Lazarus woke up in the middle of the night and couldn't move. His room was dark, but there were even darker things within it. The darkness felt like it was alive.

He lay there, eyes open. His shirt clung to him with sweat and his peripheral vision blurred, his heart pounding so furiously he wanted to put his hands over his ears to quiet the noise.

Suddenly, Lazarus snapped his eyes open, and he was in his bed. His heart wasn't beating fast, and he wasn't sweating. The experience had been in his mind.

He rose and went to the medicine cabinet in the bathroom, but he didn't feel like taking any of the meds he'd been prescribed. The current medications did nothing but prolong the hallucinations. When he first got government health insurance, he had seen any doctor who would get him in about sleep paralysis. It seemed as much a mystery to them as it was to him.

A doctor had once asked him to describe it, and he said, "It's like I'm locked inside my coffin and somethin' is in there with me."

The description wasn't an exaggeration. The first time sleep paralysis occurred, he was a teenager and thought he was dying. That everything his mother had said about the damnation of souls was coming true and he was being punished by God. It wasn't until he ran from that place and found his own life that he realized it was a common, but not understood, phenomenon.

He slid on some jeans and shoes, grabbed his keys and gun, and left the apartment.

He drove along the Strip, something he didn't normally do. The lights were stunning for the first few minutes, but slowly a nausea would build in him. A discomfort, like being trapped somewhere and knowing there was no way out.

Partially nude women were on street corners posing in photographs for cash, and they waved to him and he waved back. People sometimes felt sorry for them, but he knew how much cash they pulled down from the horny tourists and frat boys. Some of them made more than him.

He drove past several gleaming casinos and a black pyramid that shot light into the sky. There was a turnoff that led to the Old Strip, and he preferred the bars there.

The Last Chance Saloon was his favorite, not just because of Bass and not just because they ordered Midnight Porter specifically for him, but because nobody cared who anybody was there.

He sat in a booth and looked across the room and saw Manny hanging out with Bass and a couple of other men. Lazarus ordered some absinthe and told the waitress to send shots of tequila over to them. She took them the shots and pointed out who had bought them. Manny stood up and came over, then sat and lit a joint.

"It's Bass's birthday today. You should come party with us."

"My partying days ended a long time ago, brother."

He inhaled and held it a second before letting it out. He passed it to Lazarus, who took a hit.

"You find what you were lookin' for?" Manny said, taking the joint back.

He shook his head. "No."

"Too bad."

"It is. Lemme ask you somethin'. You're too old to be running around doing B and Es. What keeps you in the club when you know it's time to get out?"

He thought a moment. "You get used to things and don't wanna change."

Lazarus nodded and sipped his absinthe, lost in thought. He clicked his teeth together a few times.

"You ever seen a home invasion when they were already in the house?" Lazarus said.

"Already in the house?"

He nodded.

"Nah, man. Too risky."

"You'd need a real good reason to do it, wouldn't you?" he said, his gaze glossing over as he stared at the green fluid in his glass. "Hiding in somebody's house and waiting for 'em."

Manny hit the joint again. "Sounds like you're lookin' for a ghost."

After he and Manny chatted for a few minutes, Lazarus wished Bass a good birthday and then sat in his car, listening to music. What Manny had said wouldn't leave him. It stuck to his ribs. *Sounds like you're lookin' for a ghost.*

Ghosts don't break in. Ghosts are there.

Lazarus drove the surface streets until getting on the freeway, avoiding the neon forest of the Strip. He got to the Grace home and parked in front. He watched it a second, then got out of the car.

The Realtor had locked up the home. The alarm had been cut off, so he forced open a window and climbed in.

The house was warm and still. He took his flashlight and held it up in front of him and ran the beam around the home. He walked over to the entrance where Sophie had found her family. He ran the flashlight up and down and tried to picture what the girl saw. He pulled up photos of the scene from the LVPD server and compared it to the area he was standing in. Some of the furniture and decorations were gone, probably in preparation for the eventual sale of the home.

He looked over to the shadowy corner where Sophie said she saw her attacker.

The air was dry as Lazarus went back to the trunk of his car and opened it. He pulled on a mask he had left over from COVID and some latex gloves.

The home was a black shape against the night sky blanketed with stars.

The crawl space—a cramped area beneath the floor of the house—was barely high enough to get on hands and knees, so he had to be flat on his stomach, the dirt and dust kicking up into his face, choking him through his mask.

The flashlight illuminated the cramped space like a candle in a crypt. The light wasn't powerful and didn't extend far, so all the corners were in darkness.

A dusty, cobweb-covered hatch was before him. He gripped it, pulled it open, and crawled inside with his flashlight. The CSI unit had been down here on the night of the murders, conducting a hasty grid search for evidence. Cobwebs adorned the space, revealing that they hadn't examined the entire area very closely.

He had to pause; the dusty air was stifling him. The space reeked of mildew and mold, damp and decaying. He lowered his mask and coughed. Skittering noise from somewhere in the darkness. Mice. At least he hoped it was mice.

As he pushed forward, cobwebs clung to his face and tangled in his hair. The flashlight flickered, plunging him into momentary darkness. In the confined space, the only sounds were the creaking of the house above him and his own breath.

Lazarus shook the flashlight, and the batteries clinked and light returned. Crawling into the main enclosure, he scanned it with his flashlight, but it couldn't reach the far side.

Lazarus was already out of breath, and wondered if it was the crushing claustrophobia or actual exertion. He crawled slowly, holding the flashlight in front of him and creating a tunnel of light. He thought to himself that there was no way a random forensic tech would crawl around here when the murder victims were in the home and there was no reason to think anyone had been down here.

Scattered leaves, twigs, some pieces of insulation, and shreds of old wallpaper.

Drawing closer to the wall, he spotted a clump on the ground. A candy bar wrapper and an orange Fanta can. He doubted these were Sullivan's: even with his powerful Mag flashlight, it was too dark down here for a kid to want to hang out in.

He shook his head as irritation grated him. "Nice job searching, guys," he muttered under his breath.

Lazarus carefully bagged the two items and secured them in his knapsack.

After getting out from the crawl space, Lazarus removed his mask, coughed, and dusted off his clothes.

He stood outside, taking deep breaths for a while, then went back inside the home.

32

The home felt like it was holding its breath. Lazarus stood in the living room and took off his button-up shirt, which was caked in dirt and cobwebs, revealing his white tank top underneath. He began searching the rest of the house. He started with the bedrooms.

The master bedroom belonged to Emily. Lazarus switched on the light, taking in the dresser, bed, and walk-in closet. On the dresser, he noticed photos of Sophie with friends and family, all neatly arranged.

He looked everywhere: closets, under the beds, in the kitchen, basement, guest room, Paul's old study, and the pantry. Then, he went upstairs to search Sullivan's room. He stood outside the door and took a moment before going in.

Posters up on the walls, mostly movies, no sports. Several stuffed animals were shoved into the closet, probably because the boy didn't want his friends seeing them when they came to the house.

Lazarus noticed a worn-out comic book on Sullivan's nightstand. Its pages were dog eared, and a small, handwritten message on the cover read "To my brave superhero, Sully. Keep soaring high, Mom loves you."

The night was hot, and he was drenched in sweat. He went to the sink in the boy's bathroom and splashed cold water on his face and dried with a towel that was hanging up. The towel had a cartoon figure stitched to it. He folded it neatly and placed it by the sink.

Suddenly, the air conditioner hummed to life. Cold air enveloped him; it didn't emanate from the vent on the floor, but from above. It was a stray draft, most likely from the attic.

Lazarus went to the forensic reports on his phone and searched for a house layout, eventually discovering a hand-drawn one. The only entrance to the attic was through the garage.

A cover in the ceiling hid some stairs, and he needed to find a ladder to reach it and pull it down. He found one against the wall of the garage.

He pushed the cover aside quietly and smoothly. He raised his head into the attic, shining the flashlight around carefully. Old chests, clothes, and dozens of cardboard boxes covered in dust were scattered around.

The ceiling was just tall enough for him to stand, but he had to be careful of protruding nails.

The attic stretched endlessly into the darkness. Lazarus moved his hand along the wall and detected a draft about halfway toward the house. He stood quietly a long time and looked over every inch of wood.

Something caught his eye—a nearly invisible detail unless you were searching for it. A hairline crack extended from the floor to the ceiling. The wall didn't fit snugly.

As he pressed on it, the wall shifted slightly, creating a ten-inch opening. Lazarus attempted to squeeze through, but the gap was too tight. Resorting to his phone's flashlight, he recorded a video by extending his arm through the gap, scanning from side to side.

When he played it back, his heart raced. It was a cramped room, no larger than a closet, and it held a worn sleeping bag, a notebook, flashlight, and unopened cans of Fanta.

The floor creaked behind him.

Slowly, his fingers reached for his gun, feeling like time had stopped. Then, from the darkness, he heard a noise—a rough, heavy inhale, like someone struggling to breathe through sand.

He turned quickly, shining his flashlight and pointing his gun at a man who raised his dirty arms to shield his face.

"LVPD, on the floor now!" Lazarus shouted.

The figure sprinted toward the opening in the floor and leapt down into the garage, vanishing into the house. He was fast.

Lazarus followed, his heart thumping like a jackhammer.

The door to the home had been shut and locked. Lazarus stepped back and then crashed his heel into the flimsy wood, breaking it around the doorknob. The door flew open with a sharp bang, but the figure was already at a window, jumping outside before Lazarus could raise his weapon.

The figure was small and thin. Easily half Lazarus's size. He wore little more than rags, and for a moment, Lazarus thought it was a kid. But he saw the tattoo on the calf as the man jumped out of the window.

Lazarus vaulted over the windowsill and touched down on the patio. The figure was sprinting directly toward the street through the neighboring field. Lazarus dashed after him, gaining ground quickly. He wondered if the figure was either injured or deliberately waiting for him.

Lazarus kept his weapon low as he raced forward, darting through a field that led to another neighborhood. Up here, the homes were unfinished, like skeletal structures with construction materials scattered around.

The person was audibly grunting now, and Lazarus had closed the distance enough to hear it clearly. He appeared short and slender, wearing tattered clothes that hung off his body like flaps of dead skin.

The figure abruptly turned and entered an unfinished home, vanishing from view.

He took out his phone and dialed into dispatch. "This is Holloway, badge 72915. I'm in pursuit of a suspect on foot near the vicinity of 111 Oceanside Drive heading northbound toward Ash Street. Male, short height, wearing torn and dirty shorts and a T-shirt and is possibly armed. Tattoo on the right calf. Notify units in the area to be cautious, suspect is extremely dangerous."

A gust of wind swept through, causing the bare bones of the house to emit a haunting groan.

He went inside.

33

The exposed wooden structure made Lazarus feel like he was inside the skeleton of a huge creature that had swallowed him. He walked carefully, taking slow steps in the dark. The moon was a small, thin shape in the sky, providing just enough light through the unfinished roof to keep him from tripping.

Stacks of drywall and lumber were everywhere in the home, secured with plastic ties. Lazarus stopped every few steps and listened, but all he could hear was the breeze whistling through the structure.

Sweat trickled down his back, seeping into his cotton tank top and making it cling to his skin like soggy tissue. His throat was sandpaper.

There was a second floor, but the stairs were unfinished. Lazarus worried that the figure had already passed through the house and was heading for the street. He hadn't seen the man well enough in the dark to provide a good description. If he escaped, he would vanish.

"I just wanna talk," Lazarus shouted.

There was no reply, just a soft flap from sheets of plastic hung over sections of the wooden frame.

A closet was finished and the doors closed. He approached slowly. He expected rounds to come flying out of the thin wood.

He stood to the side, out of the line of fire. Leaning against the incomplete wall near the closet, he strained his ears to listen. There was no audible breathing, but the rustling breeze outside could have masked the sound.

Reaching over slowly, he gripped the handle of the closet and began opening it.

The explosion of pain on the back of Lazarus's head sent him tumbling forward into the closet door and then to the floor. He spun around just as another blow was coming and managed to get his arm up in time, blocking the hit from the slab of timber the figure was swinging at him.

The shape stood over him, feet on either side of Lazarus's body. He lifted the timber in his hands and swung down. Lazarus held up his arm again, and his left forearm took most of the blow. He ignored the pain and slammed his fist into the figure's groin, then grabbed his legs at the back of the knees and pulled. The figure stumbled backward, releasing the timber.

Lazarus found himself on his knees with no time to regain his footing before the figure came charging at him. Despite being smaller, he was significantly faster. He frantically searched for the lumber he had used to strike Lazarus.

Lazarus managed to grab it first. The figure charged at him like a wild animal, emitting grunts and growls. In a momentary glimpse under the feeble moonlight, Lazarus noticed that his face was disfigured.

The attacker pounced on him like a crazed creature, his nails clawing at Lazarus's face. In the moonlight, Lazarus glimpsed a glint of metal, a screwdriver, in the figure's hand.

The figure swung the tool down, attempting to thrust the tip into his eye. Lazarus grabbed the man's forearm, preventing the screwdriver from entering his eyeball by a few inches. The figure exerted his weight, forcing the screwdriver down. Lazarus grunted, struggling to push him off, while the man drooled and spittle landed in his mouth and eyes.

Lazarus, his muscles straining under the onslaught, twisted suddenly to the side, using the attacker's momentum against him. The screwdriver, now off its course, stabbed into the floor.

Lazarus pulled out his cuffs and swiftly cuffed one wrist to the figure and secured the other to an exposed plumbing pipe in the closet. The figure, desperate and frenzied, attacked the pipe relentlessly, yanking and pulling and grunting. Lazarus, breathing heavily, lurched to his feet as the figure lunged forward and missed grabbing him.

Sirens wailed in the distance.

34

Lazarus had to be examined by the paramedics; the back of his head bled, and they feared a concussion. They insisted he go to the hospital, but he resisted for now.

In the back of a police cruiser, the assailant sat flanked by two LVPD officers. Following a hospital visit, he would be transported to the station for booking. So far, he stayed silent.

Lazarus didn't wait for anyone to take his statement.

When the paramedics weren't watching, he slipped away to his car and then headed to the station. After retrieving the murder book from the Dungeon, he positioned himself near the interview rooms, anticipating the arrival of the man. His head throbbed, and occasional waves of dizziness washed over him, only to recede into the background.

He sat down in a chair in front of the interview rooms and closed his eyes. He opened them when he heard footsteps.

Two officers brought in the man and took him into an interview room. Lazarus didn't get a good look at him. He rose and went to the one-way glass and watched as the little man was seated at the table and the two officers cuffed him to the metal ring on the floor.

His clothes were rags, his hair roughly shaved with something dull. Some patches of hair had grown longer than others. The right side of his face was deformed from a burn. The scarring curled around the side of his head. His right eye was blackened, but not fully. It gave a discomforting appearance of the eye being burnt out of the socket.

He was small and unremarkable. He appeared soft and weak, but Lazarus had felt his strength. It didn't match his body.

The elevators dinged, and two detectives stepped off. Lazarus knew them both. Gilroy and Hobbs. Gilroy was pudgy and had a thick mustache that didn't fit his face, and Hobbs could've been his brother. Both from Homicide.

"Heard you got him," Gilroy said.

"We got someone."

"Been a bit. How you been?"

"Skip the small talk. What d'ya want?"

The two glanced at each other and Hobbs said, "We thought you could use some help, that's all."

"I don't. Thanks for stopping by."

"Don't be like that."

"You didn't mind kicking this case 'cause you had nothing, and now that I've done all the work for you, you wanna walk in here and say you got an arrest for the cameras?"

Gilroy said, "You want help or not?"

Silence a moment as the two glared at each other.

Lazarus finally said, "Lieutenant said this was mine. I'm gonna see it through."

Hobbs said, "Have it your way," and gave him some papers. It was a booking sheet.

Lazarus watched them get back on the elevator. They wouldn't have tried to take this from him without the lieutenant's approval. But it didn't matter what the lieutenant wanted. The reason the case was taken from Homicide was because Judge Dawson had asked the lieutenant to give the case to him. The lieutenant was a climber, and Judge Dawson was a good person to have on your side if you wanted to climb.

Lazarus read the booking sheet.

Owen Alistair Whittaker.

Twenty-nine years old. A rap sheet longer than Lazarus had ever seen. The charges were from all over the country. There were criminal histories from Louisiana, Georgia, Colorado, Idaho, California, Florida, and Texas. Over eight hundred arrests in his short twenty-nine years, mostly crimes related to homelessness. Camping in a public place, public indecency, public intoxication, resisting arrest. A burglary conviction back in '05 and an assault with a deadly weapon charge in 2016, but nothing that would have him locked up for long.

Lazarus murmured under his breath, "You ride the trains, don't you, my man?"

Then he went to the vending machines and bought an orange Fanta before going into the room.

He liked the interview room cold. The few times Lazarus had seen a cop drama on television, cops always seemed to be messing with the temperature to get people to talk. Though that was certainly a tried-and-true tactic—alternating extreme temperatures, withholding food and drink or providing as much as the perp wanted and then withholding the bathroom, sleep deprivation, sitting or standing in uncomfortable positions . . . he knew and had studied them all, and found them all ineffective. Too many false confessions, too many cases reopened later. He preferred more civilized—if there was such a thing—means.

He shut the door behind him and set the Fanta on the table.

He sat down and watched Owen Whittaker. The man was looking down at the cuffs on his wrists.

"You know what happens next?" Lazarus said.

Owen didn't reply.

"You're gonna be held in the holding tank until we're done. Then you're going down to the jail, and that's where you'll be for your trial. When you're sentenced, you'll get transferred to death row."

The man lifted his gaze slowly. The eye marred by the burn had a milky gray iris. His head seemed oddly small for his body, his arms strangely long. Everything about him was disproportionate.

"The bloody chef tattoo on your leg, that real or fantasy? You ever actually done it?"

Owen went back to staring at his cuffs.

Lazarus reached into the murder book. He took out the color photo of Ava Mitchell smiling for her college ID. Then he pulled out another photo and placed it next to that one: her on the medical examiner's table.

He pushed the photos closer to make sure Owen could see.

"She was beautiful, wasn't she?" Lazarus said.

Owen gazed at the photo of her corpse, his burnt eye lagging a fraction of a second behind the other when he blinked. His voice was raspy as he said, "I like her more this way."

Lazarus nodded once and leaned back in the chair. He took out his cigarettes and placed them on the table but didn't light one. "I figured you would."

Owen swallowed and was so thin Lazarus could see the full movement in his throat. He took out photos of Emily and Sullivan Grace and put them in front of Owen.

"Two years between Ava Mitchell and the Graces. Why so long?"

Lazarus watched the man in silence. The way his mouth pulled back from his face because of the heavy scarring created the appearance of a skull with skin wrapped around it.

"I got a history on you. It's quite a journey round the country. Looked like a train route to me. You ride the rails?"

Owen blinked slowly.

"I knew a guy, successful lawyer, who took a month every year to ride the rails. Wouldn't take any money with him. Said it kept him human. Reminded him there was somethin' still to live for."

He pulled the cigarettes closer to himself and lit one. He held it out to Owen, who didn't move.

"Take it, it'll relax you."

Owen simply blinked.

Lazarus took a drag and said, "Two years is a long stretch if you're itchin' to kill. I wager we dig into some of those missing persons cases along those train routes, we'll find some of your work, won't we?"

Owen moved his hands, and the cuffs rattled.

"I carried Ava's photo for a time. I'd stare at it to see what you saw, but I couldn't see it. Only thing I could come up with was that you're a man who likes making beautiful things ugly."

Owen took a breath, and Lazarus could hear the gravelly sound of scarring in his lungs.

"Where you from, Owen? Least tell me that."

"Hell," he whispered.

Lazarus exhaled smoke through his nostrils. "They speak Creole in hell? 'Cause I know bayou when I hear it. I'd say Terrebonne Parish."

Owen remained silent, his breath continuing to rasp in the quiet room.

"I started as a cop in N'orlins when I was eighteen, and that was the drinking age on account a' Mardi Gras. Governor figured if you're old enough to get drunk, you're old enough for a badge. So, I hitchhiked from Utah to N'orlins with a hundred bucks in my pocket, got hired the day I arrived, and was sent to the academy the next week. Fate."

Owen was staring at him now, giving his full attention.

"N'orlins had the highest rate of police corruption in America at the time. A system more corrupt than the criminals. It was like somethin' dark had crawled out of the city . . . rotting it from the inside."

He paused, staring at the smoldering ashes on his cigarette.

"Katrina destroyed everything. Police force had to be rebuilt 'cause so many people left the city. I'm sure they all think it'll be better, but there's no such thing as *better*, is there?"

He hesitated.

"I noticed the Bible in your belongings. It was worn out. You a man of faith?"

Owen grinned now, his dry lips cracking as they spread wider.

"You hid in the Mitchells' cabin. Some campers saw you the week before hiking up there. How long you hide in the Graces' house for?"

Owen looked back down to the table, losing interest.

"Why is Sophie Grace still alive? You killed everyone else, why not her?"

Owen said nothing, and Lazarus could see the interest fading.

"Some native tribes here used to believe if you murder someone, they'll be your slave in the afterlife. What do you believe, Owen?"

Owen blinked, the lid of his burnt eye looking like it scraped down the flesh as it closed. Then he leaned back and sat motionless. Lazarus knew Owen wouldn't be talking again, so he left the room. When he looked back through the glass, Owen was staring blankly at the can of Fanta. He wasn't there anymore.

35

Piper rushed to the station. She went to the Dungeon and then the detective's bureau but couldn't find Lazarus.

The space was buzzing with activity. Small groups of officers mulled around and whispered about who the media had already dubbed the Creeper, because of his living in the homes of the victims before attacking them.

Lazarus entered the detective bureau, where a few detectives approached to offer their congratulations. He exchanged handshakes with a couple of them, looking massively uncomfortable, before making his way through the crowd. Eventually, he spotted Piper and headed over to her.

"What are you doing here?"

"You kidding me?" she said. "It's all over the news. They're calling him the Creeper."

A detective came by and said a quick comment about the good work Lazarus had done, and they shook hands.

"Let's get outta here," Lazarus said. "I've had enough glad-handing."

They went down to the Dungeon. The lights were off, and Lazarus turned only half of them on. He sat down at his desk. Piper noticed more photos and bits of evidence taped to the board. Red, blue, and green marker-scribbled notes took up the white spaces in between.

Piper sat down.

"How'd the media find out already?" she said.

"They pay for tips. And I have a feeling I know which detectives tipped 'em."

She crossed her arms as she watched him. "Did you interview him?"

"Yes."

"What did he say?"

"Not much."

"How are you sure he stayed in the victims' homes?" Piper asked.

"The second CSI sweep turned up signs of someone staying in the crawl space, attic, even inside the walls. I bet we'd have found the same at the Mitchells' cabin, if we'd looked closer initially."

"Did he say why he did it?"

"No."

Piper took a moment, absorbing the information. "So, he was living in their homes . . . watching them?"

He nodded. "Seems like an extreme form of voyeurism."

"What kind of person does that?"

"I'll show you."

—

Piper followed Lazarus up to the holding tank on the first floor. They had to go through metal detectors, and Lazarus stopped to chat with a watch commander.

The holding tanks were a series of cells to temporarily hold defendants who were traveling from the jail or prison to the courthouse or station. The cells were small but clean, with steel sinks and toilets. A cot that always had to be made if the prisoner wasn't sleeping. No decorations were allowed.

In the last cell, Owen Whittaker sat on the edge of the bunk and stared at the empty wall.

She had to swallow because her throat felt dry.

He was shorter and thinner than her, but something about him made him loom larger than he was. The revulsion she felt tasted like rancid milk in her mouth.

Owen slowly turned his head and saw her.

He slid his tongue out of his mouth and onto his cracked and bleeding lips.

Lazarus said, "He'll have a lawyer soon, so if you wanna talk to him, now's the time."

Piper watched him a moment.

"I have nothing to say to him," she spit before heading back to the elevators.

36

It was past eleven when Piper got to Sophie's high school.

Piper entered the school and approached the front desk, asking the location of Sophie's class. After verifying her credentials, they gave her a visitor hall pass.

Sophie was in physics, and Piper waited in the hallway. Sophie sat at the back, staring out the window with her backpack at her feet. Her books, pens, and notebooks were all still tucked away, and she was just gazing out the window. It didn't appear like she was paying attention to anything but whatever was outside.

The bell rang, and students poured out of the classrooms. The cacophony of youth filled the halls as everyone went to lunch. Sophie was one of the last to leave the classroom, and her gaze was down to the floor. She glanced up long enough to recognize Piper and her faced changed, a slight upward motion to her lips. Not quite a smile, but not indifference either.

"I was never good at science," Piper said. "I liked history more."

"I like science. I thought I wanted to be a doctor."

"Not anymore?"

They began strolling together down the hall.

She shrugged. "It doesn't seem important anymore."

Piper watched her tuck a strand of hair behind her ear, and for some reason it made her sad.

"You wanna grab a smoothie? It's on me."

"I'd like that."

They went to a nearby smoothie shop, a colorful space of neon pinks and blues with smoothie flavors like Skittles & Sherbet.

"I used to go somewhere like this in law school," Piper said. "They knew I didn't have much money, so they would let me sit and study all day without making me buy anything."

"Was law school hard?"

"It was hard learning to think the way a lawyer has to think, but the workload was okay. My grandma used to be a nurse and taught me some studying tricks. She was good at making things easy to remember."

They ordered and sat down. Sophie took a drink and seemed to be lost in thought before she said, "Where's your grandma now?"

"I still live with her."

"Why?"

"Because she took care of me, and now it's my turn to take care of her."

She nodded. "I took care of Sully. He was always getting in trouble, and my mom would yell like crazy. She didn't know how to get him to listen, but I did. You just had to be nice. People thought he was a bad kid, so they never talked nice to him anymore."

"You sound like you're a good big sister."

She had to swallow. "I was."

They sat in silence awhile, listening to a loud conversation from a group of high school students in the corner.

"They think I'm, like, cursed," she said, watching them. "They're not mean, but they don't want to be around me or look at me."

Piper leaned forward, resting her elbows on the table. "They're learning what to do, too. This is going to be a hard adjustment for everybody, but you know what I've learned? Time really does heal. Time and laughter. Unfortunately, I'm not very funny."

She grinned. "I like you."

"Thanks," she said.

They drank brightly colored smoothies in silence a few moments.

"I didn't just drop by for a smoothie, Sophie. I have some news and I've been debating where the best place is to tell you. Maybe back in your room?"

"No, you can tell me. I don't cry as much anymore."

The remark saddened Piper, and she had to clear her throat before speaking. "They, um, caught him. That detective that was with me when I met you? He caught the man that killed your family."

Sophie said nothing. Tears formed in her eyes, but she didn't make a peep. Piper knew she had made a mistake telling her in front of other people. She might not cry. When the body wanted to cry, you had to let it.

"I have to go," Sophie said suddenly and rose.

"I'll drive you back."

"No," she said. "I can walk. I wanna be alone."

37

Piper sat in the packed courtroom at eight in the morning two days later. The air was stifling, carrying the odor of sweat and bodies. The media occupied most of the seats, forcing some attendees to stand at the back. The outside temperature soared to 110 degrees.

She sat behind the prosecution table, where twenty-seven cases were listed on the court docket for today, but everyone was there for Owen Alistair Whittaker. The name on everybody's lips. Piper wasn't sure what he was—serial murderer, mass murderer, spree killer; all the same to her—but she knew he was an oddity that piqued the public interest more than she would have wanted.

The prosecutor was someone covering arraignments and wouldn't be the assigned prosecutor.

"All rise, Eighth District court is now in session," the bailiff said. "The Honorable Maria Covey presiding."

A woman with dark black hair and glasses came out. She sat down and looked over the crowded courtroom a moment before saying, "Please be seated. Let's call the matter of Owen Alistair Whittaker, number twenty-three on the docket."

The bailiffs brought Owen out in an orange jumpsuit and white slippers with no laces. He looked clean, and she wondered if he willingly showered or if they had to hose him down. He glanced to Piper and then was stood at the lectern.

Judge Covey said, "Mr. Whittaker, am I correct in understanding that you are currently without residence or employment?"

He gave no response.

"Mr. Whittaker, I do need a reply. Are you currently without residence or employment?"

He didn't answer.

"Well, for now, I'm entering not guilty pleas on your behalf then, and assigning the Clark County Public Defender's Office to represent you in this matter. They will have someone come visit with you today. We'll set this matter for a scheduling conference two weeks out. Bail is denied at this time. Thank you."

Piper watched as he was led out of the courtroom. His eyes met hers one last time, and she felt a wave of disgust. Then, he was gone. As she prepared to leave, she spotted Lazarus standing at the rear of the courtroom, watching.

"I've never seen so many reporters," she said.

"Wounds attract flies."

Camera crews swarmed outside the courtroom. When the doors swung open, they surged forward, clamoring for a shot. The people exiting the courtroom were pursued by reporters, and as they spilled into the hallway, the cacophony of voices swelled.

Lazarus and Piper decided to take the stairs rather than the elevator.

"I gotta meet with the DA's office," Lazarus said once they got to the first floor.

He seemed distant, distracted. She thought that catching this man would have offered some relief, some perspective. It didn't seem to.

"You okay?"

"Fine," he said without turning around. And then he was out the doors and gone.

38

Russo Maria Bianchi woke in a strange bed and took a moment to orient herself. She sat up, her nude body slender in the dawn's light coming through the open window. Beside her, a young man lay asleep—his skin, smooth and unblemished. The skin of youth.

She traced her fingers delicately across his back, savoring the warmth of his youthful flesh. Rising gracefully, she collected her scattered clothing from the floor. Her long chestnut hair came down to midthigh, and she found her elastic and pulled it back. She heard the man in the bed inhale as he woke and rolled over onto his back, watching her. She pulled on her black thong and then her business suit, putting the pinstripe jacket on and looking at herself in a full-length mirror by the bed.

"Why do you have a full mirror by your bed?" she said.

"I like to look at myself when I get up."

She shook her head. "Youth really is wasted on the young."

He sat up, and the sheets rustled. "I thought we could grab some breakfast."

She turned and looked at him. He was easily half her age, and the brightness in his eyes was captivating. Life hadn't touched him yet. No crow's-feet or ulcers from a cheating spouse, no lessons in solitude from raising two children as a single parent working full time. He was sweet and innocent, and she wondered how long that would last.

She cupped his beautiful face in her hands and kissed his forehead before whispering, "Oh honey, you only have one good trait, and I've had my fill of it. I don't need you anymore."

He sat quietly on the bed, shocked, as she got her bag and left the apartment.

The hallway was dirty and smelled like mold. She had lived somewhere similar through law school. An old mental institution that the owner couldn't sell and instead converted to student housing.

Since it had a past as an institution, especially back when the mentally ill were treated worse than livestock, Russo thought people might have died there, either by their own doing or others'. She heard things at night, odd sounds and movement, but the rent was so cheap, she convinced herself it was noise from the other apartments; looking back she knew they weren't. She had the luxury now of accepting the truth. Truth wasn't always a luxury life afforded.

She got into her Porsche and rolled the top down as she slid her sunglasses on. A text from her assistant buzzed her phone. It said Our office got assigned a new case. It's all over the news!!!

She clicked on the link her assistant had sent, and it opened up an article.

The Creeper's Origins: A Dive into Owen Alistair Whittaker's Tumultuous Past

By Rachel Stowers, Staff Writer for Las Vegas Ledger

Las Vegas has borne witness to numerous harrowing tales over the years, but the story of Owen Alistair Whittaker, chillingly christened "the Creeper," has unquestionably shaken our community.

Hailing from Terrebonne Parish, Louisiana, Whittaker's early life played out in a boys' home known to some in our area with Louisiana roots—a place spoken of in hushed tones due to its troubled history. The tragic event at the hands of some older boys that permanently scarred young Owen, leaving half his face burned and rendering one eye sightless, has become a defining chapter in his unsettling narrative.

Beyond these physical scars, Whittaker grappled with a rare condition diagnosed when he was just ten. This ailment seemed to freeze Owen in time, trapping him in a childlike physique.

After departing the boys' home, Whittaker took to wandering. Sources at the freight train circuits who didn't want to be identified have reported spotting him boarding trains in his youth, possibly marking the start of a sinister trail across the country.

Law enforcement agencies, just beginning to put pieces of a grim puzzle together, have started tracing his movements by linking him to an escalating series of crimes centered around rail stops. While some of these offenses started off as mere petty thefts—stolen goods from nearby establishments or unsuspecting passengers—it wasn't long before his transgressions took a more menacing turn. Records have revealed Whittaker's potential involvement in more grievous and harrowing acts, painting a portrait of a man who might have harnessed the anonymity of the railways to unleash a reign of terror.

However, for us in Sin City, the nightmare truly began with the Ember Lake incidents. The memory of the senseless loss of Adam Mitchell, Sarah Griffith and college student Ava Mitchell during what was meant to be a leisurely vacation still casts a long shadow over our city. As if that horror wasn't enough, the tragedy surrounding Emily Grace and her young son, Sullivan, further magnified the Creeper's menace. Investigations into these episodes paint a macabre picture: Whittaker, exhibiting almost supernatural patience, would stake out homes, hiding within walls or basements, before emerging with malevolent intent.

The ordeal faced by the Graces, particularly the unsettling revelation of Whittaker's prolonged covert stay within their home, has sent shock waves throughout our neighborhoods.

As Whittaker's impending trial looms, many in Las Vegas are left grappling with uneasy questions. How did a boy from a distant parish in Louisiana come to instill such terror in our community? And in this city of bright lights, have we unwittingly overlooked the shadows that lurk among us?

Russo texted back: The writing's garbage.

Who cares??? It's huge. It's all over insta!!!

Over what?

Instagram.

OK.

She sat there a moment, debating. She could head home, but something about the article stuck with her. It piqued her interest, and not a lot of things did after forty years of practicing criminal law in one of the most crime-ridden cities in the world.

She started her car and headed for the county jail.

39

The Porsche raced along the highway, the wind loud in Russo's ears.

The county jail was a monstrous building that tried to appear less monstrous on the outside. Russo had been here so much over the decades that it felt like a second home.

The public defenders had "jail days," where they were assigned to go to the jail that day. Usually, it meant your friends in the office would send you to explain to the clients what's going on with their cases, sometimes with the files and sometimes with nothing but bullshit. It wasn't the public defender's fault: the police and prosecutor's offices had huge says in what the budgets would be for the public defender's office and how many attorneys she could hire. Who would vote for more money and resources for their opponents?

She used to dread the jail days when she was a trial defender because all she wanted to do was be in court making arguments. Now, as director of the Clark County Public Defender's Office, she barely got to do that. It was all bureaucracy and lunacy and backstabbing. Because the PD's office continued to grow, given how much crime had been jumping recently, it was now a noticeable part of the county budget. Which meant most of Russo's job was fighting off politicians from reducing it.

She checked in and had to be wanded after going through the metal detectors.

"Do you wand the prosecutors too?" she said to the guard.

"Yeah. I don't trust no lawyers."

"Smart man."

She went into the private attorney-client room and took a seat at a steel bench. The room's floor was bare cement with white outlines indicating where visitors could stand and where they were too close to the barriers.

The door unbolted and opened, and Owen Whittaker was brought in. The media piece didn't capture accurately how small he really was. Short, but more thin. Emaciated. Like a snake standing on two legs.

The guard sat him down in front of her and left.

She noticed that his injured eye had patches of milky white and deep tar-like blackness. He moistened his lower lip with his tongue and fixed his gaze on her.

"The media doesn't do justice to how unique you look," she remarked, extracting a cigarette case of Italian imports and a lighter from a specially lined compartment in her bag, designed to avoid setting off metal detectors or security wands. "They're calling you the Creeper," she said, lighting the cigarette and putting the case and lighter back. "It fits."

He watched her with an uneven gaze, his blinks creating an unsettling rhythm.

"What?" she said. "D'you expect me to come in here and piss myself like a teenager reading about you in *Cosmo*? Please. I've lived too long and seen too much to care about you. Honestly, I don't like you. But here's the thing, Owen, if I was your lawyer, I wouldn't want you to go to prison. Do you know why? Because I love winning more than I dislike you."

She allowed the smoke to whirl around her. "That moment when the jury foreman glances at me with a little grin, like we're old friends, like we really know each other . . . that's when I know I've won. And Owen, there's no feeling in the world like it."

The two watched each other in silence a moment.

"Even though you belong in prison, I'm going to do everything I can to see you don't go there. Because it's about me, not you. So keep your mouth shut and do everything I tell you. First time you don't listen to me, I drop you. Then I assign your case to whatever new law school graduate can utter two words in front of a judge without passing out. We understand each other?"

She reclined in her chair, drawing on her cigarette and exhaling the smoke through her nostrils.

He watched her a long time, and then gave a slow nod.

"Good." She crossed one leg over another and retrieved a yellow legal pad and pen from her bag. "Start from the beginning."

40

On a cloudy Wednesday at the gym, Piper thought about the case.

There were still missing pieces, like how Owen Whittaker had managed to get into the house without being noticed. Sophie hadn't known someone was living there, but her brother had once said he thought the house was haunted because of strange noises at night. Now that comment felt eerily important.

The two weeks to Owen Whittaker's scheduling conference grinded along slowly.

When the day came, Piper dressed in a simple black suit and put on silver earrings that matched her necklace.

It was in court that Piper saw the assigned prosecutor and public defender for the first time. The prosecutor she recognized, a short man with light-red hair and a round, cherubic face named Kyle Lounger. The surname was fitting because he had a habit of leaning way back in his chair, almost like he was ready to take a nap.

At the defense table was a woman Piper had seen a couple of times but never spoken with. She sat straight in her chair with her hands folded neatly over one knee. Her suit was immaculate, her nails clean and shiny, her long hair came down behind her and cascaded past the chair and nearly to the floor.

The assigned judge on the case was Grant Billings, a man Piper knew little about.

"All rise," the bailiff bellowed as Judge Billings walked in. He was pudgy and looked like he was angry.

"Please be seated. Bailiff, bring out the defendant."

Owen emerged in an orange jumpsuit with his gaze to the floor.

Judge Billings booted up his computer and coughed, taking time to pour some water into a mug and take a sip. Then he swallowed and said, "We are here for the matter of Owen Alistair Whittaker, case number CR-2371897, for a scheduling conference. Counsel will state their appearances."

Lounger rose and said, "Kyle Lounger for the State."

The woman at the defense table stood gracefully, in stark contrast to Lounger's lumbering movements.

"Russo Bianchi for Mr. Whittaker."

"And what are we doing today, Counselor?"

"We'll be filing a motion challenging competency to stand trial, Your Honor."

She took three documents out of her satchel and held one out for Lounger, who was forced to go get it because she didn't walk over to hand it to him, and instead of asking the judge's permission to approach, she held the third copy out to the bailiff, who took it and handed it to the judge. It was apparent she was in command of the room.

The judge said, "Then we will have Mr. Whittaker evaluated for competency. Ms. Bianchi, I'm assuming you have your own experts in mind?"

"I do, Judge."

"Mr. Lounger, I assume the State will want their own experts for evaluation?"

"Yes, Your Honor."

"Then let's set this out and get those evaluations done."

The dates were set before the judge asked if there was anything else and then thanked the lawyers and called the next case. Piper watched the way Russo interacted with Owen Whittaker. She held no fear of him. Maybe some revulsion—how could she not—but she didn't show it.

Russo put her hand on his shoulder as she whispered something in his ear and he nodded, and then was taken back to the holding cells.

Lounger turned around from the prosecution table.

"Haven't seen you in a while," he said.

"Been around," Piper said.

He glanced at Russo, who left the courtroom without acknowledging him.

Lounger said, "Just another day, another psycho with mommy issues, right?"

"Suppose so," she said with a forced grin before she rose.

She went back to the Dungeon because she needed to be somewhere without a lot of people right now.

Seeing Owen Whittaker had unnerved her.

The room was dark, and she flipped on the light and saw Lazarus sitting at his desk with his feet up, his fingers steepled on his stomach as he stared at a transparent evidence bag. The case number and other information were written on a sticker across the front. Inside was a long screwdriver with a thick handle.

She said, "Is this what you do when I'm not around?"

"He put this in Ava Mitchell's neck eleven times," Lazarus drawled. "All the way through. Small guy like that. How you figure that is, Danes?"

She didn't respond.

"You know where the word *panic* comes from? The old god Pan. He would scream in the forests, and his scream would drive the animals insane with lust and rage. *Lust and rage . . .*"

He looked at her now.

"Did you see him in court?" he said.

"Yes."

"What did he look like? Happy, sad, angry?"

"Happy? No, not happy. More like it didn't matter where he was and court was as good a place as any."

He nodded as though he knew exactly what she was talking about. "You gonna be there every hearing?"

"Yes."

"Why?"

"Because Sophie would be if she could."

He turned his eyes back to the screwdriver. "I asked him why he let Sophie live. There's no reason to leave a witness alive."

"There's no reason for any of this," she said, reclining in her chair and propping one foot up against the edge of the desk. "What do you know about his lawyer?"

"Russo? She's the director of the PD's office. She's much smarter than Lounger, and he's not a great trial lawyer to start with."

"You sound like you have experience with him."

"I'd collared a man that attacked his friend with a machete. Tried to really chop him up. Lounger was the prosecutor and got several facts, simple facts like time of day, wrong, because he hadn't reviewed the reports recently. The jury acquitted."

"You can always talk to the DA about assigning someone else."

He shook his head. "They don't care what I have to say." He looked at her. "They might care what you have to say."

"No."

"Why not?"

"Because it's not my fight. I'm not with the prosecution or the defense. It wouldn't be appropriate."

"Appropriate," he muttered.

She let out a long breath and decided she should go home. It seemed like Lazarus wanted to be alone.

"I'm tired," she said, rising. "You look pretty beat, too. When was the last time you slept?"

"I don't know," he said with his gaze fixed on the screwdriver.

She could tell the conversation was over and began to leave when he said, "Danes? It's not sittin' right. Watch your back."

41

Six weeks later, Piper was notified that both defense and prosecution had completed their evaluations of Owen Whittaker. The defense had used three different experts: a psychologist, forensic psychiatrist, and neurobiologist who specialized in brain injuries. The prosecution had used the two clinical psychiatrists they frequently worked with.

County and district attorney's offices used the same experts over time, which made the cases a stable part of the experts' income. And though any DA would deny it, if the experts suddenly started testifying to things that didn't help the prosecution, they ran the risk of potentially receiving less work. It created a system of *government experts* and *defense experts*, which Piper had always found ridiculous. The facts should speak the same from either side. Without consensus by equally qualified experts, the results of the hearing were in doubt. No one could predict which way it would go, and it frightened her.

Piper was dressed comfortably in shorts and a T-shirt in the backyard, doing paperwork. She had felt restless with only one case and called Tom Williams at the office and told him she was going crazy. He said he would send her some overflow work, so now she worked from home, and it at least occupied her mind for short periods.

"Piper?" her grandma shouted from somewhere in the house.

"Yeah?" she yelled back.

"Someone is here to see you."

Piper took off her reading glasses and placed them next to her laptop as she rose and went to the door. Judge Dawson stood in the foyer in a black suit, cut to trim. Her arms hung casually at her sides, and she wore little makeup.

"Hope you don't mind I looked up your address," the judge said. "It was on your CV Tom sent over."

"It's fine. Um, Grandma, this is Judge Dawson that I told you about."

Her grandmother smiled and held out her hand, and they shook. "Lake Danes. Nice to meet you, Judge."

"It's Hope. This is a lovely home you have."

"Oh, thank you. Would you like some water or an iced tea?"

"Actually I need to speak to your granddaughter for a moment, if I may."

Lake glanced at Piper, a little disappointed, and said, "Well, I have some gardening to finish up, so I'll leave you to it. Nice to meet you, Hope."

"You as well."

When they were alone, the judge looked around the house with her hands behind her back.

"I know this area. Mostly retirees and not many children. Must've been lonely for you."

"I got by."

"I have no doubt." She stopped, lightly touching a photo of Piper and her grandmother at a birthday party. "Do you have somewhere we can talk?"

They sat out on the patio, watching a couple of older men on the golf course, and sipped iced tea that Lake had brought out for them.

"Did you read the evaluation reports?" Judge Dawson said.

"I did. Did you?"

"I may have taken a peek. We judges don't mind sharing with each other. We've got our little clique, too. So what do you think?"

"Delusional personality conduct disorder is a mouthful. Sounded like stretching to me."

"Maybe." She sipped her iced tea. "Dr. Brown said it stemmed from his brutal upbringing coupled with serious brain injuries while in his youth."

"Do you think a jury will be sympathetic?"

"I have no doubt that once Russo Bianchi gets through explaining his upbringing, that jury's going to be in tears."

The judge tilted her head slightly, almost like a shrug. "But what do I know? I've been in juvenile court my entire career and never had a jury."

"Do you wish you did?"

"No." She set her iced tea down on the table. "Are you going to cross-examine the doctors?"

"I don't know. Guess we'll have to wait and see what comes out."

"Pay attention to how Russo presents her case. You could learn something."

42

Lazarus sat at the saloon, having already finished his beers and now nursing a bottle of absinthe. The liquid like green fire in a bottle.

He watched the people here, some knocking back a few before going home to spouses they didn't want to be with and children they didn't like. The bottle was an escape, but it never lasted and left things worse than before. He'd seen more people destroyed by the bottle than anything else.

A young woman sat at a table by herself. She wore a jean skirt and a red tank top with cowboy boots, and her brown hair came to her shoulders. Lazarus called the waitress over and said he would be picking up the girl's tab. When she was told, the girl looked back and waved, and Lazarus nodded once. She came over.

"I just wanted to say thanks," she said.

"You're welcome. This seat's not taken if you wanna sit."

She sat down without hesitation. Lazarus watched her a moment.

"No way you're older than nineteen. What you doin' in a bar like this?"

"I'm twenty-two."

"And I'm not your daddy."

She smiled at him. "How'd you know?"

"I'm police."

The smile went away. "I'm having one beer and a sandwich and leaving. You really gonna bust me for that?"

"I just paid for your meal, so clearly not. I'm more curious why a nineteen-year-old is drinking alone in a place like this." He took a sip of absinthe. "See those three men in the booth across the bar? The one with prison tats crawling up his neck has been eyeing you since you walked in. If you weren't sitting here, he would've come up to you and offered to buy you a drink. One of them would've distracted you, and he would've slipped something in it, and they would've carried you outta here like nothin' happened."

"Um, paranoid much?" she said playfully.

He grinned. "You're not paranoid enough. I can assume the worst about folks, be mistaken, and nothin' happens. You assume the best and end up with the worst, that's a onetime mistake." He topped off his glass with the green liquid and took a sip, forgoing the dilution with water and sugar that was customary with absinthe. Sweat trickled down the back of his neck, soaking into his collar. "How long you been in town?" he said.

"How do you know I'm not from here?"

"Because no local girl would be in here by herself."

She glanced back to the men. One of them said something quietly to another one when they noticed her looking.

"You don't need to worry about them anymore," he said. "How long you been here?"

"A week. I'm staying at the hostel next door."

Lazarus leaned back and lit a cigarette from the pack he had out on the table. He handed it to her and she took a drag and said, "That's good."

"I rarely smoke, so I smoke the finest. Best pleasures make up in height what they don't have in length."

She inhaled another drag and blew it out. "You don't talk like any cops I know."

"You know a lotta cops?"

"I've been in trouble here and there."

He looked down to the red tip of her cigarette. "Where you headed?"

"Nowhere. Here. I'm an actress, or tryin' to be. People said Vegas is the new Hollywood, so I thought I'd give it a shot."

"Wherever you're from, you should go back."

"Why?"

"Because there's no such thing as running away. Life don't work like that."

"Really? Then how does it work, *Dad*?" she said with a smile.

He looked to the three men, their faces hard and cold. "People like you become prey for people like them."

She glanced back at them again.

"I grew up around people like them," she said.

"Then you know they got great big holes right in the middle of 'em. No matter what they do, they'll never fill 'em, but they damn sure are gonna try."

She sat in silence awhile and then said, "You sound like you know a lot about it. Having a hole in the middle."

Lazarus took her cigarette, drawing in a slow drag before exhaling the smoke through his nose.

"You got it, too," he said, handing the cigarette back. "That's why you can see it in me." He was staring at the men now, and they were staring back. "People like us, we know hurting other people don't fill the hole, so we hurt ourselves."

She remained quiet, smoking and gazing across the bar. She rested one arm under the other, the cigarette poised between two fingers, a posture that resembled a woman who had been smoking for fifty years.

She said, "And what do you do when the people that are supposed to protect you have that hole inside 'em, too?"

Lazarus pulled out the switchblade he kept in an ankle holster.

The girl's eyes widened, and she froze. She'd had a blade pulled on her before.

Lazarus pressed a silver hitch, and the blade slid out with a whisper, flicking the light off the polished steel. "I bought this in Mexico from a weapons dealer who got it off a dead cartel brujo. It's like a sorcerer, or a witch. The handle's made a' bone, not sure what kind. Maybe human. But it's light and sharp as a razor."

Lazarus expertly flipped the knife with the blade now pointed to the floor and the handle in his fist. "Somebody's hurting you, you bury this in his stomach. It'll slide in like wet clay. When it's up to the hilt, you twist hard and pull out. Rips it open so it won't stop bleedin'. Then you run."

He retracted the blade and extended the knife toward the girl. She cautiously took it.

"Buy a bus ticket and go home. If you stay in this city, it'll eat you. The world'll eat you anyway, but you're young enough you can keep a spark alive. Even a spark can set forests on fire if you keep it alive long enough."

Lazarus rose and went to Bass, who had watched the interaction.

"You sure you wanna give her that? That's a good knife."

Lazarus took out the last of his cash and put it on the counter.

"What's that for?"

"Any damage."

He turned and went over to the booth the three men were sitting in.

"Evenin', gentlemen," he said.

One of the men opened his mouth to speak, but Lazarus grabbed a beer bottle off the table and slammed it into his jaw. The bottle didn't break, but it knocked the man to the floor, his mouth bleeding badly.

He swung the bottle back and caught the second man in the face with a sickening crunch, glass shattering and blood spraying. The man fell to the ground, clutching his face and hollering in pain. The third man in the booth froze, his hands raised in surrender.

"Easy, man!"

"Get your boys and get outta here."

He took a step back and waited until the men left the bar. He looked back at the girl, and she stared at him with wide, fearful eyes.

Lazarus left without saying anything to her.

He got into his car and turned up the air conditioner as far as it would go. The stale, warm air swirled around him before the AC finally kicked in and began to cool the car. He turned on the stereo, and a song he didn't recognize blared through the speakers.

"Off to the hills, let's make our way,
While the world behind us falls away."

Bass appeared at his window and draped his forearms over the open door.

"You're tanked, brother. Sleep it off here. We got a room in the back with a good couch."

"I'm all right."

"I don't think you are. You shouldn't be drivin'."

"I'm police, Bass. I can do awful things and get away with 'em."

Bass opened the door all the way. "You're still sleeping here. Come on."

With a weary nod, Lazarus gave in, nearly stumbling out of the car.

43

Piper sat in court on the first day of the competency hearing and waited for everyone to file in. Courtrooms were mostly waiting rooms for her. She'd seen some trials, even cross-examined a witness once, but she wasn't a courtroom brawler like a good prosecutor or defense attorney was. As confident as she tried to appear, she was nervous in court.

Russo came in with no notes, books, or documents. She sat straight and folded one leg over the other. Piper noticed the court staff watching her.

Journalists and camera crews crowded the courtroom, their equipment jostling for space. The crowd pressed against the walls and spilled into the aisles, creating a claustrophobic feel.

Kyle Lounger came in and sat at the prosecution table. He leaned over to Russo, but Russo held up her hand, indicating she wasn't interested.

"All rise, Eighth District Court is now in session, the Honorable Grant Billings presiding."

Judge Billings came in and told everyone to sit down. He looked over the crowd and grew visibly agitated.

"Counsel, approach."

Russo and Lounger approached the judge's bench, and Piper followed. She wasn't a party to the case, but she felt Sophie was. Still, she stood behind the other two attorneys and let them do the arguing.

The judge said, "I don't like this many cameras in here. I'm thinking of closing the courtroom."

Lounger said, "I'd be fine with making this a closed court, Judge. No reason to have all these gawkers in here."

Russo said, "I'd like them to stay."

"Why?" Lounger said.

"Because you don't."

The two glared at each other, and it seemed like Lounger was at a loss as to what to say.

The judge said, "I don't agree, Counsel. I think a closed courtroom would be for the best. Ms. Danes, as the guardian for the surviving victim in this case, you have a say as well under the Victims' Rights Act."

"Whatever the Court deems best will be fine by Ms. Grace, Your Honor."

"Then I'm ordering the courtroom closed to the media. We'll take a minute and let them clear out. Have you two talked yet?"

Russo said, "The stage is a bit too early for that, Your Honor."

He sighed, disappointed, and said, "Head back."

When the attorneys were away from the bench, the judge said, "Ladies and gentlemen, our courtroom is a little too crowded for the matter we have before us today. As such, I am closing the courtroom to all spectators and media—"

Grumbles went up from the crowd, particularly the cameramen and reporters trying to get a clear shot for the evening news.

The judge raised his voice over the noise and issued a few more instructions, and the bailiffs called for extra help to get everyone out. Piper had never seen so much interest in a case before, and she had a feeling it had little to do with Sophie Grace.

When the courtroom was cleared, Judge Billings said, "In my chambers, Counsel. You too, Ms. Danes."

The three attorneys followed the judge as he led them through his office area, passing by his clerks' cubicles. The office was adorned with numerous old photos and memorabilia, showcasing his accomplishments and media mentions. Piper couldn't spot any family or children's photos.

He removed his robe and settled into his desk chair; he was dressed in shirtsleeves and a simple tie. As he leaned back, the chair creaked under his weight. Russo and Lounger occupied two leather recliners facing him, while Piper chose to sit on the distant couch. This situation wasn't uncommon for her; she often felt more like an observer than a participant.

"What is going on between you two?" the judge said to Russo.

"I don't know what you mean, Judge," Russo said.

"I mean you two haven't even talked yet? What are you looking for in this?"

"I'm looking for the best outcome for my client."

"Cut the tripe. What do you want?"

"I want him to be declared incompetent and sent to State View."

Lounger didn't say anything.

"Mr. Lounger?" the judge prodded.

"Dr. Brown is the recognized expert in this area in the western United States. If he says he's competent, he's competent."

"I know it's very early in the case, but have you thought about what you would be willing to offer?" the judge said to Lounger.

Piper noticed the judge was eager for a plea deal and wondered what specifically about the case didn't appeal to him: the attention, the amount of work, or simply the length of time because he had other plans?

"Murder one without parole."

"How the hell am I supposed to take that to him?" Russo said. "We might as well roll the dice at a trial. It couldn't get any worse."

"I could ask for the death penalty."

"Oh please, Kyle, you don't have the balls. You're not the type that's going to fight through crowds of anti–death penalty protestors every day."

The judge sighed and spoke in a manner that conveyed he understood he had lost this fight. "Just work it out if you can. There's no reason to have a circus for the next year."

After a few minutes of discussing the order of expert testimony, they went back out to the court, and Piper took her place behind the prosecution table. Russo sat at the defense table as Owen Whittaker was brought out.

The judge made some announcements for the benefit of the record about the hearing, the date, and some of the issues.

"The floor is the State's," Judge Billings said.

"The State would call Dr. Augustine Brown to the stand."

Piper had dealt with Dr. Brown before. He was the State's top expert on mental disorders, being used by almost every county. He was a professional-looking man, someone you'd see maybe on Wall Street. He wore an expensive gray suit and had thick glasses, a plain but expensive-looking watch on his wrist. He sat in the witness stand like an aristocrat about to give a lecture. He was brilliant but gave off a snake-oil-salesman feeling that Piper guessed juries didn't find pleasant.

"Your Honor," Lounger said as he took to the lectern, "we would like Dr. Brown recognized as an expert in mental health and mental disorders as per our motion."

"Ms. Bianchi, do you stipulate?"

It was a routine request, and Piper had never seen someone say no.

"No," Russo said.

Lounger looked annoyed as he said, "Dr. Brown, please outline your qualifications."

Dr. Brown tilted his head slightly as though surprised and said, "I'm a board-certified psychiatrist with over three decades' experience in clinical and forensic psychiatry. I'm a proud alum of Johns Hopkins University, where I taught psychiatry for a number of years before going back into private practice."

"How many patients would you say you've evaluated in your career?"

"Thousands. I really couldn't count."

"You've been qualified as an expert for the State before, correct?"

"Yes. I've testified in over two hundred trials."

Lounger looked at the judge and said again, "We would qualify Dr. Brown as an expert in the field of mental health and mental disorders."

Russo was on her feet. "We would object on foundational grounds and ask for oral arguments."

Now it was the judge's time to look annoyed. "You know we could have done this before today."

Russo simply smiled and said, "I like spending time here, Your Honor. Feels like home."

He sighed again, this time louder as though no one had heard him before. "Let's just do it now."

Lounger put both hands on the lectern and said, "Dr. Brown, please go into more detail about your clinical experience and qualifications."

Piper watched, mesmerized. It was basically Dr. Brown bragging about himself for almost an hour. It was clearly his favorite topic.

When Lounger was done going through his years of experience, varied cases, and specific education and research, it was Russo's turn.

She rose and went to the lectern without even a glance in Kyle Lounger's direction.

44

Russo watched Dr. Brown a moment. She stepped to the side of the lectern and put one elbow on it, relaxed. She looked like she was with friends describing some interesting story rather than in court.

"You talked about your time as a clinician. Please describe what a clinician does."

"That's a loaded question, it's massively broad."

"But in general they practice the art and craft they're trained in. In other words, dealing with patients."

"That is a large part of it, yes."

"You said you taught for a time, but it wasn't just a time. You taught for over twenty years."

"That is correct."

"You were involved in a lot of research."

"I was, yes. As most academics are."

"In fact, you completed no less than eighty massive research papers during your time as an academic, correct?"

"That is correct."

"So of the thirty or so years you've been a licensed physician, two-thirds of that time was spent in academia and research, correct?"

"Correct."

"You don't see patients when doing research, do you?"

"Some doctors still continue to see patients."

"Some, but not you. You were locked in the ivory tower for those years, were you not, Doctor?"

The doctor paused. A professional witness paused frequently because they knew their emotions could influence their response.

"I did not see any patients during the time, as I was focused exclusively on research and teaching."

She stepped away from the lectern and began pacing in the well, the area of the floor between the audience and the judge's bench. The bailiffs shot her nervous glances, unaccustomed to someone approaching the judge without asking permission. "What is your specialty, Doctor?"

"I have expertise in diseases of—"

"No, no, not your self-proclaimed field of expertise, I mean what type of medicine did you complete your residency in?"

He glanced to Lounger and said, "Geriatric psychiatry."

"Geriatric? As in elderly?"

"Correct."

"How old is Mr. Whittaker?"

He glanced at Owen, who remained seated with his eyes down. Owen didn't move, react, or do much of anything except breathe and blink.

"Twenty-nine."

"Twenty-nine. So based on your specialty training, he might as well be six years old, and you would understand him just about as well, correct?"

Piper's gaze shifted to Owen Whittaker. He stared intently at the table, appearing either unaware of or indifferent to the proceedings unfolding around him.

"Objection," Lounger said as he rose to his feet.

"Withdrawn," Russo quickly said. "I'd like to talk about your published works. Now, you have thirty-six noted publications in what would be considered the more prestigious psychiatric journals, correct?"

"Yes."

"Of the thirty-six, you describe fifty-two patients in those works, correct?"

"That is correct."

"Of those fifty-two, you have diagnosed exactly thirty-six as either schizophrenic or schizoaffective, is that correct?"

"I have, yes."

"That's almost seventy percent. How prevalent are those two disorders in the general population?"

He cleared his throat. "About one percent of the population suffers from these disorders."

"One percent? And you diagnose it seventy percent of the time, is that right?"

"Yes, but the pool of patients that I gather from includes—"

"Thank you, Doctor, you answered my question."

Dr. Brown grew frustrated and looked to the judge and said, "I'd like to answer that more fully, Your Honor."

"Go ahead."

"The patients that are sent to me are the most disturbed in our criminal justice system. They're the most likely to have these disorders given the extreme nature of their crimes. So it's a loaded question to say that I diagnose my patients with schizo disorders the majority of the time."

"You've mentioned that phrase before. A *loaded question*. You've accused me of that twice. Define loaded question, please?"

"It's a question that contains its own answer within the question. It leads to misleading answers."

"Misleading? Interesting. Please tell me how I have misled this court."

"That's not what—"

"Misleading—that was your word, Dr. Brown. Not mine. Please explain to this court how I have misled you."

The question flustered Dr. Brown. A flustered witness was a careless witness.

"Perhaps *misled* was too strong a word," he finally said.

Russo smiled, but it had the predatory edge of someone who had drawn first blood. "What word fits, then? It leads to *unfair* answers?"

"Yes. I suppose that works."

"What answers have you given that are unfair?"

"That's not what I'm—"

"I'd like to talk about Dale Rogers, Dr. Brown. Who is Dale Rogers?"

The way she abruptly interrupted him and shifted topics whenever Dr. Brown tried to explain one of his answers impressed Piper. Unfortunately, Piper realized, feeling impressed only meant Owen Whittaker was edging closer to being transferred to a minimum-security hospital.

Dr. Brown was clearly articulate, insightful, and intelligent, but when his status was challenged, he got hurt and angry like everyone else.

"That information is protected by doctor-patient privilege."

Russo looked to the judge. "Your Honor, it's a closed courtroom and the good doctor's credentials are at issue. Please order the witness to break confidentiality for the purposes of this hearing."

Judge Billings said, "So ordered. Dr. Brown, you may answer."

Dr. Brown paused a moment. "I cannot."

"I'm asking you to answer, Doctor."

"I understand, Your Honor, but it would be unethical for me to break that privilege."

Kyle Lounger appeared panicked; he was losing control of the hearing and knew it. Russo leaned against the defense table and let the growing agitation of the judge toward Dr. Brown cook.

Lounger rose and said, "Your Honor, perhaps a moment to consult with my witness is in order."

The judge fixed his gaze on the doctor and said, "Doctor, when you return to this courtroom, I expect an answer to this question and any others I advise you to answer. Otherwise, we will need to consider our next steps." He glanced at Russo and announced, "We'll take a ten-minute recess."

As the judge left the courtroom, Lounger and Dr. Brown quickly retreated to the attorney-client room in the adjacent hallway.

Owen's eyes rose, and he turned his head and stared at Piper.

Russo noticed who he was looking at and acknowledged Piper for the first time. "You're the guardian?"

"I am."

"What's your take on all this?"

"Just waiting to see how it plays out."

"Then try not to forget there's a human being on this side of the room, too."

A few minutes later, Lounger and Dr. Brown came back in. The judge was called and asked what would be happening. Lounger rose and said, "Dr. Brown will be continuing."

"Dr. Brown, please take the stand and remember you are still under oath."

The doctor sat back up on the stand and held his head a little higher as though to compensate.

"Dr. Brown," Russo said as she stood in front of the lectern with her arms folded, "Who is Dale Rogers?"

"He was a patient of mine in Utah."

"Assigned to you by the district court there, correct?"

"Yes."

"You received a disciplinary letter from the state medical board in relation to Mr. Rogers, correct?"

"It was a complicated issue, but yes I did. I revealed some information about his case to a party that should not have been privy to that information. I took full responsibility and took care of the professional reprimand."

"You told a friend about Dale's case, and this friend told his buddy, who wrote for a newspaper, isn't that right?"

He hesitated. "Yes."

"And what you said appeared in the paper, didn't it?"

The doctor didn't answer right away, and Russo said, "We need an audible answer, Doctor. That's what the microphones are for."

"Yes, what I said appeared in the *Salt Lake Tribune*."

"Mr. Rogers lost his job because of it?"

The doctor hesitated, his voice lacking its earlier certainty. "He did."

"His wife took their children and left him shortly after that."

"I believe so."

"And then he bought several bottles of vodka, checked into a motel room, and drank himself to death . . . because of what you did?"

Dr. Brown didn't answer. Lounger sat silently.

Russo looked to the judge.

"Your Honor, we would vehemently object to Dr. Brown being qualified as a forensic psychiatric expert in this matter. We object on the grounds that Dr. Brown's time as a clinician primarily involved research and not patient care. Further, Dr. Brown's specialty within psychiatry is geriatric psychiatry. The defendant is a twenty-nine-year-old young man. This significant discrepancy in age groups, each with unique mental health attributes, renders Dr. Brown's specialization less relevant and potentially misleading.

"Dr. Brown's credentials primarily involve teaching and academics, rather than practicing psychiatry in a clinical setting. This will hinder his ability to provide a thorough and applicable evaluation of the defendant's mental state. Also, Dr. Brown has previously demonstrated a significant bias in his assessments, favoring certain diagnoses over others. This pattern, which is well documented in his published works, casts doubt on the impartiality of his expert testimony."

Lounger rose. "Your Honor, I would object to Ms.—"

She cut him off. "I'm not finished," she said, her gaze sharp. Lounger stumbled, his face reddening.

Judge Billings intervened. "Mr. Lounger, let her finish."

Lounger sat, visibly unsettled.

Russo turned back to the judge. "And lastly, Your Honor, we object since Dr. Brown's recent professional disciplinary action for failure to maintain patient confidentiality may indicate a lack of ethical standards in his practice. This could potentially undermine the trustworthiness of his assessment. We would ask for an opportunity to brief the matter."

Lounger was on his feet. "Your Honor, this is a time-wasting tactic to—"

"Pick a real expert and we wouldn't have to waste time—"

"—aggravate the prosecution," Lounger continued as though Russo hadn't said anything. "Dr. Brown is the foremost expert in this field. He has testified in every higher court in several jurisdictions and is a frequent contributor to television and radio programs that deal with—"

"He's a TV star, so we should take his credentials seriously? Is that what you're arguing? 'Cause no offense to the doctor, but I can find much better-looking television stars to come in and entertain us."

Piper saw the judge quickly suppress a grin.

Lounger's anger flushed his face pink. "He's a recognized expert I've used dozens of times and never once has a court found him lacking in—"

"He's a charlatan."

"Your Honor! I find Ms. Bianchi's behavior unbecoming and would ask that she be instructed to follow decorum."

Piper knew that when an attorney argued about decorum, they had already lost whatever point they were trying to make. *They're being mean* wasn't an argument judges liked to hear.

Judge Billings held up his hand and said, "The defense has requested to brief this matter, and I am granting their request. Please have your briefs filed by next Friday the eleventh, and any replies by the fourteenth. Oral arguments will be scheduled for the following Monday. That concludes today's proceedings. Court is adjourned."

45

Piper went home. She had planned to be in court all day, but it looked like that wouldn't be happening.

Lake was in the kitchen sitting at the breakfast table. She had a cup of tea in front of her and her hand on her forehead. As though in pain.

"Hi, Grandma."

Her grandmother startled and said, "Oh! Sweetie. You scared me half to death."

"Sorry," she said, coming over to the table and setting her satchel down on the floor. "You feeling all right?"

"Just a headache, nothing to be concerned about," she said, rising and turning away quickly from Piper. She took her teacup to the sink and ran the water. Piper could see there weren't many dishes in the sink, but Lake started washing the couple there were. "How was your day?"

"That case I've been telling you about was crazy today. The defense attorney wouldn't let the prosecutor get out a word edgewise. She may convince the judge that a former psychiatry professor at the top medical university in the world may not be qualified to testify about forensic psychiatry. She's fierce."

"You know," she said, glancing back, "when I was younger, I wanted to be a lawyer."

"Really?"

"I took the admissions test and did well, but back then women were discouraged from working in what were considered male professions. I went to watch a court proceeding and the prosecutor was a woman, and the judge told her that women need to wear skirts in court, not pants. I decided it wasn't for me."

"I'm not sure what I'd do if a judge said that to me."

"It was a different world back then."

Piper waited a moment. The sound of the water grew louder as it hit the bare metal of the sink. All the dishes had been washed and put in the dishwasher, but Lake cleaned the sink.

"Grandma, I want to ask you something."

"Certainly."

"Can you sit down, please?"

There was a moment's hesitation and then Lake came over, drying her hands on a kitchen towel as she sat down and said, "What is it, dear?"

"You've been getting those headaches more frequently."

"Have I? I think I'm just tired. The hot summers do that to me sometimes."

"I'm not stupid, Grandma. What's wrong?"

She shook her head. "Nothing to worry about, sweetie." She rose and kissed the top of Piper's head. "I'm going to take a shower and lay down for a bit. Love you."

"Love you," Piper said absently.

Piper had gone to the doctor a few months ago for a sinus infection, and their family doctor had mentioned how her grandmother had come in. At dinner that night, Piper asked her grandmother about it, and she said it was something routine. But her grandmother came from a generation that didn't go to the doctor until they were nearly on their deathbed. Piper knew she wouldn't go in just for something routine.

Piper changed into jeans and a T-shirt before heading to her grandmother's bedroom. She heard the shower running and quietly entered the bathroom. Inside, she opened the medicine cabinet, revealing a row of amber bottles on the second shelf. Familiar with her grandmother's medications, she examined them.

There were six medications she knew she took, but there were eight bottles. She picked up the last two: donepezil and rivastigmine. She had never heard of them and quickly googled them. They were medications to help with cognitive decline, usually reserved for people with early-onset Alzheimer's.

She put the medications back and left the room. She went to the breakfast table and googled the symptoms and progression of Alzheimer's.

When her grandmother got out of the shower, she came out in a robe and got a glass of milk she filled from a carton.

"Grandma, have you been to Dr. Wilson lately?"

"Not for a few months. Why do you ask?"

"I saw some new medication in your cabinet."

"How did you see that? Were you snooping in my things?"

"Grandma," she said with a calm voice, "are you all right?"

"Yes. I am. Not that it's any of your business. And if you go through my things again, you will regret it, Piper Danes."

She stormed out of the kitchen, leaving Piper alone in the silence of the room.

46

Piper entered the office on a chilly, gray Monday, looking for Lazarus, who hadn't replied to her messages. She pondered if Vegas's abrupt weather changes were typical everywhere in this part of the country.

Riley sat at his desk speaking on the phone. Lazarus wasn't there.

Piper sat down at her desk and waited until he was off the phone. He said, "Okay, love you," and hung up and nodded a greeting to her.

"Riley, do you know where Lazarus is?"

He shrugged. "Following something up outta town."

"Really? Where?"

"I don't know."

She hesitated. "I have to go somewhere that I'm a little nervous about," she said awkwardly. "There's a doctor that was prescribing pills to Emily Grace and put Sophie on antidepressants and a mood stabilizer. I'd like to speak with him. Since he could be, I don't know, a suspect or whatever, I thought I should have a police officer with me."

"Where is he?"

"Twin Lakes."

He nodded and rose, the chair creaking as his massive frame lifted. "You shouldn't go there alone," he declared. "I'll come."

Piper settled into the passenger seat of Riley's F-350, an imposingly large truck that dwarfed most vehicles she'd seen. She wondered if he drove it because he liked the truck or simply because he couldn't fit into anything else.

Twin Lakes was on the outskirts of the city.

Piper noticed Twin Lakes' contrast to its idyllic name. Buildings marked with graffiti and wear lined the streets. The neighborhood buzzed with life, but tension was there, a community caught between hope and crime, just on the fringes of Vegas's glitz.

To break the silence, Piper asked, "Was that your wife on the phone?"

"Yes," Riley replied, offering nothing more.

"How did you two meet?"

"High school."

She waited for more and realized there wasn't anything else. "You're not much for talking, are you?"

"Smart people only talk when they have something to say, not just to say something."

Piper reflected on his words, realizing there might be more depth to him than she initially thought.

Piper assessed the medical office, located in a residential area flanked by run-down homes and a gas station. Parking near the building, with its brown bricks and dirty windows, she doubted the legitimacy of Emily Grace's back injury. There was no reason for her to drive this far out of her way for a prescription.

After exiting the car, Piper and Riley walked across the parking lot to the clinic's entrance. Riley held the door open for her. Inside, they found Dr. Thomas Newman's office to the right, where a receptionist looked up and seemed momentarily taken aback by Riley's size.

"Hi, I'm Piper Danes. I'm an attorney representing one of Dr. Newman's patients. I was hoping I could speak to him."

"Oh, um, sure, he's with a patient right now, but I'll let him know you're here."

"Thank you."

In the waiting room, Piper took a seat while Riley stood leaning against the wall. Their presence caught the attention of a young boy there with his mother. Captivated by Riley's imposing figure, the boy couldn't help but stare. Noticing this, Riley gave the boy a friendly wink, eliciting a shy smile before the boy averted his gaze.

A few minutes later a man came out in Dockers and a button-up shirt, a stethoscope around his neck.

"Hi," he said casually, "can I help you?"

"Yes, Doctor, my name is Piper Danes, and this is Detective Riley. We're here to discuss one of your patients, Sophie Grace."

"Oh, well, okay, come on back."

Dr. Newman guided them to a small, cluttered office at the back. The disarray wasn't due to an abundance of medical literature or books; it seemed haphazardly untidy, as if little care was given to appearance.

Piper and Riley took their seats as Dr. Newman settled behind his desk, watching them with a faint smile. Piper sensed an effort in his demeanor, as if he was trying to project a calm he didn't feel.

"Dr. Newman, part of my responsibility is safeguarding Sophie's welfare. I've noticed that you're the one who prescribed medications to both her and Emily Grace. Is that correct?"

"That's right, yes. I knew them for some time. But I can't discuss their records without the consent of the next of kin."

Riley said, "They don't have any next of kin."

The words hung in the air.

Piper said, "I'm Sophie's legal guardian right now, so you can discuss anything with me that you could have with her mother."

He shook his head. "You'll have to get a warrant."

"I don't need a warrant; a court order is just a phone call away," Piper asserted, pausing briefly. "Can you at least share what you feel comfortable discussing about Sophie's treatment?"

Dr. Newman shook his head. "There's not much to say. Teen depression and anxiety are rampant these days. They occasionally need medical help, and that's all I provided."

"What about her mother?"

"What about her?"

"It struck me as odd that she would drive all the way out here for a prescription when a local family doctor was basically around the corner from her."

"What exactly are you asking?"

Frustrated with the indirect responses, Piper chose a straightforward approach. "You prescribed oxycodone to Emily Grace, possibly longer than necessary. However, my concern is Sophie. Let's focus on her. If you talk to me about Sophie, I won't delve into her mother."

Dr. Newman glanced at Riley, who folded his arms and gave a small nod, as though letting him know it was in his best interest to talk.

Dr. Newman cleared his throat. "I'm still not sure what you're asking."

"I'm asking if she really needed these medications or if you gave them to her because her mother asked you to."

"That would be malpractice."

"Yes, it would."

The two held each other's gaze. "Her mother asked for my recommendation, and those were the two medications I recommended."

"Did Emily say what was going on in Sophie's life that she required these medications?"

"She said she was depressed and moody."

"Having a mother addicted to opioids can do that," she said with a bit more anger than she had meant to.

The doctor swallowed and finally got the courage to say, "I think you should probably speak to my lawyer at this point."

"There's no need, I think I got the answer I was looking for. Thank you for your time."

As they were walking outside, Riley said, "That was a waste."

"No, not really. I just wanted to know if Sophie really needed to be on those meds, and I don't think she did. Her mother wanted her on them, and the doctor just saw dollar signs. A lot of medicine is about money now."

"Everything's about money."

"You sound like Lazarus."

"Even he's right sometimes."

47

Navigating his way to the Mitchells' old cabin, Lazarus took a few wrong turns amid the dense forests, streams, and scattered boulders. He recalled reading the area's Wikipedia page when he first caught Ava's case. Ember Lake was steeped in lore about a wildfire fifty years ago, which had ravaged the surrounding woods but mysteriously spared anything near the lake. Locals talked about supernatural forces shielding the waters and preserving the nearby greenery.

The cabin, now with a fresh coat of paint and updated decor, still kept its original essence. After the Mitchells sold it, a real estate management company had taken ownership, turning it into an Airbnb destination for tourists.

Exiting his car, Lazarus took in the midday scene. Sunlight filtered through the trees, casting a patchwork of light and shadow on the ground, reminiscent of a painting. The lake lay still and empty, its waters untouched by any boats or bathers, accompanied only by a gentle whispering of the trees.

He admired the tranquil setting briefly before moving toward the cabin's porch.

After entering the door code provided by the manager, Lazarus hesitated before stepping inside. The cabin greeted him with new furniture and paint, a superficial attempt to mask what had happened here. Lazarus imagined he could still smell the coppery scent of blood but knew it was in his head.

The cabin's interior, with its cozy decor, evoked an image of a family haven where pies might be baking and children playing. But to Lazarus, it felt haunted. Steeped in a bloody history unknown to its guests.

He didn't need to consult his phone for the layout; it was etched in his memory, even appearing in his dreams, when he did dream.

Startled by footsteps, Lazarus swiftly turned, his hand instinctively reaching for his firearm. At the doorway stood an older man, plump with gray hair and a mustache.

"Who the hell are you?" Lazarus demanded.

"Who the hell are you?"

"Police."

"Oh," he said, his tone softening a little but not much. "Can I see a badge?"

Lazarus showed the badge. "Now your turn."

"I'm Norman. I do the maintenance and landscaping here."

Lazarus glanced around the cabin. "Don't look much different than the last time I saw it."

Norman brushed past him and went into the kitchen. He took a soda bottle out of the fridge and popped open the top and took a long drink before saying, "Ain't nothin' here anymore. Whatever you're lookin' for."

"You know what happened here?"

Norman's chuckle was humorless. "Everyone knows. Teens come looking for the 'murder house' and I have to chase 'em off."

Positioning himself in the kitchen doorway, Lazarus crossed his arms and leaned casually against the frame. "Is the attic accessible?"

"It's open. Why?"

"Gonna take a peek."

He shrugged. "Suit yourself."

After observing the old man briefly, Lazarus turned and ascended the stairs, feeling the man's gaze on his back. Reaching the attic door, he stepped inside. The Mitchells' belongings were gone, their space now filled with assorted items, stored without much thought.

Lazarus flicked on the switch, illuminating the unfinished attic. It was decently maintained, with a bed and rug added by the management company, likely to advertise an additional bedroom for higher Airbnb rates. The space was simple, with no closets or separate rooms, just a window framing the still water outside. He gazed out at the lake, eerily calm and deserted, resembling a dark cavern ready to engulf anyone who came near it.

Surveying the attic, Lazarus spotted a ventilation shaft positioned about six feet up the far wall. He approached, using his phone's flashlight to peer inside. The shaft was spacious, seemingly large enough for a person. Spotting a chair across the room, he dragged it over to stand on. After removing the grate, he looked into the shaft. It was filled with dust, grime, and cobwebs.

Navigating a bend in the shaft, Lazarus pushed through the cobwebs. A glint caught his eye—the light from his phone reflecting off something metallic. Inch by inch, he maneuvered closer until he could make out a faded orange Fanta can. He would have to get a warrant first and then send CSI to bag it so it could be used in court. If they ever returned his calls.

Exiting the attic, Lazarus traced the path of the central ventilation shaft that connected the entire house, realizing Whittaker could have secretly watched any room.

After inspecting all the shaft openings, he stepped outside, heading toward the water. There, he found Norman in a lawn chair, leisurely sipping his drink and scrolling through his phone.

Norman looked up. "You done?"

"I am," Lazarus replied.

"Good. Guests are coming tonight."

Lazarus gazed at the water. "You gonna tell 'em about the cabin's history?"

Norman scoffed. "Why bother?"

"Places have energies," Lazarus said. "Some might wanna know."

"What you don't know about won't hurt you."

Lazarus watched a fish glide near the pier, its skin shimmering in the sun. "I think I know one man who might disagree with you."

48

When the briefs were both filed, along with one reply from each side, Piper read them all. Both sides were excellent, and had the same tone and structure. The prosecutor's and public defender's offices pulled from the same group of fresh law students fighting for legal writing work to put on their résumés, and so the briefs looked similar.

Lounger had been caught off guard in court, but now with the briefs, his arguments were more concise and cognizant.

Piper tried not to come to any conclusions and keep an open mind as she read, but the fact was that if anybody was qualified to speak about forensic psychiatry, it was Dr. Brown. Lounger was right: this was an agitation tactic. Her trial advocacy professor in law school had called them "chameleon ruses," the idea being to subtly shift the focus of the proceedings, causing enough confusion to cloud the real issue. This was a way to show the prosecution they had a real fight on their hands. Then when Russo finally agreed to a negotiation, she would be in a position to get a better offer.

It was early morning when Piper got to court and sat down in a new black suit with tan shoes. She wore a bracelet and her necklace and had put some makeup on today, but not much.

"All rise, Eighth District Court is now in session. The Honorable Grant Billings presiding."

Judge Billings waved everyone down. He looked grumpy and had an almost comical frown on his face.

The courtroom was eerily quiet, with no cameras, media, or spectators. Owen Whittaker was led in and seated next to his attorney, the only sound the clinking of his shackles.

Judge Billings said, "We're here today for case number CR-2371897, and Mr. Whittaker is represented by Ms. Bianchi of the Public Defender's Office and the State is represented by Mr. Lounger. Under the Victims' Rights Act section II, the guardian ad litem, Ms. Danes, is here representing Ms. Sophie Grace, the alleged surviving victim in this matter. So, Counsels, I have read both your briefs and replies and am ready to make my ruling."

"Your Honor," Russo said, on her feet, "we are scheduled today for oral arguments. I would like to make those arguments."

"Do those arguments differ from the two-hundred-page brief and eighty-four-page reply you filed?"

There was a quick glance between the judge and the attorney. Piper guessed two hundred pages was too much.

"Very well," Russo said, "then I would like my objection noted on the record for appeal."

"So noted. Sit down, Ms. Bianchi." The judge looked at Owen and said, "Mr. Whittaker, do you have any questions for me before we proceed?"

Owen said nothing.

"Then I'm ready to make my ruling. I find that Dr. Brown is exceptionally qualified to speak about forensic psychiatry, psychology, neurology, or—"

"We would object, Your Honor," Russo said, on her feet again. "Psychology was not his specialty, and in fact, as the Court knows since you certainly read all of our two-hundred-page brief, his medical school records show that he only took one course in psychiatry. One. To say that—"

"Ms. Bianchi, stop," the judge said.

"I was promised arguments, Judge."

"And after reading the briefs, I no longer feel that's warranted. I'm ready to make my ruling."

"I don't appreciate having my arguments interrupted, Your Honor."

"And I don't appreciate you wasting this court's time," he said angrily. "I find that Dr. Brown can testify about psychiatry, psychology, and anything else he damn well pleases. Ruling made. Do you wish to continue with this hearing or not?"

"Yes, Judge," Russo said.

She sat down with a little grin that Piper was certain the judge didn't catch.

"Okay," the judge said, leaning back as though he could finally relax, "then Dr. Brown, please take the stand and remember that you are under oath."

49

Piper watched as Dr. Brown took a sip of water and cleared his throat. Lounger made notes at the lectern while everyone waited.

"Dr. Brown," he finally said when he put his pen down, "you have been qualified as an expert in forensic psychiatry. You have examined the defendant in this case, correct?"

"I have, yes. I had a total of twenty hours of interviews and various psychometric tests on the defendant including an IQ test, the MMPI, and the RPM."

"What conclusion did you come to after all these examinations?"

"I have come to the conclusion that Mr. Whittaker suffers from both schizoaffective disorder as well as delusional personality conduct disorder."

"Could you please tell us what led you to these conclusions?"

"Certainly," he said, crossing one leg over the other. He felt in control now and interlaced his fingers on his knee. "Mr. Whittaker presented as a twenty-nine-year-old unemployed male with a history of arrests dating back to the age of twelve, when he was arrested for severely injuring another child."

"Injuring how?" Lounger said.

"He punctured the eye of another child with a nail."

Piper briefly glanced at the defense table, curious about Whittaker's reaction. He remained motionless, his gaze fixed on the table, showing no visible response.

"What other charges did you see?" Lounger said.

"Everything ranging from larceny to voyeurism. His history is quite varied. He was raised in a boys' home after being abandoned by his parents, and from all accounts was routinely bullied to the point of hospitalization."

"Why was he bullied so much?"

"Partly, it was administrative. Some of the private prison corporations in that region of the country also own the juvenile facilities and the boys' homes. It's cheaper to not hire enough people, so the facilities are constantly understaffed, which results in juveniles being left to their own devices, so to speak. Mistreatment, unfortunately, is a common occurrence."

"Why else was he bullied?"

"When he was younger, his treating physician diagnosed him with a disorder that renders him to appear small and emaciated. In junior high school he would've resembled a third grader, so he was the target of abuse by larger boys throughout his life."

Lounger scribbled some notes. In the quiet courtroom, where the only sound was the soft shuffling of papers by the clerk, Piper's eyes found Owen Whittaker. The contrast between the man before her and the abused, vulnerable child he was made it hard for her to reconcile the two images.

"Did you find evidence of brain injuries stemming from this abuse?"

"I did. Causation for injuries that are decades old is difficult to determine, but there is one incident in particular that I think can explain a lot of the injuries I saw on the scans."

"What incident is that?"

"The incident that caused Mr. Whittaker's severe facial scarring. It involved falling from a height of about six feet onto a hot stove in the kitchen of the boys' home. The blow to his head from the fall rendered him unconscious, and he burned the flesh on his face after the boys who had pushed him over a railing ran away." He looked to the clerk. "If you could put up the images, please."

A screen came down near the empty jury box, and Lounger went through the painful process of introducing all the MRI images with Russo objecting to every single one. When the judge allowed all of them in, Lounger glared at her in victory, and she rolled her eyes.

"You see bruising here, and here," Dr. Brown said, pointing with a laser pen for the benefit of the judge. "This is at least a decade and a half old, maybe older. It's a gray zone where the oxygen to this portion of his frontal cortex didn't receive the blood it needed for that time and degenerated."

"What effects would that have?"

"This region is integral in maintaining one's personality and emotional control. Damage could result in significant alterations in personality, prompting mood swings, heightened anxiety, or changes in social and sexual behaviors."

"Is this an uncommon injury?"

"Falling certainly is not, but falling that far onto a metal stove is. Anytime you fall from a height greater than a couple of feet or get struck in the head, the brain bounces inside the skull, which causes damage. I've seen this type of bruising in many of my patients with a history of severe physical abuse."

"What other types of abuse did you find in the defendant's history?"

"Physical, emotional, sexual . . . as far as I can tell, that place was a torture chamber. It was shut down years ago by the state of Louisiana for allegations of abuse by the staff."

"When did he leave the boys' home?"

"He was let out at the age of sixteen to the custody of a foster family, who, after a few weeks, forced him out of their home. He became homeless thereafter."

Piper mulled over how Lazarus would interpret Whittaker's troubled past. She considered his early abandonment and homelessness as crucial, but not sole, factors in his spiral into violence, and was curious if Lazarus would feel the same.

"What did he do then?"

"He rode the trains once he discovered them. It's a rather common phenomenon, particularly with homeless youth."

"I'd like to talk about his specific diagnoses now if we could. Would you mind telling us about them?"

"Not at all. My first diagnosis is for schizoaffective disorder. It is a condition characterized by consistent detachment and lack of interest in social relationships. Individuals with this disorder often prefer solitude, and have little to no desire for intimacy. They usually seem cold or indifferent to others."

"What causes it?"

"The exact cause is unknown, but it is believed to be a combination of genetic, biochemical, and environmental factors. And Mr. Whittaker certainly meets the criteria for that."

"What do you mean?"

"He was a perfect combination of interior and exterior factors to create a psychopathology that is truly, for lack of a better word, terrifying."

"Objection," Russo said, shooting to her feet. "Choose a better word."

"Violent," he said with a glance toward her.

They held each other's gaze a moment before Lounger continued.

"What about his second diagnosis?"

"The second diagnosis I believe is appropriate is delusional personality conduct disorder."

"And what is that?"

Dr. Brown poured water from a pitcher into a paper cup and took a sip. The court waited.

Piper's gaze drifted involuntarily to the defense table. She attempted to envision a young, frightened boy, isolated and mercilessly bullied, with nowhere to seek help. Imagining the immense pain he endured stirred her empathy, but only to a point: rather than using his suffering for something positive, he had turned to inflicting similar pain onto others, and enjoying it.

"It's a rather new disorder. This term isn't officially recognized in current diagnostic guidelines, but it encapsulates the distinct cluster of behaviors and thought patterns we've observed in Mr. Whittaker."

"What is it exactly?"

"The disorder is characterized by delusional thinking, primarily of a persecutory or grandiose nature, that persistently influences the individual's behavior. This is combined with recurrent violations of societal norms and laws, a hallmark of conduct disorder."

"What type of behavior would this manifest as in a person?"

"Individuals with this condition may struggle with an unwavering belief that they possess extraordinary abilities or insights. This delusional thinking drives them to act in ways that are socially inappropriate, aggressive, or unlawful, as they believe their actions are justified or even necessary given their delusions."

"Does it affect how they treat people?"

"Absolutely. A major part of this disorder is the inability to empathize with others and a lack of remorse for their actions. This results from their delusional beliefs, but also from an inherent lack of understanding or concern for societal expectations."

"What caused it in this case, if you had to guess?"

"Objection, speculation."

"Overruled," the judge said with a quick glance to Russo. As far as Piper knew, that objection should have been sustained. Russo remained impassive and didn't show a reaction.

"In Mr. Whittaker's case, the severity of his childhood trauma, combined with his inherent predisposition to mental illness, may have resulted in the development of this condition. The chronic neglect, abuse, and subsequent brain injuries he suffered could have significantly disrupted his cognitive development and mental health, leading to the emergence of these distinct symptoms and behaviors."

"You've seen this disorder before?"

"As far as whether I've had any patients, no, but I have studied those that are incarcerated and suspected to suffer from the disorder.

However, he meets all the currently understood preconditions: the defendant's childhood experiences combined with the existing schizoid personality disorder formed a breeding ground for the proposed DPCD. The ongoing physical and psychological torment, particularly the incident that left him with scarring and loss of vision in one eye, would've only amplified his preexisting condition, pushing him further into this syndrome. He's a unique case," he said, looking at Owen.

"How so?"

"In examining the details of the victims' deaths, we see this intersection of delusional thinking and disregard for societal norms. He lived in the walls, cellars, crawl spaces—almost merging with the homes of his victims, watching their lives. The extraordinary belief that he could not only exist unnoticed in these tight spaces but could also control the lives of those living there showcases the depth of his delusional thinking. And the crimes themselves, the murders, show a shocking lack of remorse or empathy. I believe my diagnosis to be medically accurate."

"Can you be medically certain?"

"No, certainty doesn't exist. All I can do is point to the disorders that the defendant could be suffering from and make a judgment about whether they legally understand the nature of their actions."

Lounger asked, "And with all that in mind, Dr. Brown, do you believe that Owen Whittaker is competent to stand trial?"

With a sip of water, Dr. Brown shifted his attention back to the prosecutor.

"Given my assessments and understanding of the disorders, yes, I believe he is," Dr. Brown replied.

"But he has been diagnosed with severe mental disorders, how can he be deemed fit for trial?"

"Competency for trial is not about whether or not a defendant is mentally ill," he said. "It is about whether or not the defendant understands the charges against him, the court proceedings, and whether he can assist in his defense. Owen Whittaker, despite his severe mental disorders, has consistently shown an understanding of these factors throughout our evaluations."

"Can you clarify that, Doctor?" Lounger asked.

"Mr. Whittaker understands he is charged with multiple murders. He understands that if found guilty, he could spend the rest of his life in prison or be sentenced to death. He is able to discuss his case with his lawyer and participate in his defense. These are the legal standards of competency."

"He has delusions, though. Doesn't that impact his understanding?"

"His delusions are mostly centered around his living situations and his relationship with his victims," Dr. Brown responded. "They do not affect his understanding of the trial proceedings or the consequences of a guilty verdict. While Owen Whittaker is severely mentally ill, he meets the legal standards of competency to stand trial."

"Thank you, Dr. Brown. I have no further questions."

Russo got up and smiled at him. He didn't smile back.

50

"Ms. Bianchi, your witness," Judge Billings said.

Russo smoothed the front of her suit jacket. Her dark eyes homed in on Dr. Brown with an intensity that made him shift in his seat.

"Dr. Brown, in your years of experience, how many times have you diagnosed someone with delusional personality conduct disorder?" Russo asked.

"It's a rare condition," he admitted.

"So it's safe to say that DPCD isn't your area of expertise."

"I wouldn't say—"

"You're not an expert in it," Russo cut him off. "You're not extensively published in the area, and you haven't led any research studies on it, correct?"

"No, I have not."

"So the prosecution's expert witness in a case where DPCD is a key issue isn't an expert in the disorder."

"I doubt there are many experts. As I said, it's a relatively new diagnosis."

"Right," she said with a bit of glee in her voice. Piper had a feeling the doctor had said exactly what Russo wanted him to say.

"So since it's so new, and since, as you say, there are no experts that understand it—"

"I didn't say that. I said there are only a few recognized experts. There are only a few recognized experts on the Galápagos Island blue-footed booby as well. Doesn't mean we can't study it."

"Who's the most recognized expert in the world on this disorder?"

"I wouldn't know that off the top of my head."

"So that would likely mean there are consequences and implications of the disorder that you are unaware of? Since no one even knows who the experts are that can tell them about it?"

"Something this new, we're going to be learning about it constantly and adapting the current medical standards."

"Dr. Brown, in your analysis, you noted that Mr. Whittaker experiences hallucinations and severe paranoia, correct?"

"Yes, that's correct."

"And you attributed these symptoms to DPCD?"

"Yes, those symptoms are often associated with the condition."

"And schizophrenia, would that not also cause hallucinations and paranoia?" Russo asked.

"Yes."

"Schizoid personality disorder?"

"Yes."

"But instead of playing a guessing game as to which disorder is causing what, couldn't we say those symptoms also align well with the trauma Mr. Whittaker experienced in his childhood? His abusive upbringing, the incidents of bullying, the torture and disfigurement . . . Could these not also result in social withdrawal and difficulties with relationships?"

"Yes, absolutely."

"Dr. Brown," Russo said with a little more speed, "in all your experience, have you ever diagnosed DPCD before this case?"

"No. The disorder was too recently identified and classified."

"So, it's a brand-new disorder, one you have never encountered in your private practice?"

"I've studied—"

"Have you encountered this disorder before in your private practice?"

"No," Dr. Brown finally said. "I have not."

"Is it possible then, Dr. Brown"—Russo's voice was almost a purr—"that you might have jumped at the chance to identify this new disorder, to be one of the first psychiatrists to publish a research paper and identify yourself as an expert in this area? Particularly with a defendant so unique?"

"Objection," Lounger said without looking up from some papers. "Compound question."

"Sustained."

Dr. Brown, clearly affronted, answered the question despite Russo having the objection sustained against her for asking it. "I would not risk a misdiagnosis for the sake of—"

"Dr. Brown, do you recall the tests you performed to identify the disorders present in Mr. Whittaker's psyche?"

"Yes, we performed a battery of tests including MMPI-2, Rorschach test, CAT scan, the Raven's Progressive Matrices exam, and extensive interviews to understand his state of mind and history."

"Could you tell the Court about the reliability and validity of these tests? Especially the Rorschach test and the MMPI-2?"

Piper knew the tests, as many underage victims of crime were given batteries of examinations to determine the help they needed. But she didn't always trust these tests. The mind was good at keeping its secrets hidden.

"Well, these tests have been used for decades and have shown significant results in identifying various psychological conditions—"

"Isn't it true"—Russo cut him off—"that the Rorschach test has been criticized for having a low validity in diagnosing specific mental disorders?"

"Yes, some have criticized the test. However, it still remains a useful tool in a comprehensive psychological evaluation."

"And isn't it also true that the MMPI-2 can have false positives, meaning it can suggest a mental disorder where none exists?"

"There is a possibility for false positives in any medical or psychological test, but it happens less than you'd assume."

"Oh, I assume it happens a lot, Doctor. It's like finding water with a divining rod, isn't it?"

"Objection."

"Sustained."

Russo began walking the well now, almost circling in front of Dr. Brown. "Would you say the Rorschach test and MMPI-2, they're subjective?"

"They have a degree of subjectivity, but—"

"And wouldn't you agree, Doctor, that any degree of subjectivity could possibly lead to inaccurate diagnoses?"

"The tests have standardized scoring and interpretation systems, which minimize subjectivity."

"It's still possible for a misdiagnosis to occur, isn't it?" Russo said. "Could a patient with, let's say, a horrifically traumatic past possibly be misdiagnosed due to the subjectivity of these tests?"

"It's certainly a possibility."

Russo nodded. "And the CAT scan you performed, could it detect psychological disorders such as DPCD?"

"No, it is used to detect physical changes or damage in the brain, not psychological disorders."

"So, you diagnosed Mr. Whittaker with a disorder that can't be physically detected and used subjective psychological tests to get that diagnosis?"

"You're simplifying this far too much. The mind doesn't exist in physical reality, as far as we know. It is a construct in our brains. Detecting disorders of the mind and treating them, or even coming to conclusions about them, is a field that you will not have certainty in. It's not difficult to detect injuries to the brain, but injuries to the mind are far more elusive."

Russo pivoted swiftly, still owning the courtroom. "You said in your report that Mr. Whittaker was likely dealing with a combination of inherent mental illness and the results of brain injuries from his abuse in childhood, correct?"

Dr. Brown nodded. "That's right."

"And that childhood abuse and trauma can significantly affect a person's mental health and behavior, right?"

"Absolutely. Childhood trauma is linked to a variety of mental health disorders."

"Trauma, which includes being bullied relentlessly, living in fear, being physically and sexually assaulted, suffering severe burns and mutilation—this would all have a massive negative psychological effect, correct?"

"Yes, that level of trauma would certainly have a severe impact."

"So Mr. Whittaker's alleged conduct could have been a manifestation of his traumatic past rather than a reflection of his inherent mental state?" Russo asked.

Piper's eyes flicked to Whittaker, who sat with his head oddly tilted toward the table, seemingly in discomfort. Lounger had set aside his pen and notepad and was now focusing intently on Dr. Brown's testimony.

"It's possible that the trauma could exacerbate preexisting conditions or even trigger new ones, but it's unlikely to be only trauma considering the severity of the organic injuries."

"Dr. Brown, I want to talk about the competency evaluation now. Could you tell the court how many times you personally examined Mr. Whittaker?"

"Twice," Dr. Brown said, straightening in the witness stand.

"And during these examinations, did Mr. Whittaker seem lucid to you?"

"Yes, he did."

She nodded. "So, according to your professional opinion, based on only two visits, a man with a traumatic childhood history, with inherent mental illness and brain injuries so severe that you state physical, emotional, and sexual abuse would not alone explain his behavior, you're testifying that an individual like this is perfectly capable of understanding the proceedings and assisting in his own defense?"

Piper pictured a jury absorbing these details, possibly concluding that someone like Owen Whittaker couldn't have comprehended his actions. For the first time during the hearing, Piper considered that Dr. Brown might not understand Whittaker's mind as thoroughly as Russo seemed to.

Dr. Brown shifted uncomfortably in his seat. "That's a simplified way of putting it, but . . . yes."

Russo's lips curled into a smile that wasn't friendly. "So you'd wager a man's life on two visits?"

"Objection, Your Honor," Lounger interrupted, standing from his seat. "Counsel is badgering the witness."

"Sustained," the judge said. "Please rephrase your question, Ms. Bianchi."

"Very well. Dr. Brown, in your professional experience, can the mental state of a person with such a complex and severe psychiatric profile as Mr. Whittaker's be accurately assessed in just two sessions?"

Dr. Brown hesitated, then admitted, "Not extensively, but—"

"*But.* There's that word. Experts love that word because it hedges their bets."

"Objection."

"Withdrawn. Dr. Brown," she began, her gaze locked onto his as she paced, "you've spent a good amount of time explaining these mental disorders to us, correct?"

"I suppose so," Dr. Brown replied.

"And you've mentioned that you've only had two opportunities to interact with Mr. Whittaker, is that correct?"

"Yes, that's correct."

"Just two visits to diagnose not one, but two severe mental health conditions. One of them being newly recognized, is that right?"

"Yes—"

"In your professional opinion, is it beneficial for someone suffering from such disorders to be subjected to the stress of a criminal trial?"

"Well, it depends—"

"Depends?" Russo cut him off. "On what, Dr. Brown? The level of their suffering? The severity of their condition?"

She didn't wait for an answer. "Dr. Brown, isn't it true that trials can be severely traumatizing, especially for those with preexisting mental conditions?"

"Yes, they can be."

"And yet, you believe that Mr. Whittaker is competent to stand trial?"

"Yes, I do."

"But you've also admitted that it's possible that your diagnosis could be premature or inaccurate?"

"That is correct about any diagnosis."

"So the most accurate conclusion to draw from all this is that you're not exactly sure how someone with a severe and unique history like Mr. Whittaker will respond to various stimuli. You have no idea how the trial would affect him, no idea how this new diagnosis affects him, you've spent almost no time with him, and you, by your own admission, do not specialize in the treatment or identification of his specific disorders. I don't know, Doctor, seems a bit more like charlatanism than medicine to me."

"Objection!" Lounger said.

"No further questions for now, but I retain the right to recall Dr. Brown."

"So ordered." The judge looked to Piper. "Ms. Danes, the Nevada Victims' Rights Act does give the guardian the opportunity to cross-examine witnesses. Would you like to cross-examine Dr. Brown?"

Piper thought back to her trial advocacy class in law school, and realized her mind was blank and she couldn't remember anything from it. She swallowed and stood up, clutching her files tightly because she knew her hands would be trembling otherwise.

Piper turned to glance behind her and spotted Lazarus standing at the back of the room, casually leaning against the wall with his badge clipped to his belt. He nodded once, and she grinned in turn.

"Yes, Your Honor," Piper said nervously as she turned back to the judge. "I do have some questions for the doctor."

51

Piper cleared her throat as she brought the files to the lectern. She tried to adjust the microphone, and it caused loud feedback that she was certain made her blush. She cleared her throat again and said, "Dr. Brown, my name is Piper Danes, and I'm the guardian ad litem for Ms. Sophie Grace. I'd like to preface this by saying that I respect your work. You've given some valuable insight in your publications on complex mental conditions in children."

"Thank you," he responded with polite indifference.

She cleared her throat again and realized she'd done it three times now.

"Um, so you agree that mental disorders, like schizoid personality disorder and DPCD, are incredibly complex?"

"Absolutely."

"And as such, Doctor, these disorders can lead to a variety of behavior, but they are not the sole determiners of behavior, correct?"

"I would agree, yes."

"Thank you," she said, unsure of her own voice. "I've been thinking about the defendant's moniker in the press. Are you aware of what that is, Doctor?"

"Yes, I believe they used the term Creeper or something similar."

"Where did that moniker originate?"

"Keep in mind I only heard this secondhand from a staff member of mine, but I believe someone online stated something akin to that he lived among the filth of the victims, like a cockroach, and that somehow developed into the Creeper."

Russo rose. "I object to this whole line of questioning."

The judge looked at Piper, who said, "I didn't hear a legal argument in that objection, Judge."

Russo glared at her. "How about improper character attack for one?"

"That does not apply to—"

The judge flinched when her voice boomed through the courtroom, and she knew she had spoken too close to the microphone.

"Sorry," she said with a shy grin. "Um, subsection 2(a) clearly states that the guardian is not technically a party to the matter at hand, but is the spokesperson for the victim, and as such is given certain privileges not enjoyed by either party. Like allowing hearsay or leading questions on direct examination."

"I'll allow it. But let's keep that in mind; you are not a party to this matter. Keep it brief."

"Of course." She looked back at her notes. "Cockroaches are described as survivalists, correct?"

"Objection, he's not an entomologist."

Piper quickly said, "He can testify as to the general understanding of cockroaches, I believe, Your Honor."

"Overruled."

"They are survivalists?" she said to Dr. Brown. "And by that, I mean they adapt and thrive, even in extremely hostile conditions?"

"I suppose so," he said, his curiosity piqued.

"The moniker, we could say, is fitting then to Owen Whittaker, correct? Because despite the cruelty he faced in his life, he survived and adapted."

"He did. But that doesn't justify—"

"I'm not trying to justify anything, Doctor. I just want to understand. And I want the Court to understand. Can you confirm that mental illness can influence someone's actions?"

"Certainly it influences it, yes."

"Severe mental illness makes survival more difficult, correct? For example, last month a transient man was found dead from exposure. He had been diagnosed with schizoaffective disorder."

"Yes, it would make survival more difficult than someone without such disorders."

"But Mr. Whittaker obviously didn't die. He survived his brutal environment and is here with us today."

"He is."

"And you would have to have a high level of competence to survive the conditions Mr. Whittaker has survived, wouldn't you? The man who died from exposure did not survive. Mr. Whittaker's survival shows us his capacity to make decisions, and to plan and execute ideas that helped him survive, correct?"

"Yes, it would take the ability to plan ahead at least somewhat to survive the life that Mr. Whittaker has."

"Thank you. I'd like to ask about the Graces specifically now. Despite this disorder, Owen Whittaker hid undetected in the Grace household, correct?"

"Correct."

"So he was able to understand and adapt to his surroundings, even strategize to avoid detection. Could that be indicative of competence?"

"Objection." Russo was on her feet now. "This is all speculative."

"Overruled."

"Judge, why don't you pull out the needle now and stick it into my client's arm."

"Ms. Bianchi, I will tolerate a lot but I will not tolerate disrespect. Is that clear?"

"Crystal," she said, keeping her eyes locked on him as she sat back down.

Piper said, "It's all right, Judge, I only have a few more questions. Dr. Brown, in your professional opinion and based on the testing done, do you believe Mr. Whittaker understands cause and effect?"

"I do. He did not wish to be detected and developed various methods to get around the homes at night. We believe he got into the Grace home when the door was left unlocked and the alarm system off because the family was home, which by itself would take planning, foresight, and stealth. So yes, I believe these actions show an understanding of cause and effect."

"Do you believe he understands the consequences of his actions?"

"Based on my training and experience, and my hundreds of hours with patients, yes, I do believe Mr. Whittaker understands the nature and quality of his actions."

"Thank you. No further questions."

"Your Honor," Russo said instantly, "may we have a meeting in chambers?"

"That's fine. And we might as well break for lunch afterward. Court is in recess until two."

They followed him back to his chambers again, but this time he didn't take off his robe. He sat on the edge of his desk and folded his arms, a clear indication that he did not intend to let this continue for long.

"What is it, Counselor?"

Russo said, "We need Ms. Sophie Grace to testify."

"What!" Piper said. The other three looked at her, and she felt heat in her face but didn't avert her gaze.

The judge calmly said, "Why would I let the underage victim testify at a competency hearing?"

"Dr. Brown just testified that my client knows what he's doing, that he understands the consequences of his actions. I would like Ms. Grace to take the stand and explain in detail the events of that night, and then I'd like to recall Dr. Brown to explain them to us with that understanding in mind."

Lounger shook his head. "It's all irrelevant. There's video recordings of her interviews with the police. They should suffice."

"They don't suffice. She had just seen the dead bodies of her family and was so traumatized she could hardly speak."

"What are you asking for really, Counselor?" the judge said.

"We do not have a good grasp of the exact actions of my client for that night because Ms. Grace hasn't given a proper interview. If Dr. Brown is going to testify that my client understands cause and effect and the consequences of his actions, then we have a right under the Sixth Amendment to cross-examine Ms. Grace and determine what exactly his actions were that he allegedly understands the consequences of."

Lounger looked to the judge as though he were done and wanted a ruling, so Piper stepped forward and said, "Ms. Bianchi wants to get a preview of Ms. Grace's testimony and rattle her for trial, as well as show the prosecution that their case isn't as strong as they think with a traumatized minor. Forcing Ms. Grace to testify is all upside for the defense. This has nothing to do with preserving Mr. Whittaker's right to cross-examine his accusers."

Russo said, "Well, luckily, whether this is upside or downside for us doesn't matter. What matters is what the law says, and I would cite *Harold v. Thomas*, which held that the defendant has the right to cross-examine a victim at a competency hearing if the victim's testimony is relevant to the ultimate issue of the defendant's mental state. I would say how Mr. Whittaker acted that night, his actions, what he said, are enormously important to understanding Mr. Whittaker's ultimate state of mind at the time of the offenses he's charged with."

The judge tapped his fingers against his biceps. "Any counter from the State?"

"We would submit to the Court, Judge."

Piper stared in disbelief at Lounger. "*Harold v. Thomas* also held that the right of a minor victim's well-being had to be weighed against the defendant's right to cross-examination and gave a two-pronged analysis, the most important prong being the safety of the minor child. I can attest as her guardian that being cross-examined at this point and time after the murders of her mother and brother would be devastating to her psychologically."

"Nonsense," Russo said. "Ms. Danes is not a mental health professional. We have no idea what the impact will be on Ms. Grace until she actually testifies."

The judge thought a moment. "Here's what I'm going to do. I'm going to examine Ms. Grace in camera myself first. I'll gauge her ability to answer questions at that time. If Dr. Brown agrees that it is not detrimental to her mental state to be cross-examined at that juncture, I will allow the parties to ask questions. Now if you'll excuse me, I'd like to enjoy lunch by myself."

Piper left the judge's chambers and picked up her satchel on the way out of the courtroom. Lazarus leaned against the wall sipping coffee out of a plastic cup. They began walking down the hall together toward the elevators.

"Lounger is one of the worst prosecutors in that office," Piper said. "Why would they give it to him?"

"When you work for the government, you don't want high-profile cases. If you win, you get nothing, but if you lose, the stigma stays with you. Lounger was probably too lazy to get out of it."

They rode the elevator down. The front entrance swarmed with people hurrying to lunch, and two vendors sold fruit smoothies and sandwiches. They ordered two sandwiches. There were a few tables out, and they found the one that looked the least dirty. They ate their sandwiches in silence a moment before Lazarus spoke first.

"Russo's good," he said.

"She is."

"You think she actually has a shot of having him declared incompetent?"

"I don't know. His disorder's so new I'm sure her expert will testify that he's not competent. I don't think Judge Billings will buy it, but Russo will file an appeal, and you never know what an appellate court will do."

He took a bite of his sandwich and chewed a moment. "If he's declared incompetent, there's a chance he could get out at some point."

"Not a huge chance, but a chance. He'll also be in a minimum-security hospital, which may not be the best place for someone like him."

Lazarus sighed, setting down his sandwich. "It's more than just this case, Danes. If he gets out, he'll be in the wind. We'll never see him again. Who knows how many bodies someone like him could rack up before he's caught again."

The two sat in a silence a moment before Piper took a drink and said, "Riley said you went out of town the other day."

"I did."

"Where'd you go?"

"The Mitchells' cabin."

"Really? Why?"

"We gotta be sure, don't we? Worst thing that could happen is Whittaker is working with someone else who's still out there."

"What'd you find?"

"I found a Fanta can in a ventilation shaft. CSI checked the rest and found food scraps he'd taken and an old blanket. He was there. What about Sophie? You really gonna let her get up on the stand?"

"I don't have a choice. But I can't believe the judge is making her do that. I'm thinking of filing a judicial complaint."

He thought a moment. "I'll be there watching."

"Why?"

"I want to see how Sophie acts."

"You wanna see if you think she had a part in this, you mean."

"Whatever you wanna call it."

"She had nothing to do with this."

He took another bite of his sandwich and said, "We'll see."

52

That afternoon, Piper waited outside the courtroom for the bailiff. Lazarus was there, speaking quietly in the hallway with someone. Russo came up the elevator and checked her watch when she saw that no one had been let into the courtroom.

The doors opened, and Piper was the first one in. She sat at the bench behind the prosecutor's table. The judge was already out in his robe.

"Afternoon, Counselor," he said.

"Afternoon, Your Honor."

Russo and Lazarus came in, and Dr. Brown and Lounger walked in together afterward. Lazarus stood in the back of the courtroom. Dr. Brown sat down in the pews, and Lounger took his place at the prosecution table.

"Looks like everyone's here," Judge Billings said. "Detective Holloway, I notice you snuck in."

"Just consider me a fly on the wall, Judge."

"Well, it's good to see you. Anybody have a problem with the detective being in the courtroom? Okay, then let's get started. Hank, bring in Ms. Grace, would you?"

A moment later, the bailiff appeared with Sophie and Carol, who had her arm around Sophie's shoulders. Sophie looked scared until she saw Piper.

"Ms. Grace, my name is Judge Billings. Please have a seat."

Carol brought her over, and she sat down in the witness chair. Carol whispered something to her and then left the well and sat in the audience pews. Piper had seen in camera judicial interrogation before. It was a practice that was common in juvenile court where the judge felt the need to ask questions of a witness in private. The process affected children differently than adults: even if they were the victims, once they were put on the stand, they felt they were the ones that had done something wrong.

The judge said, "Bailiff, please bring out the defendant."

Piper said, "Your Honor, there's no reason to have Mr. Whittaker in the room while Ms. Grace testifies. It would be too upsetting."

Russo was on her feet. "While I sympathize, clearly the defendant has a right to be in here to hear his primary accuser's accusations. Why have a trial if we can't even agree to that?"

"I agree it is Mr. Whittaker's right to confront his accuser, but Ms. Bianchi, it's a short leash."

"I understand."

"Then Bailiff, please bring him out."

Owen Whittaker was brought out of the back. When he saw Sophie, he did something he'd never done before. He stopped. So abruptly that the trailing bailiff ran into him and shoved him to keep going. He couldn't get his eyes off Sophie on the stand.

Sophie was fidgeting and staring down at her lap, unable to look up. Piper glanced behind her and saw Lazarus sitting in the audience section, carefully watching Sophie.

Once Owen was situated next to Russo, the judge said, "Ms. Grace, do you understand that you're required to tell the truth in a court of law?"

"Yes," she said nervously.

"Okay, well, I'd like to ask you some questions. Will that be all right?"

She nodded.

"Good."

Piper quickly said, "Sophie, you're not in any trouble. We just need to find out exactly what happened. Okay?"

"Okay."

She glanced at the judge, who looked back to the girl and spoke in a soft voice. "Do you understand what was said, Sophie? Do you understand why you're here today?"

Her gaze kept to her lap. "To talk about the man who killed my mom and brother," she murmured, her voice barely audible.

Piper's jaw tightened.

"I know this will be difficult, but we need to understand what happened that night so that we can best protect you. The courtroom is closed and we're not recording anything, we're just talking to determine how best to move forward. So please answer these questions honestly. You do know the difference between truth and a lie, correct?"

Piper said, "She's fifteen. She understands, Your Honor." Anger at the question. Sophie wasn't five.

The judge gave her a sideways glance and then turned back to the girl. "Can you tell us what you remember about that night, Sophie?"

She nodded and swallowed.

"My mother and brother were watching a movie," she began, her voice barely audible. "I was supposed to watch it with them, but there was a school dance. My friend Jason picked me up, and we left." She hesitated. "That was the last time I saw my mom and Sully."

The courtroom was silent. She glanced at Piper for reassurance.

The judge said, "What happened when you got home?"

"I opened the door and shouted something, like 'I'm home' or something. No one said anything back. I turned to go into our family room, and that's . . . when I saw them. They were dead."

Her voice was trembling now.

"Did you see anything else?" the judge asked. Piper was grateful he didn't ask her to describe what she saw in detail.

She nodded. "I saw a man in my house."

"Where in the house?"

"He was standing in the room, in the corner so I couldn't really see him. Then he came out of the dark and I saw some of him. He had a lot of blood on him. I tried to run and he came after me so I ran up the stairs to my room. I got to the window and didn't have time to open it so I had to jump out. I don't really remember anything after that. I went to the hospital and people were asking me questions."

She sat still on the stand, showing no tears or emotions. Just seeing Owen Whittaker made her go blank.

"Sophie," Piper said, "if at any time you feel uncomfortable, you tell us, okay? If you don't want to talk or need a minute to yourself, you say something."

Russo rose. "I get that she's here to protect her, Judge, but Ms. Danes can't simply interrupt questioning, even if it's done by judicial interrogation."

The judge looked at Piper, his stern look saying everything he needed to say. Then he turned to Sophie. "Please go on, Ms. Grace."

"I couldn't see all of his body, but I know he was naked and had blood all over him. It was everywhere. He looked like . . . I don't know. Dead, I guess. I didn't look back. I don't even know if he was chasing me when I jumped out the window. I was just trying to get away."

The judge eyed Dr. Brown, eyebrows raised. Dr. Brown, watching Sophie, nodded.

"I think we can open questioning," the judge said. "Sophie, I'm going to let Ms. Bianchi and Mr. Lounger ask you some questions, okay? But your guardian is in the room, and if you have any questions, you can always ask me or her. Do you understand?"

Sophie nodded, her gaze still on her lap.

"Mr. Lounger. Any questions?"

"Yes, Judge." He got up to the lectern and looked at Sophie. "When you saw the naked man, can you tell us more about that? What did you see exactly?"

"I saw a man standing in the corner. I couldn't see his face but I know he was staring at me. He was breathing really hard and there was blood everywhere. I could see his legs. They were dirty and covered in blood. It was all over him, all over the room . . . everywhere. My brother and mom weren't breathing."

Lounger flipped a page in a yellow legal pad that contained his notes before saying, "Can you recall anything peculiar in the days leading up to this attack? Any strangers you didn't recognize around the neighborhood or your family discussing anything strange that had been going on?"

"I would sometimes see things move."

"What do you mean?"

"Like, I'd leave something out on the kitchen counter and it'd be moved when I saw it the next day, or I'd come home from school and some of my clothes would be missing. Like underwear and things." She gave a weak smile. "Sully said we had a ghost."

Lounger cleared his throat, and Piper was certain he hadn't really paid attention to what she had just said.

"Did you get a good look at the weapon he had used on your mother and brother, Sophie?"

"No."

"Did you see where the man went after you jumped out of the window? Did he try to follow you?"

"I don't know. I didn't look back."

Lounger scribbled a note. "When you were running away, did you see anyone else? Any passing cars or neighbors out that maybe might've seen something?"

"No."

"Thank you, Ms. Grace. That's all I had."

The judge said, "Ms. Bianchi."

Russo approached the witness box and rested a hand on its edge. She leaned in with a seemingly warm smile.

"Thank you for being so brave today, Sophie. I can't imagine what it's like to have to testify about the worst moment of your life in front of strangers. You're a brave girl."

"Thank you," she said.

Russo continued, "Have you ever had something really bad happen to you before? Like your brother got hurt and you were there?"

She nodded. "Yeah. My brother fell off his bike and cut his head. He had to get stitches."

"So you remember him falling off the bike?"

"Yes."

"Do you remember how you felt? How, when you saw your brother fall, everything was in slow motion and then after it was hard to remember what you saw?"

Lounger just sat there. Piper rose to her feet and said, "Objection. Leading."

Russo said, "Given her impaired ability to give comprehensive answers, I'd like to treat the witness as hostile for the purposes of this hearing, Judge. Regardless, I can lead during an in camera questioning."

He looked at Piper. "I think leading is appropriate here."

Russo said, "Sophie, was it hard to remember the details of your brother falling off the bike afterward?"

"I guess."

"Okay, so Sophie, had you ever seen the man you identified as being in your home that night?"

"No."

"Never seen him before that night?"

"No."

"So you saw this man's legs, but it's like when your brother fell off the bike, isn't it? Everything in slow motion."

She nodded but said nothing.

"You were in a state of shock when you saw your mom and brother. With having seen something like that, you might be misremembering details about it, right?"

"I don't know."

"Let's talk about your escape. You said you jumped out of your bedroom window, correct?"

"Yes."

"Can you describe the condition of the window when you jumped out of it?"

She looked at Piper and then to Russo. "I don't know what you mean."

"Was it closed, open, broken?"

"It was closed. I had to jump out. I felt it cut me everywhere."

"When the police arrived, they found your window broken out and suspected that you had used the chair of the desk in your room to break it out. Something you never mentioned before. Can you explain that?"

"No. I don't know. I mean . . ."

"Objection," Piper said on her feet again. "Badgering."

"Overruled."

Piper sat back down.

Russo said, "Sophie, is it possible you're mistaken about the window when you jumped out and in fact you had already broken out the glass?"

"I don't know," she said with a tremble in her voice.

"And if you're mistaken about that," she went on without acknowledging Sophie's answer, "could you be mistaken about other details of that night?"

"Objection," Piper said. "Asked and answered." She wasn't even certain if that was the right objection, but she couldn't sit there and say nothing.

The judge, with a hint of exasperation in his voice, said, "Ms. Bianchi, wrap it up."

"I'm done. Thank you, Sophie."

It wasn't a full cross-examination; it was a sneak peek for Lounger. A taste of what Russo could do to Sophie on the stand if he put her up in front of a jury. Just with questions about a broken window, Russo had rendered Sophie uncertain and confused.

She sat down. The judge looked to Piper. "Any questions, Ms. Danes?"

She went to the lectern.

Piper's gaze settled on Sophie. She looked so small and vulnerable in a witness box that hadn't been designed with children in mind.

She gave a warm smile to Sophie, who was barely able to glance up.

Piper moved closer to Russo and Owen Whittaker, trying to show Sophie she had nothing to be afraid of from him anymore.

"The man that chased you, did he seem familiar with your house's layout when he moved around?"

"I think so."

"Why?"

"He didn't hit our big coffee table when he was chasing me. Most people that come over bump into it because of where my mom put it."

Piper nodded.

"Did he do anything to you? Acknowledge you in any way?"

"I think he smiled at me."

Piper felt a cold revulsion. His smile was one of the worst things about him.

"Did he say anything to you?"

She nodded, but her gaze fell back to her lap. "He said 'Run.'"

"He told you to run?"

She nodded. "Yes."

"You said he chased you through the house, is that right?"

"Yes."

"What was the defendant doing while he chased you?"

She shook her head. "I don't know. I only looked behind me once. I think I heard him laugh."

"He laughed?"

"Yes."

"Like it was a game?"

"Yes."

"To play a game, you have to understand it, don't you, Sophie? You have to know what's going on and be able to understand how your actions are impacting the people around you, don't you?"

Russo rose. "Objection. Counsel is testifying."

"Sustained."

Piper cleared her throat. "Did he say anything other than telling you to run?"

"No."

"Did it seem to you he understood what he was—"

"Objection. Ms. Grace is not a mental health professional to testify as to how Mr. Whittaker was behaving that night."

"She's a competent witness and can testify as to general observations as to mood and behavior. Things she actually saw, not conclusions she came to."

The judge said, "The objection is overruled."

Piper said, "Sophie, what did the man that chased you seem like? Did he seem like he knew what he was doing?"

"I guess."

"What do you mean?"

"He . . . liked it."

The courtroom was in silence a moment.

"Thank you, Sophie. Nothing further."

Russo rose. "Your Honor, there's clearly more here. No one at any time before right now mentioned that Mr. Whittaker spoke that night. The defense will need time to prepare. I would also ask that, since we've had the in camera interview, we call Ms. Grace to the stand in open court."

Lounger didn't even look like he was paying attention. As he opened his mouth to say something, Piper could tell it was going to be that he would submit to the judge's discretion.

"I would object," Piper said. "The court has gotten everything it needs. There's no reason to put her through testifying at a competency hearing, and then at a preliminary hearing, and then at trial. It's too much for a young victim with this degree of trauma, Your Honor."

Judge Billings glanced over to the young teen still in the witness box. "I need to think about this. We'll reconvene tomorrow morning at eight, and I'll give my ruling. Court is adjourned until then, thank you."

53

Judge Billings left the courtroom first, not waiting for the bailiff to announce his departure. He went back to chambers and took off his robe and put it on the hook. He used to toss it on his couch until his wife, Anna, bought him the coatrack for his birthday.

He shut the door, sat at his desk, and put one of his aching feet up. Turning fifty-nine this year, he was feeling the tug of age. It felt like gravity, an invisible force slowing him down. A man had to do what he could to fight it and make himself feel young. Sometimes he did good things to feel young and sometimes not so good things.

He opened the bottom drawer and took out his bottle of cognac and a tumbler and poured two fingers' worth. He took a sip and savored the taste. His father used to drink cognac with a cigar every night before bed, and he would sit out on the porch with his father and listen to his stories while he drank and smoked.

The office phone buzzed. "Judge?"

"Mm?" His response carried a touch of irritation.

"Judge Dawson's here to see you."

He hesitated. "Let her in."

The door opened, revealing Hope Dawson dressed in a blue suit accentuated with gold bracelets. Judge Billings always thought she looked like she was running for office or about to give a speech.

"Want a drink?" he said.

"Celebratory or sorrow?" Hope said as she shut the door and then sat across from him.

"Neither. Just a drink to drink."

"I'm fine, thank you."

He drank down a swallow. "Quite the case today."

"How did it go?"

"The girl's a mess, but she's convincing."

"And the competency?"

He observed her briefly. "The debate continues."

"You have a sense of where you stand?"

His gaze held hers. "It's inappropriate for the bench to come to any conclusions before hearing all the facts."

"You're human before you're a judge. Humans naturally form views prematurely."

She had a way of unsettling him, an unease he could never pinpoint. "Brown says he's competent, and I've never seen a better forensic psychiatrist. Have you?"

"No. But I also know you're unreasonably embarrassed of being overturned by the appellate court. If Ms. Bianchi makes a well-argued case, you may side with her to avoid the embarrassment of an overturned ruling."

"I forgot, this is your baby, isn't it? Your test case. Well, lemme tell you something, I've met Allen Bishop and he's a pompous ass. You want to change people's behavior, you have to punish them. Kids included. It's the only way."

"We impose the death penalty, but murders persist. It's not severity of punishment, it's certainty of punishment that deters crime."

He sighed, reclining slightly. "What do you want?"

"I want to know which way you're leaning."

"I won't tell you."

"You already have," she said with a grin, then rose. "And I know you hate Ms. Bianchi—"

"I don't hate anybody that comes into—"

"Just keep it fair. You overrule her objections too much, and I don't want this overturned."

Judge Billings thought back to the hearing and knew Judge Dawson hadn't been there. He wondered how she knew that he'd overruled Russo's objections too much.

"What's your interest in this? What do you care about some academic's theories? There's as many legal theories as lawyers."

"Not like this. You can throw money at problems and only ever work at the edges. If you want change, it has to come from the ground up. It's too late for this generation, but maybe not for the next."

"*Change*," he scoffed before taking a sip of his cognac. "Fantastic. I'll keep it in mind. Now can you get the hell outta my chambers so I can drink in peace?"

Judge Dawson observed him, tilting her head subtly. She leaned in, their proximity allowing him to catch a hint of her perfume. With piercing gray eyes and delicate teeth, she remarked, "Valerie is quite striking. I've noticed all your clerks are young, blond, and remarkably attractive, aren't they?"

His face went slack. "What does that—"

"She's giddy every time you walk into a room. And I'm not an idiot, Grant, like your wife. But she doesn't need to stay an idiot forever."

Hope left.

Judge Billings poured more cognac.

54

Lazarus left the courtroom just as Owen Whittaker was led away, and they exchanged a single glance. Piper was speaking to Carol but excused herself and met him out in the hall.

"What'd you think of her?" Piper said.

"I probably believe her."

"Probably?"

"Certainty's a rare thing."

She reached out, gripping his arm and stopping him in place. "What is your problem?"

"What are you talkin' about?"

"You're still acting like Sophie's a suspect. I saw nothing but a traumatized girl on that stand."

"I never said I think she's a suspect."

"What then?"

"I don't understand why she was left alive, that's all."

They walked to the elevators in silence and headed down.

"Did you know he told her to run?" Lazarus said.

"No."

"Russo's going to have a heyday with it. That she never mentioned it before now."

The elevators opened on the first floor and Piper stepped off, but Lazarus didn't move. "Forgot somethin'. Catch up later."

Lazarus leaned against the wall as people with name tags got on, looking like they might be jurors. He smiled at some of the older ladies. Everyone was quiet as they rode the elevator back up, probably because a judge told them not to talk.

He went back to the courtroom and the door leading to the holding cells and knocked. A bailiff opened the door, a middle-aged man with a sloppy haircut and a large frame. Lazarus knew him.

"Hank, what you say I come in there for a minute and you go get a cup of coffee?"

He glanced back. Owen was the only one there.

"I say it takes me two minutes to get a coffee."

Lazarus pulled out a twenty and gave it to him. "Get a donut, too."

The bailiff grunted, snatching the bill from Lazarus. His bulky frame lumbered past, trailing menthol cigarettes.

Lazarus watched him disappear through the double doors of the courtroom.

Fluorescent lights flickered, casting an eerie glow across the four small adjoining holding cells. Thick bars and cloudy plastic panels separated each cramped space. All were empty except the last cell. There, Owen Whittaker perched on the concrete bench, hands cuffed, wrists raw. His pristine white slippers weren't dirty from the grimy floors yet.

Lazarus sat across from him on another bench. He took out his package of cigarettes and lit one, and held it out for Owen. The little man took it and inhaled a long pull. Lazarus lit one for himself and leaned back.

"I know there's somethin' dark in the world that lives right alongside us. It whispers. Gets us to do things we never thought we could."

Owen said nothing.

"See the thing is, the dark stops whispering and starts barking when it knows it has you. And you don't want it anymore, but it's not leaving. It's lost its taste, but the hunger's still there."

He smoked awhile.

"We're numbed nerve endings trapped in decaying flesh, being tossed around in the storms of the universe. But sometimes we have a choice. Sometimes we don't need to do what the dark whispers. You can make a choice and show mercy. Don't put that girl through a trial. You can at least do that for her."

Owen lowered his gaze, taking a drag from his cigarette, while a thin trail of drool escaped the corner of his mouth, tracing a path down his chin.

Owen discarded his cigarette and raised his gaze, revealing the grotesque burns that marred his face. The right side contorted eerily as he bared his teeth, hissing at Lazarus until he was out of breath.

Lazarus dropped his cigarette and stepped on it. He stood. "You shouldn't drag this out. The anticipation of an early death will break you. If you get the chance, you should kill yourself."

He left the holding cells and didn't look back.

55

Lazarus didn't feel like going home after court.

He headed to the Strip.

As evening fell, bright lights lit up, and rounders worked on the sidewalks to pull people into casinos. Watching them, Lazarus was impressed. They could quickly guess if someone liked drugs, booze, or a good time and then make lavish promises of what they'd find if they only went inside the casino.

The few times Lazarus visited the Strip, he avoided the flashy casinos full of tourists. He was drawn to quieter spots.

He drove past the main Strip, heading to Old Vegas. Here, the bars were older, the casinos worn, and the people carried heavier burdens. This was where he felt at ease.

He parked illegally and got out. A rounder was standing out front of a casino called Bricks. He was slim with piercing eyes.

"My friend," he said to Lazarus, "you look like I feel."

Lazarus gave a small grin. "You should go into politics with that insight."

"Man down as much as you needs something to pick him back up."

"What you got?"

"Come in and find out."

The rounder guided Lazarus inside the casino. It stank of smoke and sweat and liquor. Gamblers with glazed eyes mechanically pressed buttons at their machines, hoping their luck would change. Or did they? Lazarus wondered if hard-core gamblers cared about winning. Compulsion didn't usually care about things like that.

The rounder took him to a bartender wearing a colorful shirt. Nodding toward Lazarus, the rounder said, "Get him whatever he needs. First one on me."

Lazarus sat at the bar. The bartender said, "Got something special."

He pulled out a red bottle with writing on it in a language Lazarus didn't recognize.

"Turkish. It's made with opium. Not technically legal but . . ."

He poured a splash into the glass. Lazarus, without breaking eye contact, gripped the man's wrist, tipping the bottle until the shot glass overflowed.

"You should take it easy. Powerful stuff."

Lazarus eyed the glass, its contents dark enough that light couldn't get through. He threw it back, the taste reminiscent of soured licorice, nearly causing him to choke.

"That's the worst drink I ever had."

The bartender took a small shot and grimaced. "You know it's a ride when it's this bad."

Lazarus watched the gamblers on the floor.

"You wanna play?" the bartender said. "It'll be a bit more enjoyable."

"I don't gamble," he said, taking out his vape pen and sucking on it. "Get enough of that just being alive."

"Ain't that the truth."

The bartender started to put the bottle away, but Lazarus took it, refilling his glass to the top. He downed the drink and thanked the bartender with a nod.

It didn't take long to feel the effects of the drink. The intricate floor patterns, devised by psychologists hired by the casinos to induce confusion and hinder clear thinking, undulated. He blinked, thinking his eyes were playing tricks, but the wavy lines kept shifting.

He approached a roulette table, watching the wheel turn and the ball jump between number slots with a metallic click.

"You in, sir?" the dealer said.

He took out a fifty-dollar bill and put it on black. It came up red.

"You know they call this the Devil's Wheel?" Lazarus said. "You add up all the numbers on the wheel, it comes to 666."

"That so?" the dealer said, uninterested.

Lazarus wandered among the tables, warmth enveloping him. Soft colors blurred his peripheral vision, interspersed with flashes of light. His phone's vibration startled him. It was Riley.

"You feel like a drink, big daddy?" Lazarus said over the ding of the machines.

"You need to get down to the jail," he said flatly.

Lazarus stopped walking and put his finger in the other ear to hear better. "Why?"

"He got out, Laz. He's gone."

Lazarus knew he was too inebriated to drive, his vision still blurring and spinning, so he got a cab and guzzled coffee the entire drive to the jail, trying to negate the effects of whatever drink the bartender had given him.

He got down to the jail and jumped out of the cab. He ran inside, pushing his way past the metal detectors and guards. He saw Riley standing in a circle of guards and staff talking. An alarm was going off: the jail was on lockdown. Warden Stuart was there in his pajamas and sneakers. Lazarus saw paramedics rush past with a man on a gurney, red-soaked gauze on his neck as they tried to slow the flow of blood.

The warden looked panicked and was on the phone with someone, probably the federal marshals.

"What happened?" Lazarus said to Riley.

The big man motioned with his head to follow.

Riley guided Lazarus through the corridors with the warden behind them. Inmates peered from their locked cells while guards stood by, armed with stun guns and rifles. The twisting hallways, packed with cells, felt like a maze.

They got to a cell with chipping white bars and bare cement floors. Steel toilet and sink. Above the bed on the roof was an air vent, and the cover was off and had fallen on the bed. Lazarus went inside and examined the vent. The opening was small. It didn't look like a man could fit through, maybe a child.

On the sink, he spotted an untouched toothbrush. Using it, he swabbed the vent's interior, then sniffed the brush's tip.

"It's grease. Probably from his food. You got someone watching him while he eats?" he said to the warden, who was off the phone now.

The warden shrugged. "How would I know?"

"Because you're supposed to be in charge, Warden. He was probably starving himself so he could fit through that hole. If anyone was paying attention, they would've noticed."

"How are we supposed to know he could fit through an air vent? There was no way anyone could've seen this coming."

Lazarus gazed up at the small hole in the ceiling. "The next family he tears apart might not agree with you."

56

Piper pulled into the dimly lit parking lot of the CJC, the clock nearing ten. She had called Carol, insisting that she stay by Sophie's side until Piper arrived. When Carol asked why, there was a long silence on the other end before Piper told her Owen Whittaker had escaped.

She hurried to Sophie's room, finding Carol sitting on a chair in the hall reading a paperback.

"How did it happen?" she said, looking up from her book.

"He snaked his way through a vent by covering himself in grease. He got out through the laundry and nearly killed another inmate folding clothes. Then he vanished."

"You really think he's coming here?"

"I don't know."

"I'll wait with you."

"No, you go home and get some sleep. Detective Holloway is sending down an officer to stand guard. I'll wait until they arrive."

Carol told her she would be at home if she needed her to come back. Piper thanked her and then waited until she was alone. Then she put her ear to the door. Silence. Just in case, she cracked the door and peeked inside. Sophie was on the bed, turned away, her hair spread over the pillow. The moonlight illuminated the room enough that Piper could walk through quietly without running into anything. She checked that the window was locked and then went back into the hall and sat down. She left the door open a bit so she could hear.

Carol had left the paperback on the chair, and Piper picked it up. It had a cover of a woman being held captive by a handsome man with his shirt open.

She heard footsteps when she was less than twenty pages in. Lazarus came up the stairs.

"Been here long?" he asked.

"No, barely got here."

"I got an officer stationed outside. I'll have him come up."

"I'm okay for now. I want to stay."

Lazarus nodded and went to a window at the end of the hallway, looking down at the courtyard.

He said, "All they had to do was watch him."

He came back and slid down the wall across from Piper, his forearms resting on his knees. He took out his vape pen and inhaled.

"You know they didn't even catch him on the surveillance cameras? He's like an insect, crawlin' around without anyone noticing."

They sat in silence a moment, the only sound that of their breathing.

"Do you remember your mom very well?" Lazarus asked.

"Some. I tend not to think about it. What about you?"

He nodded as he took a drag from his vape pen, releasing a plume of gray vapor. Piper didn't like smoke, but Lazarus's had a distinct aroma, reminiscent of leather rather than cigarette.

"What did she do when she realized the man was already married?"

"Nothing. Her pride wouldn't let her go back to my father. When you're in denial, even the unbearable can seem bearable. So I grew up as a desert rat."

"So you were raised by the polygamists?"

"For a while."

"What was it like there?"

He shrugged. "Wasn't all bad. They got me training real young—bows, handguns, rifles, hand-to-hand, horticulture, divining for water . . . everything a young boy needs to survive the apocalypse.

But my favorite part was that they'd let me out in the deserts. Got to be alone a lot."

He played with his vape pen, staring out the window.

"Church services were entertaining at first. They'd hold serpents 'cause of a line in Mark that says, 'They will pick up serpents with their bare hands and the poison will not hurt them.' They'd hold diamond-back rattlesnakes, six or seven of 'em at a time, and sing hymns."

Lazarus was quiet a moment.

"I saw them lifting snakes and I thought, *These people really believe. They have skin in the game. These people* know."

He took a slow drag from the vape. "I found out they defanged the snakes before they brought them to church."

"That seems like a smart choice."

He looked at her now and said, "If they really believed it, they would've left the fangs in."

After a long silence, Piper peeked into the room to check on Sophie.

"What about you?" Lazarus said.

"What about me?"

"No one comes to religious fervor in a vacuum."

"You think I have religious fervor?"

"Do you?"

"I don't think so. I believe there's a God watching over us and that we return to him when we die. Why he lets the horrible things happen that happen, and why good people are always suffering, I don't know."

"Why do you assume suffering is bad? Maybe it makes us what we are? I wouldn't blame your God for that." Lazarus twirled the vape pen in his fingers. The hallway light cast a pallid glow over the ornate rug spread on the wooden floor.

Piper said, "My favorite book when I was a teenager was *Frankenstein*. Maybe because Mary Shelley was my age when she wrote it, and that blew my mind. But you know what I got from that book? When Victor dies at the end, the Creature chooses to die with him.

He gets lost into the frozen arctic. As distant as Victor was from him, when his creator wasn't there anymore, there was nothing left. Just . . ."

"Oblivion."

Piper watched him a moment. "Yeah."

He rested his head against the wall, lost in the dance of shadows on the ceiling.

"What finally made them take you away from your mother?" he said without looking at her.

"Um," she said with a shot of discomfort, "my mother had overdosed and gone unconscious. I called 911 and then went back to watching television on the couch with her unconscious body next to me while I waited. It became so normal I didn't even think about it. They didn't let me back with her after that, and she didn't fight for me."

"You tried to find her since?"

"No. Have you tried to find your mother or father?"

There was another long silence before he said, "I should've given the jail better instructions or—"

"This wasn't your fault. You did everything you could."

He shook his head. "If he gets away, Sophie will spend her life looking over her shoulder and thinking he's right there."

She went somber as she said, "She'll be doing that anyway."

57

Near midnight, an officer entered the CJC and went to Sophie's room, nudging Lazarus awake from the hallway floor and telling him he would take over. Piper, asleep in her chair, stirred. Lazarus gave the officer a nod as they both got to their feet. "Go home, Danes," he said.

"What are you going to be doing?"

"Visiting someone."

Lazarus exited the building and headed to his car.

The sky was clear, with the moon casting a pale glow. He drove aimlessly for some time, eventually finding himself on the streets leading to Judge Dawson's hilltop home.

He parked, went to the door, and knocked. Judge Dawson answered in silk pajamas. She looked wide awake but had no makeup. He thought she looked better without it.

"Are you drunk?" she said.

"No."

She opened her door. He stepped inside the home and went to the kitchen. A bar was there, and he poured himself some whiskey and took it outside to her patio. The city lights burned as bright as the moon.

Sin don't sleep—a sergeant of his in New Orleans had told him once. Lazarus had later heard the sergeant had hanged himself in his garage.

"You should stop coming here like this," she said, joining him on the patio with a glass of red wine. "People will say you're in love with me."

"People say lots of things."

He studied her under the moon's glow, noticing the shimmer in her eyes, her flawless nails, the gentle sway of her hair. "You look beautiful in the moonlight."

"Thank you," she said casually, as if he'd commented on the weather.

"You don't care about compliments, do you?"

"I don't care all that much for words. Most people have no insight into themselves, so the words they say are meaningless."

He moved closer, intending to kiss her, but she subtly averted her face. Settling into a chair, he took a sip of his whiskey, his gaze drifting to the railing her husband had fallen from. "You miss him at all?" Lazarus said.

She noticed where he was looking. "No."

"You know, me and you never talked about it."

"Why would we?"

"Seems odd that I didn't care, and that you didn't care that I didn't care."

"Don't overthink it," she said before taking a drink of wine. "We can talk about something else. I've given enough interviews to the police on this subject, I think."

"This ain't a cop askin'."

"A friend then?"

"If people like us can have friends, then you and I are as close as we're gonna get."

She gave a half smile. "How interesting it would be to find out who you think 'people like us' actually are."

She sipped her wine, eyes fixed on him above the glass's edge. "I told Charles I wanted a divorce that night."

"Why?"

"He was a terrible husband. I married him for expedience. My father thought it would be a good marriage. Never mind that he had a history of physical and mental abuse to all his girlfriends going back to high school. He had the pedigree and the right family name, so that was a mild issue to my father."

"You don't strike me as the type that can be bullied into anything."

"I was young. I hadn't learned yet that the most important word to be able to say to family is no. That lesson only comes after heartache I hadn't yet experienced."

"What happened when you told him you wanted a divorce?"

"He stood at the railing and said he would kill himself if I left him. I thought he was being dramatic, trying to manipulate me. I told him to go ahead and do it . . . and he did."

Lazarus thought about this for a while.

Judge Dawson was staring out over the city.

"Owen Whittaker escaped," he said, finally breaking the silence.

"I know. The warden called. How do you feel about it?"

"How do I feel about it? I feel like I wanna put my fist through the warden's teeth."

"Rather extreme reaction, isn't it? You're assuming it's over and that he's gotten away."

He finished the whiskey and put the glass down. "He hid in walls and crawl spaces for weeks. If he doesn't want to be found, I won't find him."

"You did once. You can again," she said. "What would you do if you were him? How would you describe yourself at this moment?"

"Off balance."

"So what would you do?"

"Go somewhere familiar to get my balance back. Somewhere I could hide out and think."

Cradling the wineglass with both hands, her nails gleamed under the moon's glow. "That sounds like a suitable place to begin."

"Better than blacking out at the saloon, I guess."

Despite the lingering dizziness and fatigue, he had some motivation he could use now, at least for a while.

Lazarus rose and looked out over the city from the railing. It was a sheer drop all the way down with jagged rocks on the way. "Why keep this house after somethin' like that?"

"Because to hell with him. That's why."

58

Lazarus was running on fumes. Empty Midnight Porter bottles and cigarette stubs surrounded him. He leaned on the printer in the Dungeon, awaiting the final pages.

He had mapped out Owen Whittaker's arrest sites, identifying nearby shelters. If he'd stayed at the shelters, maybe someone there knew him, knew if he had his own camp somewhere.

Only one shelter in Nevada was close to the tracks. Three blocks from there, Owen had once been nabbed for shoplifting beer.

His phone rang. "Yeah."

Piper said, "Hey. I need to run home and get my grandmother her pills for the morning. Can you come hang out at the CJC? I don't want to leave Sophie alone."

"Where's the officer?"

"Breakfast. Don't be mad, I said he could go because I was here."

Lazarus exhaled. "I can't right now. I'm heading down to a shelter."

"For what?"

"I sent uniforms to all the rail yards so he can't hop on any freights, and he's not walking outta town, so he's gotta be somewhere. Somewhere familiar to him."

"Sounds promising."

"Sounds like bullshit, but I'd be going crazy sittin' in the Dungeon waiting for a phone call."

"Well, at least be careful."

"When am I not?"

Lazarus spoke to a volunteer at the shelter, an older woman who wore a sweater though it was over ninety outside. Lazarus pulled out the booking photo of Owen Whittaker on his phone and showed it to her.

"You seen him here?"

"I seen him before. Don't know his name. He don't talk much."

"He have any friends here? Regulars?"

"I don't think so, but Brian might know something. He works here. I'll get him."

She went into a back room. Lazarus looked out over the main floor. It was covered in cots, like how cots were arranged haphazardly in gymnasiums after natural disasters. Some of the beds had men sleeping, pillows or blankets over their faces.

"Can I help you?"

He turned to see a man slightly taller than him with brown hair.

"I'm with the Metro PD. I'm looking for this man." He held up the picture.

"That's Owen. But I saw on the news that he was in jail?"

"Let's say the story was greatly exaggerated. You know much about him?"

"Not really. He doesn't talk. I think it hurts him to talk, because of the burns on his face."

"But you do know him?"

"I make it a point to get to know everyone that comes here, Officer. They're not faceless numbers, they're human beings with histories and families."

"I'm there with ya, but right now all I care about is finding him. You said he doesn't talk *much*. What has he talked about?"

"We try to get people jobs when we can, and I thought he'd be a good candidate. He'd never held a real job, not once. I thought maybe if we could show him what it was like to make money through your own work . . . I don't know. I felt bad for him. I had no idea that—"

"Did he ever mention anywhere else he spends time?" Lazarus interrupted. "Somewhere he might go where people wouldn't look for him?"

"There's a place he's mentioned before. I'd given him this nice jacket out of the lost and found and he wasn't wearing it when it was raining, so I asked him where it was. He said he'd left it at his camp."

"Where's his camp?"

"I think he was staying in the tunnels near the movie theaters on Sahara."

He handed him a card. "If he comes back here, you call me."

"I will."

Exiting the building, Lazarus got into his car and shot a text to Riley before steering toward the Strip.

He veered off into a secluded freeway alcove, near an overpass bustling with traffic. Beside him, a stairwell descended beneath the overpass, directing pedestrians safely underground, away from the speeding cars. Adjacent to the stairwell, a maintenance tunnel burrowed deep into the city's sewer system.

The day's heat was oppressive, and Lazarus cranked up his air-conditioning, waiting. Soon, Riley's truck rolled up. After stepping out, Riley fastened a Kevlar vest around himself, a hat emblazoned with "SWAT" perched on his head.

"You ready, big daddy?" Lazarus said as he got out.

"Did you know it's my wife's birthday today? It was supposed to be my day off."

Lazarus opened the trunk and strapped on his vest and grabbed two flashlights.

"Then keep your guard up, 'cause she's gonna be wicked pissed at me if you die today."

Together, the two of them descended into the dark tunnels beneath the city.

59

The tunnel began vast, stretching about fifty feet across with towering ceilings. As they went deeper into the sewers, the space grew more constricted. The sound of flowing water echoed below, its vibrations humming under Lazarus's shoes. The air was thick with the pungent mix of fecal matter and the unmistakable odor of rotting wildlife.

Riley said, "I called it in. We should wait."

"And let Tactical handle it? Aren't you Tactical? You'd just be back in here."

"But with six other guys."

"You sound like you don't trust me."

"It's hard to trust someone that's not scared of dying."

Lazarus ran his flashlight over a dark corner and saw nothing there. "Don't even know if he's here. We should make sure before we call in your Cocaine Cowboys."

Lazarus kept his pistol in the holster. People lived down here, and he wouldn't put them at risk. They'd been through enough in life without getting accidentally shot by the police.

Riley said, "I hate the dark."

"Just pretend it's light."

"That doesn't make sense."

"Being afraid of the dark when you're the size of a tank don't make sense either."

"I didn't say I was afraid. I said I hate it."

A set of stairs led farther down, and before long they were in a narrower tunnel. The rushing water was louder. He could see people lying on a sleeping bag. An older Asian woman with a man who wore a Las Vegas Raiders cap. Lazarus approached them. The woman was up and stared at him quietly.

"I'm looking for this man," he said as he showed her the picture on his phone.

She shook her head.

"He's got a camp here. You got a guess where it could be?"

She cast a brief look down the concrete tunnel to her right.

He nodded once and said, "You two need to go up. He's dangerous."

Lazarus watched as they gathered their things and left silently. He turned his flashlight to the corridor the woman had pointed to.

"Stay here," Lazarus said to Riley.

"So you can catch one in the back? No."

"If I don't see him, as soon as I pass he's gonna run, not shoot. I need you out here."

"No, this is stupid."

"You can only tell that in hindsight. This is just *probably* stupid." He double-checked the magazine of his weapon. "If I'm not back in fifteen, you head up and wait for Tactical."

Lazarus began walking deeper into the tunnel.

The corridor opened up and then narrowed again. It was an access tunnel to get farther down into the sewers. There was a pair of double doors with a padlock and a warning sign that there was high voltage behind the doors.

Farther down, the hallway split into two sections. He couldn't hear his footsteps because of the rushing water, and it was only getting louder.

He swept the flashlight from left to right. Refuse gathered in corners. A tattered sleeping bag, empty bottles of booze and used syringes. An old magazine. He moved things aside with his foot and didn't see anything else.

Lazarus walked a little farther on and then paused, straining to hear beyond the roar of water. Swiftly drawing his pistol and holding up the flashlight, he descended a set of metal stairs. They led to dim, concrete pathways flanking a river of human waste. The stench was overwhelming. Warm and putrid.

Lazarus looked at a faded red sign on the wall but couldn't read it. He slowly moved to a corner and peeked around. The corridor kept going and split into different paths farther ahead, and then nothing but darkness. He checked his phone: no signal.

Lazarus thought that if there was a hell, this might be its back door.

The corridor stretched straight ahead, allowing him to move faster. The roar of rushing water drowned out all other sounds, leaving him navigating darkness without being able to hear anyone approaching.

The tunnel ended in solid metal grates, locked with thick chains. A sign read "City of Las Vegas Personnel Only." Even a determined Owen Whittaker couldn't squeeze through the narrow gaps. Lazarus, with no other option, followed a path marked by a faded toxicity warning.

The tunnels narrowed into tight passageways. As water sounds faded, his footsteps echoed on concrete. He emerged into a dimly lit space with tents, cots, and a fire burning in a trash bin, smoke escaping through grates to the city above. Lowering his gun, he observed a few people milling around their makeshift camp.

They didn't acknowledge him, but one man paced farther away in the dark. Lazarus could see some stripes on his sneakers that reflected the firelight. Vegas had a massive homeless population living underground, and some of them were wanted men who had found a place the police didn't go. They wouldn't tolerate strangers.

He put his gun away and took out his wallet. He held up a couple twenties, all the cash he had left, in the beam of the flashlight.

"Forty bucks for whoever gives me thirty seconds of their time."

Nobody moved, nobody said anything. As though he wasn't even there.

A male voice from under some blankets said, "Turn off ya light."

Lazarus approached the voice, spotting cropped hair beneath a blanket. Pulling it back, he revealed a man with scabs on his face, wincing in the light.

"Money first," he said.

Lazarus placed the twenties next to the man. He quickly snatched them and pulled them under the blanket.

"What do ya want?"

Lazarus showed him the photo. "You seen him?"

He shook his head.

"You sure? You barely looked at the photo."

"I ain't seen him."

Lazarus scanned the large space again. "There anywhere else folks sleep down here?"

"No. It's closed off. You gotta go around and go into that side from the Boulevard."

He nodded. "Thanks."

As he left, he saw the man pacing holding something now, but it was too dark to see what it was.

Lazarus walked faster down the corridor.

60

Piper pulled her car to a stop in her driveway and got out, spotting the *Las Vegas Herald* on the front porch. Her grandmother had been a reader for three decades. She wondered why since the news only seemed to upset her.

Piper went inside and called out, "I'm home, Grandma."

She set her keys on the kitchen table and grabbed a juice from the fridge before kicking her shoes off her aching feet. Leaning against the counter, she took a swig from the bottle. She hadn't slept in a chair since college, and her neck pinched and caused a headache.

In the bathroom, she grabbed some Advil and chased it with her juice. She looked at herself in the mirror. Her hair was a mess, her skin looked pale from a lack of sun, and she had dark circles under her eyes. She washed her face and pulled her hair back with an elastic before brushing her teeth. When she was done, she went back to the kitchen.

"Grandma?" she called out. "You home?"

Piper went to the garage through the kitchen. Lake's car was still there. Her grandmother took walks every day, but those were in the afternoons. She checked the backyard to see if she was gardening. She called Lake's cell phone, and it went to voicemail.

She went to her grandmother's bedroom. No one was in there, and the bed wasn't made.

Then she called Lazarus.

"Hey," he said, breathing heavily.

"I know this is stupid, but I can't find my grandma and I wasn't sure who else to call."

"Can't find her?"

"She's not home, but her car is here and she's not answering her phone. Her bed isn't made, and she always makes her bed the second she wakes up."

Lazarus was silent a moment.

"Get out of the house."

Just as he said it, she caught the movement in her grandmother's closet. Subtle. If she hadn't been looking right at it, she would've missed it.

The darkness moved like it was alive. A shadow unfurling.

Piper forced her body to take steps back and was stopped by the wall behind her.

Seeing Owen Whittaker outside of shackles and a jail jumpsuit made her feel sick. It didn't look natural somehow, as though he was never meant to be free.

Piper, heart pounding, went for the hallway, and the sound of the closet door slamming open spurred her to run. She could hear the press of his footsteps on the carpet behind her.

As she rounded into the kitchen, the linoleum betrayed her. Her feet slid out from under her, sending her crashing to the ground.

Owen lunged, closing the distance between them in a heartbeat. With a snarl, he went down on all fours and sank his teeth into her calf. Her scream echoed through the house as pain lanced her flesh.

She yanked her leg out of his mouth and kicked him with her heel in the face. His nose crunched, and his head snapped back. She crawled out from under him and was on her knees, and then her feet.

She scrambled to the counter and flung open a drawer, grabbing the biggest kitchen knife she saw. Her heart in her throat, hands shaking, she turned to face her attacker . . . but he wasn't there.

She breathed hard and loud. The garage door was close. She moved slowly to it, holding the knife out, and stayed near the counters. Having something at her back made her feel safer.

She ran for the door.

Owen leapt from around the corner and grabbed her arm that held the knife. He twisted the knife toward her, shooting a jolt of agony through her wrist. She screamed.

Piper felt his small, leathery hands wrapped around her throat and pushing her against the door, crushing her neck. The hands felt like stone against her skin. Immovable. She dropped the knife and pulled at his fingers.

Though smaller, he was so much stronger than her. She clawed his eyes and felt her thumb plunge into the blackened wound. He didn't scream, but his face twisted in pain, revealing layers of burnt muscle. He put his hand over his injured eye and stumbled backward.

She shoved him and ran for the stairs leading to the basement. Nearly falling because she was skipping so many steps to get down. The door was open, and she slammed it behind her. There was no lock on it.

She dashed into the spare bedroom and locked the door behind her. Desperately scanning the room, she looked for something to defend herself with. As she felt sweat run down her face, she noticed a window. But when she tried to open it, it was jammed tight. Pulling hard, she accidentally cut her thumb.

Scratching outside the door. A small nightstand was next to the bed. She lifted it and started smashing it into the window. The first blow bounced off, but the second shattered the glass. She grabbed a sheet off the bed and wrapped it around her hand as she frantically knocked loose the jagged glass that was on the sill. Then she laid the sheet over it and started climbing through.

Her head was outside now. She glanced back to the door and saw it wide open.

A grip like a vise wrapped around her ankle and pulled her back inside. The sheet came off, and the glass scraped her thighs and belly.

She screamed and he pulled harder. She fell to the bed. Blood was oozing from his eye where her thumb had gone in.

He stood panting, and then looked up toward the ceiling. Piper heard it too: footsteps upstairs.

While he wasn't paying attention to her, she kicked him with both legs in the stomach, sending him flying back and hitting the wall.

Piper rolled off the bed and ran for the stairs.

61

Lazarus skidded his car to a stop in front of Piper's home, Riley beside him. They rushed out, and Lazarus withdrew his weapon.

"Get the back!" he shouted.

Riley ran around the house, and Lazarus went to the front door. A scream pierced the air. The door was unlocked and he charged in, weapon up.

He sprinted through the home, going from room to room.

Now he heard grunting, almost a growl. He ran toward the sound and saw a nightmare. A bloodied Piper Danes crawling up the stairs as something sleek and quiet rushed up behind her.

Lazarus dived past her and crashed into Owen Whittaker like a linebacker.

The two rolled violently down the stairs, a crack echoing as someone's head collided with the wall and left a hole. A whirlwind of blows and grunts and growls. They finally skidded to a stop at the bottom, breathless and dazed.

The gun was inches from Lazarus's face. As Owen lunged for it, Lazarus grabbed him tightly. Owen snapped around and sank his teeth into Lazarus's hand, blood seeping out. Lazarus didn't flinch, separating himself from the pain.

He grabbed the gun with his free hand and pressed it against Owen's temple. Owen knocked the gun away, giving Lazarus enough time to spin on top of him and put his weight on him. The smaller man, in such a vulnerable position, stopped moving.

Lazarus yanked out his cuffs, flipping Owen face down and then securing his wrists behind him. Pain pulsed through Lazarus, his breath shallow, head pounding. He cradled his likely broken wrist and, exhausted and dizzy, leaned back, resting his head against the wall.

From the top of the steps, Piper watched Lazarus cuff the bleeding man. Her breath came in ragged gasps, a mix of nausea and dizziness making her want to vomit. Tears would have come if she'd let them.

A faint whisper broke the silence. Owen was murmuring something. Lazarus leaned in close to hear, and his eyes darted to the hallway pointing to the downstairs bathroom.

"What did he say?" she said.

He didn't respond.

She made her way down the stairs. Owen was handcuffed on his stomach and got to his knees. Blood dribbled out of his eye and created what looked like bloody tears running down his face.

She looked at Lazarus and saw him pick up his firearm and holster it, then go to the bathroom door. He switched on the light, but his body obscured her view.

"What's in there?"

"Nothin'. You head on upstairs. Riley's there."

She moved nearer and saw dark-red spots spattered on the bathroom's white walls.

"Lazarus," she uttered, breathless, "what's in there?"

He turned to her. "Go upstairs, Danes."

She tried to get past, and he stepped in front of her. He leaned in close, his breath brushing her ear as he said, "You don't want this in your head."

The tears came.

"No," she said, her voice trembling.

She tried pushing past Lazarus, but he held her in place.

"Let me go!" she shouted as she broke free and ran to the bathroom.

Lazarus let her go. He glanced at Owen, who was now up on his feet with his hands still cuffed behind him. An ugly grin came to him before he licked the blood off his lips.

Turning his attention back to Piper, Lazarus saw her frozen in front of the bathroom, her gaze fixed on the tub. He approached her silently.

"No," she whispered, shuddering, tears running down her cheeks.

He gently pulled her away from the bathroom and shut the door. She stood frozen, unable to move, so he put his arm around her. He didn't notice her hand slide down to the holster against his ribs and pull out his weapon.

She lifted the firearm and pointed it at Owen Whittaker's head.

The gun shook in her unstable hands. Lazarus paused, seeing the tears shimmer in her eyes. "If you do it," he said softly, "it's murder."

"I don't care," she stammered.

He whispered close to her ear, "You're not like him. Gimme the gun, Danes."

The tears wouldn't stop, and her hands shook so much that Lazarus feared the gun might slip from them.

"I know you got faith in divine forgiveness, so you need to ask yourself: You practice what you preach? Or you just another pretender defanging the snakes?"

Gently, Lazarus eased the gun out of her hands. She collapsed into him, and he held her as she wept.

62

Riley got down to the basement and rushed Owen Whittaker like a bull, not realizing he was already cuffed. He slammed the little man to the ground and had his knee in the center of his back in a second.

Lazarus said, “I got him. Take her upstairs and call medical.”

He gave a silent nod. Piper, tears streaming, moved from Lazarus to Riley, her quivering hands covering her face. Riley paused at the stairs, glancing between Owen and Lazarus. “You good?” he asked.

“Unless he’s plannin’ on taking me down with just his kicks, I’m fine. Go.”

Riley hesitated, then helped Piper up the staircase. Lazarus lingered, only moving once the sound of the front door echoed and the footsteps above stopped.

Owen Whittaker stood, battered and heaving. His breaths were rough, like wind over old cloth. His eye was a blotchy mix of blood and marred skin; his good eye fixed on Lazarus.

“You went after Ava, Sophie . . . her,” he said, motioning with his chin toward the stairs. “You feed on their hurt, take what they love. Why? What’s in it for you?”

Owen licked his lips, smearing some fresh blood across them. “I feel less alone.”

Lazarus’s gaze dropped to the floor. They were silent a long time.

Lazarus finally spoke. “Even in the abyss, now and then a little truth seeps through, don’t it?”

Outside, a breeze whispered, causing the unsecured front door upstairs to tap gently against its wall stop.

Lazarus lifted his weapon and fired.

The bullet tore through Owen Whittaker's skull, shattering his teeth and exiting in a spray of blood and gore. Brain matter splattered the wall behind him, and droplets of blood rained down on Lazarus. The lifeless body slumped to the floor like a discarded puppet.

Lazarus set the gun down and started taking off his blood-speckled shirt as he stood over the corpse.

He had work to do.

63

The ambulance had arrived within minutes. Piper remembered bits and pieces. Riley talking to her outside under the shade of a pine tree. The sound of the ambulance and paramedics, police officers running in and out of the house.

She was already at the hospital when she heard that Owen Whittaker was dead. The police officers outside her hospital room were talking about it. He had attacked Lazarus, and Lazarus had no choice but to shoot. She didn't remember hearing a gunshot.

She felt a disconnect, like she was floating outside her own body. She would have visited Lazarus, but even the act of getting out of bed seemed too hard. Glancing out the only window, she noted it was afternoon. Had she slept at all? She couldn't remember.

Bandages wound around her calf, hiding the stitches underneath. They kept mentioning shock when she asked why she was still there. Eventually, they said she could leave but couldn't drive due to the pain medication.

Her first thought was to call her grandmother to pick her up.

Pulling together the last of her strength, she dressed and found Lazarus waiting for her in the hallway.

"I'll take ya home."

They had given her a crutch in case it was too painful to walk on her torn calf. He walked patiently with her down the hospital corridor as she got used to it.

Once in the car, he started it, and they sat there for a moment.

"I don't think you should go home by yourself. You should stay with me."

She didn't have the strength to object and say she would get a hotel.

Lazarus drove her to his apartment and then led her to his bedroom. She lay down on the bed, and he draped a blanket over her. She felt dizzy and weak, but the apartment smelled like leather and it reminded her of horses and distracted her from the intense nausea.

He left the bedroom and shut the door, and she began to cry and didn't stop.

64

It took three days before Lazarus was in front of an Internal Affairs review board, which was really just two detectives taking his statement. The men smoked and laughed and talked little about the case. They asked if he wanted his union rep there, and he declined. Then they turned on the recording equipment and asked Lazarus for his official statement.

He went through in detail what had happened in those seconds after Ms. Danes and Detective Riley had left the house.

Owen escaped the cuffs and lunged for Lazarus's gun. During the struggle, Lazarus regained control and ordered Owen down. Owen shoved him away, ripping his shirt, and charged again, and in response, Lazarus fired a single time. The bullet entered through Owen's mouth. Despite Lazarus performing CPR, Owen didn't survive.

They asked a few questions and then thanked him for his time and said that they would be in touch with their findings.

He left the building and went to his car and sat quietly a moment, in debate. Then he started it and headed to the freeway.

Lake Danes's funeral had already begun by the time he got there. He saw Piper and Sophie, and a lot of friends and relatives. He leaned on his car and kept his distance, but he could hear the words of the preacher. Words about fire and clay and the dead rising out of ash.

When it ended, Piper saw him. She walked over. She was in black and looked nice, but he didn't say anything about it.

"I wasn't sure you'd come."

"Don't like funerals or weddings. Two of the same thing if you ask me," he said, trying to make her smile.

She looked down to her shoes. "I don't think I got to thank you."

"You don't need to . . . I don't know what to say other than I'm sorry as hell and—"

"I know," she said.

He looked over to the crowd that was dispersing from the gravesite. "How's Sophie?"

"She's hanging in. We found a friend of the family in San Jose that's willing to take her. She's a director of a nice charter school there, and Sophie's going to enroll."

He looked to the small tractor that would be pushing dirt over the coffin. "You goin' back to the GAL?"

"I don't know. Judge Dawson called me to talk. She mentioned she wants me to stay. I haven't decided. I'm taking a leave of absence for a while, and I guess I'll see what happens."

"Don't take too long to decide if you're coming back or not. I'd hate to have to train someone new."

He got back into his car. Before pulling away, he said, "You need anything, you call me."

"I will."

She watched him as he drove away.

65

Judge Hope Dawson didn't like the morgue and hated hospitals even more. Her rotations in medical school and then residency were pure torture, but she wanted the knowledge and forced herself to push through. But medicine wasn't her passion; the law was. The law was power. What was prescribing medication compared to a profession that gave you the authority to have people imprisoned or set free?

Outside the morgue, she paced. The soft shuffle of her Italian handmade shoes contrasted sharply with the stark hospital basement. Her tailored Saint Laurent suit felt out of place in the sterility.

Dr. Henry Moss stepped through the double doors of the examination room. He was a friend of her father's and one of the most respected medical examiners in the United States. She had known and trusted him her entire life.

Dr. Moss's once-youthful face was now lined with wrinkles, his hair graying at the temples. Behind him, on a metal slab, lay the corpse of Owen Whittaker. Whittaker had no next of kin, and his body would be cremated tomorrow, like most unclaimed homeless individuals.

"Well?" she said.

Dr. Moss let out a breath. "Almost everything Detective Holloway stated in his review hearing about the death is accurate."

"Almost?"

"The problem is, if Mr. Whittaker shoved him away before charging at him again, as he stated, we would expect to find gunshot residue indicating a distance of about three to four feet. The gunshot residue on the cadaver indicates a distance of nine to ten feet. I doubt a simple shove from such a small individual would send Detective Holloway back ten feet. And no pathologist worth his salt would miss that. He must have people who owe him favors. If the cadaver wasn't so desiccated, I would recommend a second autopsy performed by someone outside this jurisdiction and a new report written for posterity. But you asked me if he was lying, and yes, I think he is. He was much farther away from this man when he shot him than he says. Far enough that Mr. Whittaker was likely not an imminent threat."

Judge Dawson nodded, her eyes lingering over the body on the metal slab. It was shriveled and twisted, like a withered husk. Its mouth was open, revealing rows of broken yellow and black teeth. The skin was a sickly gray, and the veins beneath it were gnarled and twisted.

"So," he said, taking off his gown, "you going to report him?"

"No," she said, her lips curling into a smile. "I have something more interesting in mind for him."

About the Author

Victor Methos's journey into the world of law and justice began at the age of thirteen, following a profound personal experience where his best friend falsely confessed to a crime after enduring an eight-hour interrogation. This pivotal moment steered Methos toward a future in law, culminating in a law degree from the University of Utah. Starting his career as a determined prosecutor in Salt Lake City, he soon established Utah's premier criminal defense firm, showcasing his prowess in more than a hundred trials over a decade.

One case in particular left an indelible mark on Victor, inspiring his breakthrough bestseller, *The Neon Lawyer*. Transitioning from the courtroom to the writer's desk, Methos has since dedicated himself to crafting gripping legal thrillers and mysteries. His exceptional storytelling has earned him the prestigious Harper Lee Prize for *The Hallows* and an Edgar Award nomination for Best Novel for *A Gambler's Jury*. He currently resides in southern Utah.